REPENTANCE

THE STORY OF KACE HAYWOOD

A BOURBON SERIES NOVEL

MEGHAN QUINN

Copyright © 2015 Meghan Quinn
bookmark: Copyright
Published by Hot-Lanta Publishing
Copyright 2015
Cover by Murphy Rae with Indie Solutions
Edited by LS King and Murphy Rae with Indie Solutions

ISBN: 1518647502
ISBN-13: 978-1518647505

Meghan Quinn

A note from Kace...

I'm a man of few words. I don't feel, and I don't make friends with anyone outside my circle. I don't talk about my past, and I don't care to hear about anyone's future. I like to seclude myself from the outside world, observe others and live my life in a self-induced solitary confinement.

I spend my days working for my best friend as a thank you for what he's done for me, for what he's covered up. At night, I think about my wrongdoings. I let it eat me alive until I end up at the bottom of a bottle, temporarily forgetting my past sins.

I've succeeded at keeping a safe distance between myself and the outside world. I'm proud that I've kept people at arm's length. At least I was...until the day I Met Lyla.

I thought I knew what love was. It was a far-off concept I'd experienced before, but fuck was I wrong. I thought I knew what it was like to be touched by a woman, to be idolized by a woman, to be lost in a woman's scent, but I had no clue until Lyla came along.

She ruined me, wrecked me, gutted me from the inside out, and not because she wouldn't love me back. No, I knew she loved me. I could see it in her eyes. She ruined me because she was a dream, an illusion of happiness I couldn't hold on to. I'm not allowed to love. I'm not privy to such a fundamental notion in life. I don't deserve love, not after what I've done, not after what I've taken away from someone else.

During the lowest point of my life, I lost control, and I've been paying the price for that three-second lapse of judgement ever since. There isn't a day that goes by I don't think about what I've done, that I don't recognize the kind of monster I've become.

Sorrow, regret, and remorse are the only emotions I allow myself to feel. Anything else is a secondary musing that is quickly washed away.

There is one moment in my life I wish I could take back, but every choice you make comes with a consequence; I'm a fucking living example of that.

Some people celebrate the day they were born. I celebrate the day my soul died. This is the story of my repentance.

CHAPTER ONE

My present...

Summer.

My least favorite part of the year. Not because of the hot and humid weather of Louisiana; no, it was the nightmares that grew heavier with each passing day during that season.

I could take the humidity.

I could deal with the heat.

I could even manage dodging the tourists visiting the French Quarter.

But the nightmares, the flashbacks, the reminders of what the beginning of summer represented to me—they were unbearable.

My days at the Lafayette Club, managing the Jett Girls, were over, and now I was in charge of the new community center my best friend, Jett Colby, was funding. When I worked at the club, helping the Jett Girls perform their dances for the city elites, I was able to hide in a hole, do my job, and then bounce.

But with the new venture, I was faced with the fact that

a sinner like myself was forced to put on a jolly fucking face and act like I was an upstanding citizen.

I was the furthest thing from an upstanding citizen.

Jett Colby, now he was an upstanding citizen. He created the Lafayette Club to help save women from a life on the streets. He named them Jett Girls and created a system where they earned not only an education but a living as well. Now, he was rotating the employees of the Lafayette Club over to the community center, which included myself and the Jett Girls. We were going to serve our community in the best way possible; offer them a free education through wellness and a second chance in life.

But the way I saw it, me serving the community was a fucking joke.

Even though I had my reservations about the idea, it was my duty to suffer; therefore, I did.

Goldie, Jett's fiancée, had made it her mission to get on my nerves whenever she could, and her newest mission was to continually shove her best friend, Lyla, into my life after I'd made it a goal to expunge her from my memory.

Lyla.

She was a unique brand of woman, a once-in-a-lifetime kind of woman who affected you the minute she walked into a room. She ingrained herself into your marrow and rested there, never leaving.

The minute I met her, I knew there was no way I was going to be rid of her, and the fact that she was linked so closely to my inner circle didn't help either.

But just like everything else in my life, I couldn't have her.

I couldn't wear this cloak of guilt and fully give myself to her, and there was not a chance in hell I would be sharing my past sins with Lyla. I couldn't take the judgment from her, not from her. I needed Lyla to idolize me, to look at me with those green eyes and cherish me.

I was a selfish bastard, but it was the one thing I held on to in this bleak fucking world.

I brought the slowly emptying glass of whiskey I was clutching to my lips. The amber burn of the liquid glided down my throat, reminding me that even though I lived in a numb state, I was still alive.

Fuck, I shouldn't be. I would be rotting in jail right now if it weren't for Jett and his money.

I pressed a hand hard into my forehead, trying to rid of the pounding headache taking over my body while music played behind me. Goldie was celebrating her first showing in an art gallery. The Jett Girls, her friends, were dancing, drunk off their asses, and Jett was sitting next to me, trying to get me to enjoy myself.

"You're bringing down the morale, Kace," Goldie shouted from across the room.

"Tell me something I don't know," I mumbled as I took another sip of my drink.

"At least Diego isn't talking to Lyla anymore," Jett whispered to me.

Yeah, thank fuck for that.

Diego, our good friend, had spent a good half of the night talking to Lyla, making her laugh, and giving her the kind of attention she deserved. It wasn't until I physically pulled him away and talked to him privately that he finally took off, feeling cock-blocked.

I'd straight up built a fortress around Lyla and let everyone at the party recognize my caveman-like gesture. She wasn't very happy about it, given the ripe mood she was in and the death glares she was sending my way. I didn't have to face her to know she was shooting daggers at me. I could feel them sticking in my back.

It was a dick move, especially since I wasn't allowing Lyla to be a part of my life. But being the dick I was, I couldn't allow anyone else near her, not until I was able to get her out of my system, which I knew deep down was going to be never.

"Good thing he left," I muttered.

"Are you going to drink your night away again?" Jett asked, always concerned about me.

"It's not like I don't do it every night. You just don't see it."

"You think I don't see the empty whiskey bottles in your room? I'm not stupid, Kace."

"Well, then act stupid," I said gruffly. "Nothing is going to change. You know that, so why do you keep trying?"

"Hoping I get lucky one day. Get my best friend back."

"What you see is what you get. Deal with it," I stated, knowing fully well I spoke the truth.

While working at the Lafayette Club, I'd found it easy to deal with the women in my life, never committing to them. But since I met Lyla, I'd felt more irritated and volatile than ever. I used to be able to hold on to a good mood for at least an hour or two, but now, knowing there was one woman out there who held me by the fucking balls and I couldn't do anything about it, it made me outright unbearable to be around.

The only distraction I had was taken away from me and in its place was Justice. Justice, the community center, where I now worked, was almost complete. The construction company was moving along quickly with the infrastructure, putting us on track with the opening. The actual main center would be available to begin arranging for our grand opening shortly. The center wouldn't be open to the general public yet, but we would be able to go inside and start organizing, something I was looking forward to because I would be able to keep the girls busy and out of my business.

But more importantly, I wanted to keep myself busy, even though I was feeling uneasy about the new venture. At first, I was excited, proud of my friend for such an idea, but the closer the opening came, the more uneasy I felt. Was I really cut out for running a community center offering second chances when I wouldn't grant myself one?

Lately, the days seemed to drag, leaving me to my thoughts, which were toxic. If I was left alone to my own musings too long, I slowly drowned myself in the what-ifs that were constantly rolling around in my head.

What if I'd handled my life differently? What if I hadn't put all my trust in one person? What if I hadn't allowed myself to be provoked?

What if I hadn't punched him?

What if I hadn't killed a man with my fists?

Would he be reading his little girl a story right now? Would he be kissing her on the forehead and tucking her in? Would she be looking at him, seeing him as the one and only man in her life?

Little Madeline. Would her life be perfect if it weren't for me?

Most definitely her life would be better off if she still had her dad, but God took the wrong man that night.

My biggest regret, a shame that would haunt me for eternity. A regret I would never speak of, for I was a private man, a reserved man, a man of few words, someone who deserved hatred rather than pity.

That was why I'd chosen to live my life as if I were dead,

because living it as if I was alive would be too painful. To experience joy would be wrong. To know what love was... that emotion wasn't deserved.

That was why I kept Lyla at a safe distance, so she could keep away from my toxic tendencies. I had my moments, my slip-ups with her, but overall, she knew I wasn't emotionally available, and I knew she was an absolute dream I wasn't privileged to ever enjoy.

I was emotionally detached, deprived, stripped bare because of my wrongdoings.

I'd chosen to live in grief.

I'd chosen misery. It was a slice of the penance I actually deserved.

I'd killed a man.

Kace fucking Haywood, washed-up boxer and short-tempered monster, had killed a man.

I downed the rest of my whiskey and signaled to the bartender for another as my demons resurfaced.

Like every other night, I grasped the only thing I knew that could ease my pain. I allowed the amber liquid to run rapidly through my blood, numbing me to the world.

CHAPTER TWO

My past...

"That was one hell of a knockout," Jett said, tossing me a beer from the fridge and taking a seat at the chrome-and-marble bar in my living room.

Looking around my house, I was pleased with how it had come out. It wasn't quite as luxurious as Jett's mansion, but it was a huge step up from the trailer I'd grown up in. Being on top of my game in the ring had paid off. Sponsorships quickly started sprouting from everywhere, and I was inundated with endorsements, tripling my bank account in a week.

Money wasn't an asset I was dependent upon. I was more driven by success, and by proving my worth to myself and to my father. But I wasn't going to lie; being able to buy whatever I wanted was kind of nice. Being able to not worry about living paycheck to paycheck was a relief, a feeling I would always cherish since I knew from experience how the other half lived.

"I was really impressed tonight," Jett said in all sincerity. "Working with Jono has really paid off."

"I agree," I said after taking a sip from my bottle.

Jono was my new trainer, and he had really beefed me up in the last couple of months, adding more muscle and working on my timing and distance. My ability to think on the spot while reading my opponent had always been a strong suit of mine, so that was why we'd spent so much time focusing on my timing. After tonight, I could tell all my hard work was starting to pay off.

Previously, I'd trained on my own, but recently I'd decided to step up my game, given the amount of talent I was showing, so I hired Jono. Best decision I'd made, because after a few short months, I was the man to beat in the ring, a hefty goal of mine.

I was on top, a feeling I would never forget.

"Still think you can take me?" I jokingly asked Jett. When we were young, we would always get in stupid fights, and we were pretty evenly matched, but with my new training regimen, I had no doubt I would own him.

"I will always be able to take you," Jett said with a smirk, letting me know how much he didn't believe his statement.

"So how are you feeling about the whole Natasha thing?"

Natasha had been Jett's fiancée, "had been" being the key word. She'd recently left him for another man. For a guy of Jett's stature, it was a giant blow to his self-esteem.

"Don't really want to talk about it," Jett curtly stated, trying to drop the topic, but I wouldn't let him off that easily.

"Are you ever going to talk about it?"

"No."

"She was a bitch anyway," I said, taking a long pull of my beer. After I put my bottle down, I looked at Jett, who had a questioning look of fury in his eyes. I shrugged. "What? You can't tell me she was a fucking dream to be around. She was as cold as a witch's tit."

Jett shook his head. "Why do people say that? Are witch's tits really cold? How did they get such a cliché term attached to their breasts?"

"Are you some kind of spokesperson for witches now?" I asked, confused.

"Just got to stick up for all witches and their warts."

"And that's not a cliché? Not all witches are hideous, you know. Take Sarah from Hocus Pocus. I would totally tap that. Hell, I would fuck all three of them. Something about fucking a broad on a broomstick does it for me."

Laughing, Jett shook his head. "There is something seriously wrong with you, man."

Silently agreeing, I pulled up the remote sitting on the bar and turned the TV to the sports channel. I was hoping to see a recap of my match, and knowing Jett wasn't going to talk about Natasha, this was perfect timing to fill the silence in the room.

"When's the next match?" Jett asked as a Lexus commercial came on.

"Now that I'm no longer an amateur, I have a few months to get ready for the next one. I'm looking at about only two matches a year now."

"Easy day at the office with a big payout." Jett leered.

"Screw easy." I laughed. "Not with the training schedule Jono has me on."

I was about to lay out my training regimen but stopped when the sportscasters started talking about my fight. I turned up the TV and listened.

"Haywood versus Crane. Can we talk about the explosive match we witnessed tonight? Kace Haywood, up and *coming boxer, has taken the boxing scene by storm, introducing his quick instincts and fast punches that result in an early knockout with almost any opponent he comes across. With his professional title in tow, he will be unstoppable."*

A video montage of my amateur and professional career unfolded while a voiceover started telling my story.

"At a young age, Kace Haywood had an interest in the sport, but it wasn't until after high school he started to take his career seriously. Born and raised in New Orleans, he self-trained in a small gym that has since been washed away by Hurricane Katrina. Prevailing through the storm, he continued to train and has now hired the infamous Jono Mills as his trainer. With Jono at his side, Kace Haywood is a lethal combination of smarts, instincts, quick feet, and impeccable timing. With the extra muscle Haywood has put on and the in-depth knowledge from his trainer, Kace Haywood will be a household name in the next few months."

Jett patted me and then squeezed my shoulder, letting me silently know he was proud of my accomplishments, of how I was able to succeed in my sport so quickly and make a name for myself.

The announcers came back into view, looking at their notes.

"Farfetched prediction or spot on?" one talking head asked another.

"Spot on. Kace Haywood has it all. The talent, the speed, and the looks. He is the total package. He will make sponsors happy, bring more female viewers to the sport, and set the standard for all boxers to come."

"I don't think they could have blown anymore sunshine up your ass if they'd tried," Jett pointed out.

"They could have talked about the punisher in my

pants." I winked.

"I tried to send them pictures, but they said it would have been too embarrassing for you. I tried to tell them you didn't mind showing off all two inches, but they refused."

"Fuck off." I laughed.

"It's always about dick size with you, isn't it?" Jett asked.

"When is it not about dick size?"

"Not sure." Jett laughed, finishing his beer.

Taking a serious spin on our conversation, I asked, "Are you ever going home or are you going to continue to pussy up and sleep in my guest room?"

"Don't want to leave you alone. I know how much the dark scares you," Jett countered.

"Seriously, man. You have to go home at some point. You have to move on."

"I know," he answered sharply. "I fucking know." He ran his hands through his hair, resting his elbows on the bar. "It's just not that easy. The place is so empty now. I miss her."

"Natasha?" I asked, completely confused.

Jett grimaced as he turned his head slightly toward me. "Fuck no, not Natasha. I miss my mom."

Ah hell. I wasn't good at shit like this. I'd never been the kind of guy who carried around a great deal of empathy, so dealing with other's emotions wasn't my bread and butter. Give me a fucking punching bag, and I could smoke the shit out of it, but emotions? I would rather get knocked out in the first round.

Jett had recently lost his mother to AIDS after reconnecting with her. Jett had grown up on the wealthy side of life. His dad was a business tycoon who'd used Jett's mother to have his child so one day, he's have someone to pass his business down to. Once she gave birth to Jett, his father had made sure that she never saw her child again, making Jett grow up without the love of his mother. Because Jett was so soured by his father's lack of affection toward his mother, Jett made it his mission to grow to be a better man than his dad.

Knowing Jett never showed an ounce of feelings, I had to man up and be there for him. He would do the same thing for me, even though we had a silent understanding that we never explored our feelings with each other.

"Damn, I'm sorry, man," was all I could think to say.

"Me too," Jett agreed. He took a deep breath and said, "I just wish I could have done more for her. I wish I'd had more control over the situation. I hate not having control."

"I can understand that," I said lamely. Digging deep, I continued, "I need control too. I need control over everything. I think that's why I trained myself for all those years and why it took so long for me to hand over my future to a trainer. Without control, I feel lost, almost confused."

"Exactly," Jett said, pulling a little harder on his hair. "I feel anxious, like I can't breathe."

"Like someone is sitting on your chest, clouding your thoughts and ripping your very instincts out from under you," I added.

"Do you think I could have saved her?" Jett asked softly.

Wanting to sound as sincere as possible, I cleared my throat and placed a hand on his shoulder. "No, Jett, I don't think you could have. I think you gave your mom a loving end to her life. She left on a good note, on a happy note. That is something you should focus on, not the other side of things, because if you focus too much on what you could have done, you will just drive yourself to an early death. It's not healthy."

Jett nodded as he looked at his empty bottle. Taking a deep breath, he sat up and chanced a glance at me. "Shit, things just got profound." He chuckled.

Knowing I could easily make a sarcastic comment, I decided not to and agreed with him. "They did, but don't ever think you can't talk to me. I know I can be an emotional void at times, but I'm here for you, man. Always will be."

"I appreciate that," Jett said, getting out of his chair. He took a look at his watch and let out a long breath. "I guess I'll be heading back to my place."

"You can stay if you want." I shrugged, not caring either way.

"Nah, I think it's about time we put this little live-in situation we've got going on, on the back burner. I think it's about time we both get some pussy."

"Speak for yourself." I winked.

A slow smile crept across Jett's face. "Bullshit. When?"

"Locker room," I said with pride.

"From who, Jono?"

"Fuck no!" I said, laughing. "One of the ring girls."

"Catch her name this time?" Jett asked, shrugging into his jacket.

"Not quite."

"Classic Kace." Jett shook his head. With a serious look on his face, he added, "Seriously though, I'm proud of you, Kace. You've come a long way. You can only go up from here."

"I hope so," I said with a smile.

I had a house, I had a job, I had a purpose and a goal to maintain. My life was just beginning, and I couldn't be more excited about what my future held for me.

CHAPTER THREE

My present...

Right hook, left hook, upper cut, upper cut.
   Right hook, left hook, upper cut, upper cut.
The vibration from hitting the bag in front of me ran through my body as I continuously tried to knock out the bag swinging from side to side. I repeated the cycle over and over in my head at a rapid pace, my arms flying at an uncontrollable rate until I couldn't breathe anymore.

   Sweat dripped off my face, burning into my eyes, fogging my vision, but I didn't let it or my shortness of breath stop me. I continued to smoke the bag, to take out my frustration, to help forget. I was always trying to forget.

   Right hook, left hook, upper cut, upper cut.
Breathing became labored and the burn running through my muscles was more than welcomed by my body. I lived for the burn, for the numbing agent that temporarily eased the sear in my soul.

   Upper cut, upper cut, upper cut....
"Fuck!" I shouted as I cross-punched the bag, sending it

into the air for a moment of relief. With one last spin, I dodged the bag and threw another right hook into it before tearing myself away.

Catching my breath, I leaned against the cool wall of the training room in Jett's hotel only a select few had access to.

The door opened and Goldie popped in, wearing her typical workout gear of short shorts and a tank top.

Goldie unfortunately was one of the people with access.

Lyla followed, wearing a sports bra and shorts, looking more provocative than Goldie.

Lyla was another person with access to the gym. Fuck me.

The one woman who haunted my dreams was a constant presence in my daily routine thanks to Goldie, my best friend's girl.

"Oh, sorry. I didn't know you were in here," Goldie said, startled by my appearance. "Are you done?" she asked, taking in the scene in front of her.

The hanging bag continued to sway from my forceful punches, sweat marked the mats in a ring around the bag, and my entire body was on fire from my workout. I abused my body every chance I got, and today was no exception.

"I'm done," I answered curtly, tearing my gloves off with my teeth.

"I thought you worked out at night," Goldie said as she stepped up on the treadmill and started pressing buttons.

"I do."

Avoiding Lyla's glare, I tore off the tape encasing my hands, wadded it up, threw it in the trash can and grabbed my water. I didn't want any drama.

Seeing Lyla was inevitable, but fuck if I didn't want to bump into her every day, just to see her beautiful face. It would be like running into your ex every damn day, but the funny thing was

Lyla and me had never been in a relationship. We just suffered from explosive sexual tension, which in my opinion was worse. My body craved hers in every way possible, but I wasn't allowed to have her, and fucking someone else wasn't even a quick fix. It just made the urge to make Lyla mine even more demanding.

I was heading for the door when Goldie called to me. "Don't you want to boss me around in here? You never pass up the chance to make me sweat."

The sexual innuendo in her tone did not escape me.

I enjoyed training others, torturing them on the treadmill and then forcing them to do plyometrics until they were ready to collapse. Goldie was the most fun to train because she was a sassy, stubborn woman who always put up a fight, so forcing her to do burpees on command was a real pleasure. But with Lyla in the room, I really wasn't in the mood.

Without turning around, I shook my head and said, "Not today."

"Kace, what's wrong?" Goldie asked, sounding sincere.

"Nothing," I shot back, making it to the door and ignoring the troubled look on Lyla's face.

I grabbed a towel from a shelf on the way out and wrapped it around my neck to absorb some of the sweat that continued to trickle down my soaked skin.

The physical exertion I'd just put my body through was now a giant waste of time because the stress I'd been trying to reduce had come back full force the minute Lyla walked through the doors.

Our last real conversation that didn't involve fighting ran through my mind on constant replay. All she wanted was a little something from me, a little give. She wanted to know who I was, why I didn't lead my own life, why I refused to accept happiness. But what she wanted I couldn't give her because that meant explaining myself, and explaining myself wasn't an option.

I'd asked her to let it go, to not worry about it, but that wasn't good enough for her. She needed more; she needed a man with a heart, with the ability to share his life, something that was impossible for me to do.

The touch of her small hand against my bare chest still branded me. I could still feel her soft body pressed against mine, the weight of her full breasts resting against my skin, her hardened nipples grazing me ever so slightly.

Fuck!

I shook my head, downed the rest of my water bottle, and started toward my room. I had some plans for the community center to go over before we were allowed access into the building. I wanted to make sure it was as safe as could be before I allowed the employees inside.

When Jett had approached me with the idea of managing the place, I'd accepted the opportunity. It was a job I was more than willing to take on because the act of helping others appealed to me. Even though I wasn't the most approachable person, I still felt the need to help others achieve their dreams since mine were gone.

"Kace," Lyla called, making my entire body go numb.

Why? Why couldn't she leave me the fuck alone?

I didn't turn around. I couldn't. I couldn't look her in the eyes, the beautiful green eyes that haunted me at night.

"Kace, can I please talk to you?"

No, I thought.

I didn't want to talk. I just wanted to fuck. I needed to fuck her out of my system. That's what it was. I just needed one more moment in time with her legs wrapped around me, crying my name in the throes of ecstasy.

That's what I convinced myself of at least. Well, tried to convince myself.

"I have things to do, Lyla," I answered.

"Turn around," she said softly and pulled on my shoulder.

My stomach sank from her tone. I clenched my jaw and willed myself not to turn around and push her up against the wall so I could take what I wanted.

Taking a deep breath, I looked her in the eyes. Her face was full of concern and questions I had no intention of answering.

"What?" I asked, rather rudely, but better to be rude than put my heart on the floor for her to stomp on.

Caught off guard for a second, she searched my eyes. "Can I just talk to you for a second?"

"Sure, talk." I gestured for her to continue.

Gaining courage, she said, "I want to apologize for last night. I wasn't very nice to you at all, and I shouldn't have been throwing myself at other guys while you were there."

Last night, another way our paths had crossed. Our lives were tangled together because our best friends were engaged. It was an unfair circumstance I had to live with.

"I don't care what you do with other men," I lied.

In fact, I'd ached last night watching her engage with someone other than myself. Lyla was my crutch, a pleasure I couldn't allow myself to have. My life was going nowhere. She didn't need to be sucked into my void. I couldn't offer her the things she deserved.

She gave me a pointed look. "That's why you interrupted my conversation with Diego?"

She had me there. Diego was my friend, and I'd taken it upon myself to educate him on my unreasonable expectations when it came to Lyla. Basically I couldn't be with her, but I didn't want anyone else to be with her either.

"He's bad news," I lied again. Diego was probably one of the most upstanding guys I knew besides Jett. He would never do anything dishonest. The minute he'd found out about my situation with Lyla, he backed off immediately.

"Sure." A small smile spread across Lyla's lips, her soft and full lips.

"Is that all?" I asked.

"I just wanted to apologize. I know you're going through a tough time...."

"What?" I asked, anger starting to boil up inside of me. "Who told you I was going through a tough time?"

"I was talking to the girls, and they were saying something about the summer—"

"Don't fucking talk to them about me," I gritted out, interrupting her. Goldie and the Jett Girls loved to gossip and push my buttons. Of course they would talk about me to Lyla. "They know nothing about me, so it's best you all mind your own fucking business. Got it?" I tried to contain my rage, but it was hard not to get in her face, to startle her enough to leave me alone. She didn't need to be snooping around in my past. That was the last thing I wanted her to do. She didn't need to be exposed to my weaknesses.

She took a step away from me, a little shocked from the anger pouring off of me. Guilt ran through me from startling her so much. I didn't want her to see this side of me, this bitter, hateful man, but I didn't know how to be any other way. It was rare when I could really be myself and those moments were usually with Jett, who knew my sins, knew the demons I faced every day.

"Why won't you just talk to me?" she asked.

Rubbing my face with the towel, I tried to stomp out the frustration I felt before I lashed out in a way I knew I would regret later.

"Lyla, it's none of your business. You've made it quite clear I'm not the man for you, so why can't you just drop it?"

"Because I think we have something in common."

The woman was delusional. I shook my head and draped the towel over my head, forming a faux hood. I pulled on the ends while I looked at her. "You couldn't be further from the truth. We have absolutely nothing in common."

The cautious woman who'd confronted me morphed into one of defiance now. She poked my bare chest and said, "You know, Kace, you're not the only one with a shitty past. You're not the only one suffering, so stop acting like it. There are plenty of people around you who've had as much misfortune as you, maybe even worse. I mean, what really happened? You can't be a boxer anymore? Big fucking deal. There are worse things than that."

I shook my head and didn't allow her to provoke me. I knew she was trying to get the truth out of me, but what she didn't know was I've been holding my truth in for so long, I'd become a master at denying and deflecting.

"You act as if you're troubled, Lyla," I stated coolly.

She crossed her arms and stuck her chin up in the air, a defiant stance I knew well, thanks to my interactions with Goldie.

"If I was I wouldn't be telling you."

It was almost cute how she was trying to hold back, but what kept me from pushing her buttons some more was the darkness that shadowed her eyes. At that moment, I remembered that in fact, there really was something troubling her. Something deep, something that penetrated her surface and hit her hard, a kind of trouble that only one who was fighting the same kind of demons would recognize.

My face softened some as I took her in. "If you want to talk about it, I'm here," I stated.

"You can't be serious. Do you really think I would talk to you about anything? Ugh, you're so frustrating," she said, turning away, clearly needing space. I watched her long legs move gracefully down the hallway before she stopped and turned back. "I don't get it, Kace. I really don't. I thought we had a connection. I thought there was something between us. I don't understand why you keep pushing me away when I can see in your eyes how much you want me. Why are you denying yourself?"

"You know why." I spoke softly.

"I really don't," she shouted. "But I fucking wish I did."

Not giving me a chance to respond, she returned to the gym, most likely to vent to Goldie. I could only envision what my night was going to be like when Goldie confronted me later about treating her friend poorly. There was one thing you could always count on when it came to Goldie; she spoke her mind.

I needed to cut that conversation off before it even had a chance to happen, so instead of going back to my room, I went to Jett's office. I never needed to schedule a meeting to see him.

Since the Lafayette Club, Jett's old club for city elites, was non-existent at the moment, Jett's office was in the same apartment as his living space, making it very uncomfortable to pay him a visit since most of the time he had Goldie on his desk, eye-fucking her and making her promises about what he was going to do to her later.

Luckily for me, Goldie was working out, so I didn't have to be a witness to the engaged couple who had yet to set a date.

Not bothering to knock, I pushed through Jett's door and headed toward the little room in the back where he housed his office. Jeremy, his assistant, was just exiting. Jeremy took in my shirtless appearance and didn't bother to cover up the blatant perusal he gave me. What did I care? It was flattering when someone checked me out, guy or girl.

"Mr. Haywood, what a pleasure," he said with a smile, an almost wicked grin on his lips.

"Jeremy, nice to see you. Is Jett in his office?"

"Yes. Can I get you anything? Maybe another water bottle?"

"I'm good. Thanks though," I said politely and pushed past him into the office. The pleasantries were over.

I walked into Jett's space to find him sitting at his desk, running his hand through his hair as he looked over some documents in front of him. He looked up at me briefly and nodded a welcome.

I took the seat in front of his desk and leaned forward so my forearms were resting on my thighs.

"Forget to put a shirt on?" Jett asked without looking at me.

"Nah. I just know how much you like it when I walk around shirtless. Really gets your dick twitching."

"Ah, so you're in a better mood now than you were last night," Jett pointed out. I'd been a drunken ass last night. I chalked it up to another night of living with my friend, the whiskey bottle.

"Not really," I admitted. "Just ran into Lyla in the gym. Why does she have access again? It's kind of hard to move the fuck on with my life if I keep running into her all the time."

Jett placed the papers he was looking over on his desk and lifted his gaze to me. With a serious face, he said, "She's in trouble, Kace. She's taking a step backward in her life by going back to Kitten's Castle, so if offering her gym time and a possible place to stay...."

"Hold up," I said, raising my hand. "Place to stay?"

Lyla had been working at the Lafayette Club with Goldie, making a positive change in her life, until she'd decided she didn't need the help and went back to her old job, stripping at Kitten's Castle on Bourbon Street.

Nodding, Jett sat back in his chair and said, "I offered her residence, and she's considering it since we're so close to the Quarter here. It would get her back on the right track, and maybe with the girls convincing her, we can get her away from the pole and offer something more substantial for her future. I thought that's what you wanted."

"No," I lied. "Fuck. I mean, of course I want her to have more, but I was just starting to get past the fact that she wasn't living under the same roof as me anymore and now she might live here? Fuck, Jett, it's hard enough as it is, running into her all the time."

"Not my problem," Jett said heartlessly. "Maybe it's time you grow a pair and face your problems instead of hiding behind them."

"Face my problems? You really think I can make a switch like that and decide to let all my sins come to the forefront of my mind and deal with them?" In a menacing tone, I said, "I fucking killed a man, Jett. It's not like I was beaten as a child or have some kind of drug problem. I physically killed someone with my fists. That's something you never get over."

"You can't keep living the way you have been. You're not experiencing what this world has to offer. You sulk around your room, take care of tasks related to your job, and work out. There is nothing else in your life. It's unhealthy."

"And like you have the authority to tell me what's healthy? Fuck, Jett, you just came out of the hole you were hiding in a couple of months ago. And because of that, you now think you know everything there is to chasing your demons? You know nothing." I inched closer and pressed my finger on his desk while I spoke. "Until you know what it feels like to be stripped of your life, of everything you'd worked toward, you have no governance over my life. I would appreciate it if you and the girls would just leave me the fuck alone when it comes to my personal life because as far as I'm concerned, I have none and I want to leave it like that."

"Kace—"

"No." I stood up, not even remembering why I'd come to see him in the first place. "Just stay the fuck out of it. Oh, and thanks for the heads up about Lyla. Looks like I'll be looking for a new place to stay."

"You're not moving out," Jett said sternly.

"You have no control over me. I can do whatever I damn well please, and if I want to move the fuck out, I will. I don't work at the Lafayette Club anymore. I work for the community center, which requires my attention. It would do me some good to live closer so I can focus on the construction and plans to come."

Blowing out a heavy breath, Jett shook his head and pinched the bridge of his nose. "If that's what you really want to do...."

"Honestly, I don't really want to fucking do anything. What I want to do is drink myself into oblivion. It would be so easy to just shoot one up my cranium, be done with this scorching pain that runs through my body every day, but that would be too easy, and I swore I would make my life a living hell. No, my true punishment is living every fucking day on this miserable earth, replaying what I did over and over in my head as a reminder that I'm a monster who deserves nothing more than to be tortured until my dying day." I took a deep breath and turned toward the door. Before I left, I said over my shoulder, "I'll be looking for a place as soon as possible. I'll keep you informed of my search."

"Thank you," Jett said without another word. He knew when not to push me, and after my little drama queen rant, he knew the conversation was over.

With newfound purpose, I strode to my room to start looking for a new place on my computer. Maybe this was the little freedom, the little change in my life I needed. My days hiding behind Jett's doors were over. It'd been long enough that no one would be able to tell I was the man who shamed New Orleans. It was time to try to separate myself from the man who'd covered for me and try to justify my existence.

CHAPTER FOUR

My past...

A soft hand brushed my chest just as the morning sun peeked through my curtains. My body was stiff, thanks to three rounds and a few choice punches to my ribs from my opponent, but I welcomed the pain and the toll it took on my muscles. It reminded me of another fight I'd won, of another goal I'd accomplished, of the path I was continuing down.

"Mmm...," Lindsay moaned as her hand slowly made its way down my chest to my waist. She'd been a late-night pickup at a bar I frequented. She'd been trying to get in my pants for weeks now, and last night, I'd needed to blow some adrenaline and steam. She'd been in the right place at the right time.

She was fucking hot—I would give her that—and she had huge tits I'd had fun with last night, but she wouldn't be a forever kind of girl for me, and I didn't think she saw me as a relationship kind of guy, which I appreciated.

Her hand started to slip dangerously close to my cock, and I thought about stopping her, but the idea of a morning blow job appealed to me.

The light touches she was making along my torso, and the way her breasts pressed against my side, made the blood start to pool at the base of my cock. With the final reach, she grabbed a hold of my dick and rubbed it up and down, and that was all it took. I sank into the mattress and let her do her work.

"Good morning," she whispered into my neck, kissing my skin.

"Morning," I answered gruffly, unable to control the deep timbre of my voice.

"Were you already awake?" she asked as she propped her naked body up. Her breasts swayed with her movements. It was the little things in life.

"Just woke up," I responded, putting my hands behind my head and preparing for what she had in store for me.

"Good," she grinned and shifted her body down. I spread my legs so she could set herself up comfortably.

She gripped my thighs and lowered her breasts so her nipples grazed my cock. I was fully erect within seconds of her little maneuver.

She continued to slowly graze my dick with her nipples, her hair lightly brushing my thighs. It was a tangled mess but sexy, because I knew my hands were the reason she wasn't beauty queen perfect this morning. Her makeup was slightly smeared under her eyes, something I could ignore given the fact that she was about to suck me off.

Not the best fuck I'd ever had given my detachment, but she was hella good, the perfect ease for the ache between my legs.

"You're so big," she complimented me, making me feel uncomfortable. What does a guy say to that? Thank you? I grew it myself? Instead of responding, I grinned like a self-righteous chump.

Satisfied with how big I was, she crouched and lifted my cock with her hands. She brought the tip to her mouth and in one big gulp, practically swallowed me whole.

I nearly flew off the bed from how deep she took me.

"Ah fuck," I groaned as my eyes shut and I sank farther into the mattress.

She sucked me hard, licked me up and down, and juggled my balls with precision. My hand fell over my face as I let her take charge. It didn't take long until my legs started to tingle, my gut started to bottom out, and my entire body coiled, ready to explode.

She tightened her grip on my cock, letting me know she was ready. Her tongue flattened on the underside of my cock, and then she sucked the very tip as she squeezed my balls, and that was it. I pounded into her mouth, and she took me. She took every last inch of me until I was done.

"Christ," I shouted, my head flopping on the pillow. I glanced down at her, and there was a satisfied smile on her face. Fuck, I would be proud of myself too if I'd just made someone orgasm like that.

She crawled up my body and placed her hands on my chest and then rested her chin on her hands. She studied me as I tried to wash away the euphoric look on my face. I tried to act cool around women but after a blow job like that, it was hard not to smile.

My hands ran up her sides and then back down where I gripped her ass. Her pelvis thrust into mine, letting me know she was wet and wanted some attention as well.

"Best way to start your day is with an orgasm." She smiled.

"You hinting at something?" I snaked my hand around her ass and spread her legs. I felt how wet she was already, which only turned me on again.

"Oh God, please," she said, moaning.

I was never one to only take, so I flipped her on her back and hovered right above her. She spread her legs wide and ran a hand through her hair as if to say she was baffled about what I was about to do to her.

I trailed my fingers across her chest and around each nipple just as my phone started to ring. I looked over and saw that it was my agent calling. He could wait.

Her breathing picked up as I played with her nipples. I pinched them hard. I'd found out last night she enjoyed it a little rough, and I wasn't opposed to making her wishes come true, especially when I found myself fucking her up against my bedroom wall.

"Kace, please don't tease me," she groaned as my phone rang again.

My agent. What the fuck did he want, and why was he calling me so damn early?

Once again ignoring the call, I trailed my hand down her stomach. Her hips thrust into the air, encouraging me to move down farther, but I was a man who liked to take his time, to worship a fine body when I had one in front of me, so I didn't give in to her little demands.

I grazed her pubic bone, making a guttural groan pop out of her mouth, but I didn't continue south. Instead, I ran my fingers back up her stomach and was about to suck her breasts when the phone rang again.

"Son of a bitch," I spat as I gave her a sorrowful look and grabbed the cell off my nightstand. "This better be fucking good," I said into the phone, skipping all pleasantries.

"Kace, have you looked at the news?"

"No, Dale. I actually have a woman between my legs at the moment, something I'm sure you're not familiar with."

Dale was a good guy but fuck, he had bad timing.

"You might want to ask her to leave."

"Why the fuck would I do that?" I asked as the hairs on the back of my neck started to rise.

"Please, for the sake of your future, ask her to leave."

The tone Dale was using startled me. It was a warning—a warning that I was sure I wasn't going to like what I was about to hear.

"Be kind and say you forgot you had a radio interview, but get her out as soon as you can."

"Okay," I said while I cleared my throat.

"Call me back when she's gone."

I disconnected the call and stared at nothing for a second as my mind raced. What could be so bad that Dale didn't want anyone in my house when he told me?

It took about five minutes and ten apologies to get her dressed and out of my house. Surprisingly, she was pretty cool about leaving and not getting off. Maybe she was more easygoing than I'd thought.

I dialed Dale back while I started pacing the length of my house. There was no way he was going to be delivering good news. It wasn't possible from the tone of his voice.

He answered on the second ring. "Is she gone?"

"Yes. Now tell me what the hell is going on." I started to visibly shake.

"You might want to sit down," Dale warned.

"Just tell me what the fuck is going on," I shot back, my patience wearing thin.

"Kace, I got a call from the federation today. Your drug test was positive."

"What?" I practically shouted. "It's a mistake. What did I test positive for?"

"Human growth hormone. It's a banned substance, Kace."

"I know it's a fucking banned substance!" I yelled, running a hand down my face. "This can't be happening. Dale, I've never taken any kind of growth hormone. Someone switched the samples. There is no way I could test positive for HGH."

"The Anti-Doping Agency wouldn't switch. They take their jobs very seriously."

"So you think I took steroids, then?" I asked, shocked my agent didn't believe me.

"Do you take supplements?" Dale asked, his voice wavering.

"The only supplements I take are vitamins. I've never once done any kind of steroid. I've worked hard to get to where I am. Why would I chance it by taking steroids?"

"I don't know," Dale said. "Has Jono changed anything since you've been training with him?"

"No, we've been doing the same...." I paused as it hit me. "Holy fuck."

"What?" Dale asked.

Ignoring him, I ran to my kitchen, set the phone down, and rummaged through a cupboard until I pulled down a bottle of supplements Jono had recently given me. He'd told me it was a combination of natural products to help me wake up in the morning and get the best workout I could. He'd claimed the pills were cayenne pepper, green tea, and some kind of other holistic supplements.

I searched for the ingredients, but the label was blank. *What the fuck?*

Dale screamed into the phone, asking me what was going on. I picked up the cell and said, "I'm so fucked."

"What is going on?" Dale asked breathlessly.

"Jono gave me some supplements to wake me up in the

morning. I've only used them a couple of times, but fuck, Dale. They have to be laced with HGH. It's the only explanation."

"You can't be fucking serious," Dale practically growled in the phone. "I knew he was a bad idea. His reputation was tainted for a reason. He couldn't be trusted. Fuck!"

"Dale, what does this mean?" I asked, panicking now, not knowing what my future was going to look like, what my future held for me.

"It's over," Dale said flatly.

"Wait, what?" I asked as I slid down the cabinets of my kitchen and sat on the cold tile floor.

"You're banned from competing, Kace. They don't take substance abuse lightly. It's over."

This could not be happening. Dale was pulling some kind of joke on me; that's what it had to be. There was no way everything I'd worked toward in my life was coming to an end just when I was getting started, just when I was making a name for myself. This couldn't be happening.

"Dale, please tell me you're kidding."

"I wish I was, kid."

"Can't I dispute this?"

"You won't be able to prove it wasn't your fault. Who takes supplements without a label, Kace?" The disappointment in Dale's voice made my stomach turn over.

"I trusted him," I said softly as I sank farther into the cold ground.

"You can't trust everyone, Kace."

Advice that had come a little late, I thought, resting my head against the hard oak of the kitchen cabinets. The tightness in my throat constricted my ability to talk, and the throbbing in my head was almost overpowering. A lonesome tear ran down my cheek as the realization hit me that I was done. The one true thing that gave me happiness was over. My boxing days were finished.

"What's going to happen?" I asked, not really wanting to hear what Dale had to say.

"A story is going to run shortly. Your sponsorships are already pulling. You're cut from the circuit, and your title has been stripped. You're boxing days are over. I'm sorry, Kace."

"I'm sorry, too," I said right before I ended the call and buried my head in my hands, knowing fully well I'd lost everything I'd ever worked for.

Meghan Quinn

CHAPTER FIVE

My present...

"Would you like another?" the bartender asked.

I pushed my empty glass toward him. "Yeah," I mumbled, not making eye contact.

Finding a place in New Orleans to live that wasn't overpriced or mildewed or infested with rats was proving to be harder than expected. I'd looked over six different options, and none of them came close to what I was looking for.

Thinking about going back to the hotel where I would be pestered by the girls almost made it tempting enough to shack up next to the local rat's nest, but I did have my standards. I wasn't about to trade in the posh life for one that was far below what I was used to. I wasn't a princess by any means, but fuck, a little hot water would be nice.

The bar was empty other than two men playing pool off to the side. It was a bar I came to when I wanted to get away from it all. From the nagging of the girls I worked with, the control issues Jett had, and the hustle and bustle of the French Quarter.

Tourists got annoying quick. Add the fact they were usually

drunk and high-risk projectile vomiters, and it was hard for me to enjoy the unique nightlife New Orleans had to offer. Plus, with my past haunting me, I still ran into the occasional know-it-all of the boxing world. Their favorite thing to do was harass me about my past. What little they knew.

That was why I liked it in my quiet bar: no tourists, no Jett Girls, just peace and quiet.

"I knew we would find you here," a voice came from the entryway of the bar.

Diego and Blane, my friends, approached. So much for peace and quiet.

"How's our boy?" Diego asked, slapping me on the back and pulling up a chair next to me. Blane did the same.

"Your boy wants to be left alone," I replied, grabbing my drink from the bartender and taking a large gulp.

"What do you have there?" Diego asked, leaning over and sniffing my cup. To my dismay, he stuck his finger in the liquid and then tested it on his tongue. "Ahh, whiskey. I'm surprised it's not bourbon."

"Bourbon is Jett's thing," I mumbled while the tumbler was cradled between my hands. I kept my head down so Diego would get the hint I didn't want to talk.

"Where is Jett? Is he here?" Diego asked, looking around.

"No."

Grabbing the bartender's attention, Diego responded, "Fuck, you're in a mood." Turning his attention to the bartender, he said, "Can I get two fingers of whiskey and a Stella for the douche?" Diego said and pointed his thumb toward Blane.

"Thanks, snookums," Blane joked.

"You ordering drinks for him now?" I asked. I continued to look into my glass, wishing it would refill on my demand.

"You're living together, you're ordering for each other—what's next? Are you going to start fucking on center stage?" Diego owned a club called Cirque du Diable where he employed Blane. The place was actually fascinating, with its old-school circus theme. Once it opened, it would probably sell out every night.

"Who says we haven't?" Diego responded casually, causing me to lift my gaze to him.

"Dude, don't go spreading rumors," Blane chastised, clearly insulted.

"Got the miserable ass to look at me, didn't I?"

"There is something seriously wrong with you," I admitted.

"Come on, what's got your dick turning inside out?" Diego asked, thanking the bartender for his drink.

"Nothing." I shut down, not wanting to talk.

"It's that hot piece of ass from the art gallery, isn't it." Diego leaned over to talk to Blane and said, "You should have seen the massive cock block Kace threw down at the gallery. Dude straight up built a dam around this girl's pussy."

"Watch it," I practically snarled.

"See." Diego laughed and pointed at me. "I can't even talk about her without being threatened. So what is it? Why are you so fucked up over this girl?"

"I'm not," I stated casually, downing the rest of my drink. I pushed the empty glass toward the bartender and motioned for another. The man was hesitant at first, but I glared at him, letting him know I would tell him when I was done.

"Kind of seems like you are," Blane said with his beer bottle halfway to his mouth.

"Why the fuck are you guys here?" I asked, growing irritated.

"We were trolling for pussy and thought you might want to join us," Diego replied. "It's a humid night. The girls are loose and ready."

"What is wrong with you?" I shook my head.

"Just trying to lighten you up." Diego nudged me. "Come on, man. Have some fun for a change."

"I don't know what fun is," I admitted.

I really didn't want to be having this conversation, especially with Blane sitting next to me. We'd known each other growing up, but we hadn't been involved in each other's lives. He didn't know anything about me, and I only knew a little bit about him. Diego had a general understanding of my past, but he was just as clueless, and I wasn't about to divulge my life story to these two idiots.

"Just tell me about the girl. Do you like her?" Diego asked, almost sounding desperate. He was trying; I had to give him that.

Feeling like I owed Diego something, I nodded. "I thought I liked her. It's just too complicated. She wants things I can't possibly offer her."

"What? A relationship? Dude, you can give her one of those. You just have to loosen up a bit."

"Yeah, might do you some good," Blane added.

"It's not that," I said.

"Then what is it?" Diego asked.

"She wants the truth, the truth about me, and I can't give that to her. She wants to dig too deep to a place I don't even go."

"So you are going to allow your past to dictate your future?"

"I don't have a future," I responded, pushing back from the bar and itching for the bartender to finish pouring my drink. He was taking way too long.

"Dude, what happened?" Blane asked, curiosity lacing his

voice.

"None of your fucking business," I responded menacingly as the bartender came by with my drink.

"Drop it," Diego mumbled to Blane, who nodded. "So, I heard you were moving out."

Rolling my eyes, I huffed out a heavy breath and rubbed my right eye with the palm of my hand. "Jett call you?"

"No, Goldie did."

"Goldie?" I asked, surprised.

"Yeah, she said you and Jett had had a dispute and you were going to move out. She was really concerned about you. Should she be?"

For a brief moment, my heart warmed at the thought of Goldie being concerned about me. It was nice knowing that even in this dark and fucked up life of mine, there was someone out there who actually cared for my wellbeing... besides Jett, that is.

"I'll be fine," I answered. "Looked at a couple of places. I have options."

"Do you really?" Blane asked. "Because all the housing out there is pure shit."

"So true," Diego agreed. "Sometime you wonder, is it better to live on the streets or in one of the pieces of crap around the city?"

"They weren't too terrible." I tried to convince them, but I couldn't even convince myself.

"Not buying it," Diego said.

"You're right, they were shitty," I said with a smirk. "Didn't know it was a requirement in the Quarter for apartments to come with cockroaches and blood stains on the walls. There are some really classy establishments around here." There were some pretty nice places actually, but there was no way I would be able to afford them.

"Fuck, I hate cockroaches," Blane shivered.

Diego leaned closer to me and nodded at Blane. "Thor over there is a little pussy when it comes to bugs. Do you know what the asshole does when he sees one in his room? He puts a Tupperware bowl over it until I either take care of it or the damn thing suffocates. I didn't know this was how he handled things until one day I'm looking for a damn bin to put my leftovers in, and when I ask him why there are none in the kitchen, I find six bowls on his bedroom floor. Fucking idiot."

"What do you expect me to do? Stomp on them? Oh fuck no," Blane defended.

"That's kind of a puss-bag thing to say," I said to Blane, almost giddy over the fact that such a giant man could be so scared of a bug.

Blane was the biggest of us all. He could have passed as a professional bodybuilder with his ripped biceps and strong shoulders. Dude was pumped. He also did a fine job attracting the opposite sex with his blonde hair and Australian accent. Diego was thinner than Blane and me, but he was just as cut. His caramel skin and blue eyes made him a rarity, and he used that to his advantage when it came to bagging women. Both men had demons just like me. Both didn't talk about them, so it surprised me they pressured me so much. Assholes.

"Fuck you. They could crawl into my orifices," Blane shouted, defending himself against his bug phobia.

"Such a dipshit." Diego laughed and took a sip of his drink. "So, do you want to come live with us?"

"Whoa, that came out of nowhere," I responded, taken back by the offer.

Diego shrugged. "I have the extra room. You can live in the room Goldie stayed in."

"Might want to have that place disinfected first," Blane suggested. "After the one night we had to hear Goldie and Jett go at it, I bet you there are little Jetts all over the walls."

Diego cringed. "Dude, seriously. That is nasty."

"Wow, between the cockroaches and Jett's jizz all over the walls, you're really making it seem like a step up from the places I saw today," I sarcastically replied.

"Don't listen to him," Diego said, excusing Blane. "He's just mad that I won't let him lead an act for the show we're preparing for the club, so he's taking it out on me."

"You butt hurt?" I asked Blane, starting to feel a little lighter thanks to the booze running through my veins.

"No. Diego is just so self-absorbed, he doesn't know a good thing when he sees it."

"My club, my show," Diego stated.

"He's got a point." I thumbed at Diego. "Plus he used to be in a gang. Don't fuck with him."

"Dude!" Diego chastised me while hitting me in the arm. Oops. My tongue got loose when I was drunk, and sometimes secrets slipped out.

"What?" I shrugged.

"That's not public information."

"A gang? Really? You don't seem like the gang type," Blane said, trying to push Diego's buttons, and at the way Diego was fuming next to me, it was working.

"Don't judge what you see on the outside," I responded. "The boy has some mad knife skills."

"Huh, never would have thought that."

"Are we done with this conversation?" Diego asked, visibly uncomfortable. I was glad I wasn't the one uncomfortable. "Because I think we should talk about how Kace used to be a professional boxer."

My head snapped up and my gaze fell on Diego. It felt like fire was spitting out of my eyes as I stared him down.

"Or maybe we don't," Diego retracted, getting my message loud and clear.

Uncomfortable eeriness settled over us as we all leaned on the bar with our elbows propped up and drinks in our hands. We didn't talk, we didn't look at each other. We stared straight ahead and tried to let the awkward moment pass.

"So, want to live with us?" Diego finally asked, breaking the silence with a dickhead smile.

"Why the fuck not?" I answered, already regretting my decision.

Blane clapped me on the back. "Thatta boy. Maybe you can even be a part of the show."

"Nope." I shook my head. "Not going to happen. You couldn't pay me enough to get up on stage and prance around in leather vests and top hats."

"We don't prance, we stride," Diego said.

"Yeah, so much better." I rolled my eyes. I cleared my throat. "In all seriousness, thanks for the offer. It will really help getting out of the hotel. Plus your place is closer to the community center, which will be convenient."

"Why don't you just get your own place?" Diego asked. "I'm sure you have enough money in that stacked bank account of yours."

What little he knew. Yes, I had a stacked bank account, but the money didn't belong to me. I gave it to someone else every month. I lived on the bare minimum and was okay with that.

"Not in a position to have a place of my own right now," was all I said.

"Fair enough," Diego responded.

"How's the community center coming along?" Blane asked.

"Great," I answered, liking the change in subject. "We should be able to get in there soon to start getting it ready. The girls are excited. They're starting to get stir crazy. Jett has them on a strict study regimen right now, to educate them as much as possible on business management before running the center."

"Babs was telling me about it the other day," Blane said. "He has them going through all sorts of non-profit education." Babs was a Jett Girl who had fallen quickly for Blane. From the far-off look in Blane's eyes when he mentioned her, I could tell he felt the same.

"It's good for them," I said.

"What about your girl?" Diego asked. "The hot gallery chick."

"Lyla?" I assisted him.

"Yeah, Lyla. What is she doing?"

"Working at Kitten's Castle. She doesn't want anything to do with Jett's offer to work at the community center."

"She's at Kitten's Castle?" Diego almost sang. "We're going." Quickly, he pulled out his wallet, dropped a hundred on the counter, and got off his bar stool.

"The fuck we are," I responded, not budging from my chair.

"Lighten the fuck up," Diego complained. "She won't even see us. Come on. I haven't gone to a strip club in so long."

"You own one, you ass nut," I said.

"I mean a skeezy one," Diego responded, grabbing me by the neck and pulling me off my stool. "You're coming because shit, you need to loosen up a bit. Stop brooding all the time. It's depressing to be around you."

He led me out the door while Blane brought up the rear.

"If you don't like my attitude, then leave me alone," I tried to reason.

"Can't do that, sorry."

We made our way to Bourbon Street, which was packed with street performers and drunken idiots. There was a bachelor party on every corner, inebriated women holding on to each other for their dear lives, older couples enjoying the younger scene, and show girls at the entry of every strip club, enticing those who passed by to have a little look inside their establishment.

Diego and Blane dragged me along the cobblestone walkway of the closed-off Bourbon Street to the hot-pink neon sign of Kitten's Castle. The last time I had been here, I'd been recruiting a new Jett Girl with Jett for his club. That was when I'd seen Goldie for the first time.

Even though Kitten's Castle was a dirt hole, Goldie had stood out. She was exquisite. From the first moment I'd seen her handle herself on the floor, I'd known she was going to be a spitfire. Fortunately my best friend was able to tame her. Well, slightly tame her.

"Hey, sexy. You want to come in?" a girl at the door asked, shaking her hip at me and trying to entice me, but I was not biting. She was wearing fishnet stockings that had a tear in one leg and a pair of scuffed heels, her lipstick was smeared, and her bra was fraying on the straps. They must have been suffering for employees because when Goldie had worked at Kitten's Castle, this kind of appearance wouldn't have been acceptable.

"Not really," I muttered to her as Diego and Blane dragged me inside.

A mixture of sweat and booze attacked my senses, and the pounding bass assaulted my ears. The room was humid, dark, and the air was thick, almost so thick I couldn't breathe.

No one was on stage at the moment, but there were plenty of girls out on the floor. I checked my watch and saw it was only a little past nine. There was no way Lyla would be working now—at least I assumed she wouldn't be. She liked the late shift; it was when she got the most tips.

"Score. Front row seats." Diego pumped his fist in the air as he went over to the stage.

The moron acted like he'd never been to a strip joint before, let alone owned his own sex club.

"Can you clam the raging hormones and present yourself in a semi-cool manner?" I asked. "You're acting like a total tool bag."

"Just trying to fit in with the crowd, man. What would it say about us, being locals and hanging out at a strip club? People will judge us."

"Unbelievable." I shook my head, wishing for this night to be over.

Looking around, Blane leaned over and whispered, "These chicks are kind of... skanky."

I took a gander myself and had to agree. They weren't the most well-put-together women I'd ever seen. A lot of them were melting from the humidity, their faces sweaty and their makeup smeared, making them look almost ghostly in appearance. They moved around the club on autopilot, interacting with the customers like they'd been taught, bending and smiling at the right times but never getting too close unless they were paid to.

I hated that Lyla worked here, hated it to the point that I started to heat up from the thought. She was so much more than this. She was so much better.

"What are you doing here, Kace?" Lyla asked behind me, her voice smooth.

Shit.

CHAPTER SIX

My past...

Another phone call from Jett. I disregarded the ten missed calls displayed on my phone and pressed ignore once again.

From my ESPN notifications, I knew my story had broken through and I was now considered one of the biggest hometown disappointments.

A bottle of Maker's rested in my hand, the plush couch I'd had for a few short months formed to my sated body as I waited for the one phone call I was dreading. It was going to happen; there was no way in hell I wouldn't get the call. The matter was when.

Numb was all I felt looking around my house, taking in the framed pictures of me in the ring, of my accomplishments that were awarded to me. All of the hard work, the sweat, the blood I poured had all been for nothing.

All I had ever wanted growing up was to prove my worth, to show my city even though I grew up in a trailer park, watching my parents raise our family on the barest of wages, I could make something of myself. I hadn't needed help from anyone; I had just needed my determination and will to set goals and achieve them.

Much good that did me.

The ringing of my phone broke the eerie silence in my home. Across the screen read my father's phone number. I took note of the time; he was just getting off of work.

With a deep breath, I answered. "Hello, Pop."

"Tell me it's not true, son." My dad's gruff tone rang through me. No matter how old I was, I would always be put in place by the deep timber in my father's voice.

"What do you think?" I asked.

My father thought boxing was a waste of my time. He wanted me to work on the factory line just like him, making an honest living. Gaining an education was a waste of time in his mind. Taking the workforce on like a man was what he expected from his only son. Earning a wage and putting in a true day's work were his expectations even though such ideals had landed him in a beat-up trailer with a belly full of beer and no retirement plan.

"Don't you play games with me, boy. I told you wanting to be a professional boxer was a waste of your time, that you wouldn't be good enough to earn a decent living. Now you've taken steroids to get to the next level? What for? To prove me wrong?"

"Would you even believe me if I told you the accusations were false?" I said, rubbing my forehead, wishing this day would be over.

"I highly doubt reports from the Anti-Doping Agency are accusations. They don't take such things lightly. Why on earth would you jeopardize your family's well-being like this?" My dad's voice grew tighter as he said, "You should hear what the men down at the warehouse are saying. You have disgraced your family name."

"Pop, it's not true," I defended, trying to think of a way to explain this mess to my dad.

"The least you can do is tell me the truth, Kace."

Placing my bottle of alcohol on the coffee table, I rested my forearms on my thighs. "It's true about the steroids in my system but I didn't take them on purpose. I didn't know I was taking them. My new trainer laced some supplements with—"

"I don't need to hear anything else," my dad said, cutting me off.

"Pop, I didn't know they were in there." I pleaded, wishing my dad would understand.

Silence stretched on the phone, letting me know my dad was about to give me one last blow to the gut. It was the typical conversation I received from him when he was disappointed, and according to his standards, he was disappointed a great deal.

"From the moment you were born, I've raised you to be a leader, someone who takes pride in their job and receives respect from others for their hard work. I've spent countless hours demonstrating the attributes of a real man but instead of taking my lead, you skipped around with that Colby kid, defied my wishes, and cheated the system. It's a shame you carry the Haywood name and I'm forced to call you my son. Maybe one day you will learn that determination, strong ethics, and that solid, realistic goals will bring you respect. Until then, I pity your soul."

With that, my dad hung up the phone.

I sat on my couch, lifeless and unable to move.

What little the man knew about my actual life, how much energy I put into proving him wrong, how many countless hours I spent in the gym, throwing punch after punch until I couldn't feel my knuckles anymore. He refused to acknowledge my efforts and now that my name was tainted, there was no chance he would ever believe what I was able to accomplish.

One of the worst things a man can hear is disappointment in his father's voice. Not only had I disappointed him, but I'd tarnished our name and casted an air of ugly around my achievements. If I hadn't already thought my days were over, I would believe it now.

Tossing my phone to the side, I downed a large gulp of Maker's and headed for my door. It was time to drown my sorrows.

CHAPTER SEVEN

My present...

With slow deliverance, I turned around to find Lyla standing behind me, hand on one hip, wearing a pair of shorts cut high on her legs and plastered against her skin. Her shirt was cut short, so from my angle, looking up at her, I could see the underside of her breasts.

I wanted to cover her up so no one else could look at her, but another part of me wanted to rip her shirt off and fuck her right there on stage.

Images of her sultry body writhing beneath me played in my imagination. That one night with her was one I couldn't get out of my head, I didn't think I would ever get over the feeling of being buried deep inside of her.

"Hey, I asked you a question," Lyla said sternly.

"Yeah, the lady asked you a question," Diego encouraged with a smirk.

He was two seconds from getting a beat-down.

Taking a deep breath, I glanced at her and said, "Looking for some entertainment." Even though I didn't want to be sitting in Kitten's Castle and shouldn't have been pissing her off any more than I already had, I couldn't help myself.

I was an asshole. It just came naturally.

Her green eyes flamed with rage. "You're looking for entertainment?" Lyla asked, anger lacing her voice.

I nodded while looking around the room. Fuck, I wouldn't let any of these women come near me. Most likely they had some kind of knarly undercarriage. Why Lyla thought she belonged here was something I would never understand.

"Fine," she said and gestured to the DJ. The song switched immediately, and the steady beat of "Earned It" started to ring through the speakers. With the lift of her foot, Lyla pushed both Diego and Blane away, giving her plenty of space to work my lap.

Fuck me.

Slowly and methodically, she shifted around me, lightly brushing her hand against my skin, sending chills down my spine. Like second nature, my legs spread apart and my hands fell to my side. I bit my bottom lip as she stopped in front of me and started to move with the music while running her hands up her beautiful mocha-colored skin.

She was so fucking gorgeous with those piercing green eyes and soft features. The way her hair fell over her face was mesmerizing. The way she ran her hands over her body was hypnotizing, making me forget I was in the middle of a slummy strip club. Right now, it was just me and Lyla.

Right when I thought she was going to just stand in front of me the whole time, she stepped between my legs and bent over so I could see down her cropped shirt. The heaviness of her breasts peaked through and just like that, I was fucking gone.

Her hands found my thighs and her body made wave-like movements into mine, sending her vanilla-scented lotion into my nose, a smell I now associated with her. Her mouth grew close to my ear and with a light tug, she bit down on my earlobe while her hands ran up my chest.

With each beat of the music, she moved her body seductively. I was hard as a fucking rock from watching her.

Her hands travelled up my chest to my shoulders where she gripped tightly and pulled her body onto mine. Her ass rested on my lap and my head was inches from her breasts that were dangerously close to falling out of her shirt. Her hands wrapped around my neck as an anchor to her hold and her pelvis started to thrust into my lap with each beat of the song.

In fascination, I watched as her body rocked off of mine, how her stomach swayed with her movements, making me harder than I could possibly imagine. She was working me and I enjoyed every last minute of it.

The pressure of her ass on my crotch was almost painful, I was so hard, but I wasn't about to stop her. My hands went to her thighs where I ran them up to her hips and to her toned stomach.

The intake of air from her chest was unmistakable as I ran my hands up farther where I stopped just before I reached her breasts. Fuck did I want to touch them. I wanted to feel her pebbled nipples between my fingers. I wanted to feel them on my tongue, but I knew my limits in public so I stopped.

Her eyes were closed, her head thrown back and her neck exposed. Her hips continued to roll on my lap, increasing the pressure on my cock, and her one hand that wasn't wrapped around my neck was now snaking around my thigh.

She was eating me up and I wasn't sure how much more I could take.

The pause of her rocks against my cock shook me out of my stupor as I tore my eyes away from our connection and looked up at her. She shifted off of my body, leaving me wanting more, but right when I thought she was going to leave me hard and aroused, she backed up against me and settled on my lap so her back was against my chest. Her right hand connected to the back of my neck and she started to dance to the music again.

I leaned my head over her shoulder and took in the movements of her body against mine. My hand went to her bare stomach where it slowly found its way up to the cut-off hem of her shirt. Her breathing grew heavy and my heart beat against my chest. One more inch and I would have her fully in my hand.

"Fuck," I drew out, not being able to hold back the feel of her ass against my crotch. It was like fucking magic, rubbing against me, enticing me.

Unable to help it, my mouth found the dip of her neck where I started to nibble on her sweet skin. She tasted so fucking good.

Diego and Blane cheered me on like barbarians, but I ignored them and continued to work my mouth up and down the column of her neck. Her hand found my cheek and she pushed me away slightly right before she bent down in front of me, placed her hands on my shoes, and started twerking my dick. Her shorts rode up and exposed her beautiful ass, allowing me to watch her sexy cheeks ride against my lap.

The image in front of me was too nostalgic, too fucking erotic for me to let go, to not teach her a lesson about what she was doing to me.

Not able to take it anymore, I grabbed her stomach and pulled her up. She squealed when I wrapped her against my back, but I ignored her shocked cries and turned her so I spoke directly into her ear.

"Take me somewhere private... now."

The seriousness in my voice had her moving quickly off my lap and grabbing a hold of my hand. She led me away from a hooting and whistling Blane and Diego and directed me out of the humid air of the main room. I followed her down a dark hallway until she hit a door off to the side. She looked both ways and then pulled it open.

The room was dark when we first walked in, but she quickly turned on a light that cast a red glow in the room. It wasn't very bright—it was actually more dull than anything— but it set the mood for what I was about to do to her.

Sin was about to take place. I just hoped she was ready for it.

The moment she turned to face me, I hauled her into my chest and then pushed her up against the door. I reached behind her and found the knob, which I quickly locked. I didn't need any unexpected and uninvited guests barging in on us.

"Kace...," she said breathlessly. "What are you doing?"

Not so tough now, I tried not to smile, but it was damn hard. "Do you think you can fucking ride me like that and get away with it?" I asked with my hands on either side of her head and my right leg inching her feet apart. "I want you to feel how hard I am."

"I already know how hard you are." She smirked, gaining some of her confidence back.

"Fucking feel me," I gritted out. "Place your hand on my dick, and tell me how hard I am."

Her eyes went wide for a second from the menacing tone in my voice, but she was quickly shaken from her thoughts as her hand traveled down my stomach to my waistband.

She started to feel me from the outside of my jeans, but I shook my head and said, "No, fucking feel me. Pull my cock out of my pants and feel it."

Nodding, she undid my belt and went to work on the fly. I kept my hands trained to stay on the wall, encasing her head so I wouldn't be tempted to help her. I wanted her to do it on her own, even though she was working at a snail's pace, most likely on purpose.

"Take your time, babe. I have all fucking night."

She visibly swallowed, boosting my confidence even higher.

Finally, she worked my jeans down, along with my briefs, allowing my cock to spring free. It was hard, so fucking hard that when she touched it with her fingers, it almost ached. I needed release, and I needed it badly.

"Tell me how fucking hard I am," I demanded as I leaned over and spoke directly into her ear. In the dim red light, I saw the goosebumps that rose on her skin from my proximity.

"Kace," she moaned.

"Tell me," I gritted out.

"You're so fucking hard," she whimpered. Her deftly skilled hand ran up and down the length of my cock.

"You did that to me. Your fine-ass body, the way you pressed against me, the heat of your pussy on my lap—you made me this hard, Lyla, so tell me, what the fuck are you going to do about it?"

My mouth was against her ear as I spoke, and my chest was inches from hers, moving rapidly up and down. She pulled away to look me in the eyes, to see how serious I was. What I wanted to convey to her was I was beyond serious. I needed her, right here, right now.

"Well?"

Her hands dropped from my cock and captured my face with her hands. With brute sexual force, her lips landed on mine, causing me to push her harder into the door. Instantly my mouth opened to hers, granting her access to everything I had to offer.

Her tongue slipped in and out of my mouth, playing with my senses, lighting me on fire.

"Do you want me?" I asked, pulling away from her kiss and running my tongue along her neck.

"More than anything," she confessed.

Pride beamed in my chest, and that was all it took. I was hanging myself over the edge for this moment and this moment alone. I just wanted one more taste of her.

My hands left the door behind her and found her hips. I pinned her against the hard wood and then ran my hands up her stomach, but this time, I didn't stop below her shirt. Instead, I connected with the underside of her exposed breasts and found her hard nipples. Her breasts were fucking praiseworthy. They were more than a handful and so fucking round and perfect I wondered if they were augmented in any way, but from the feel of them, I knew they were natural, making it that much harder to forget this gorgeous woman.

"God," she cried as I gripped her breasts hard, playing with her nipples. I squeezed them, plucked them, rolled them until I didn't think I could take the feeling of her breasts in my hands any longer.

My dick twitched as her body occasionally grazed it. I needed more. I was ready to explode. I was done teasing.

"Grab my wallet from my back pocket," I said into the side of her neck. She listened well and did what was told. She didn't even need to be directed further. She knew what to do. She opened my wallet and pulled out a condom.

Quickly, she put my wallet back in my pocket and pulled the condom out of its wrapper. Without asking, she sheathed my length in record time and then looked up at me.

"Take your sorry excuse for shorts off," I demanded.

"Sorry excuse?" she asked with a quirk of an eyebrow.

Leaning forward, I said, "Do not fucking play with me. You know those shorts are too revealing. Now take them off."

Without another word, she pushed them off and toed them away. Her bottom half was naked, only a pair of heels gracing her feet. I looked up at her shirt and with a shake of my head, pulled it up, exposing her breasts. My mouth quickly found her nipples and I sucked.

Her head flew back, hitting the door, but she didn't mind as she pushed her chest further into my mouth. Slowly, I ran my hand down her stomach and hovered right over her pussy. She made little pelvic thrusts into my hand, letting me know exactly what she wanted.

Knowing I needed the same thing, I gave in to her demands and pressed my fingers inside her heated core. Instantly I was hit with how wet she was, for me. Heat blazed through me from the knowledge that I was able to turn on such a gorgeously beautiful woman like Lyla.

Not wanting to take my time anymore, I grabbed her thigh and wrapped it around my waist, lifted her, and then guided my dick inside her. One thrust was all it took. I was fully inserted. We both groaned at the same time from our connection. With the way her chest was moving at a rapid pace, I knew this wasn't going to take long.

I grabbed hold of her face, looked her in the eyes, and then descended on her mouth once again. With each thrust of my hips, my kisses grew deeper. Her hands simultaneously ran through my hair, making me feel dizzy from the way her nails scraped against my scalp.

A heady combination of lust, yearning, and something deep I didn't want to explore at the moment hit me, and it hit me fucking hard. My thrusts started to become uncontrollable, and her cries grew louder and louder with each passing connection.

"I'm going to come," she announced just before she called out my name and bit my bottom lip with her teeth. I tasted blood as she came around my dick, but I didn't care because at that moment, I went into a euphoric state of mind and came so fucking hard, I thought I was going to pass out.

"Fuck," I mumbled. My forehead found her shoulder and my hips continued to thrust into her until there was nothing left in me.

Her hands found my neck again as she held on tight. Lightly, she kissed my cheek until I was able to regain my strength and pull far enough away to look her in the eyes.

The red glow of the light in the room made her look like a dream, like she wasn't actually in my arms. Her eyes searched mine for answers I didn't have, and right now, in this moment, I wished I had something intelligent to say, but nothing came to mind. All I wanted was to bury myself inside her once again, forget everything around us, and live in the moment with her, but I knew that wasn't plausible. There was a world outside that door, waiting for us.

"Kace, why are you keeping us apart?" she asked in a small voice I'd never heard her use before.

"You wouldn't understand," I spoke softly.

"You don't know that."

"I do, Lyla. You deserve more than me. You deserve more than this life you've chosen for yourself."

"Sometimes you don't choose your life, Kace. Sometimes it's chosen for you."

Fucking words of wisdom right there. I hadn't chosen anything in my life. It had all been chosen for me, and because of someone else's bad decisions, I was living the consequences. I refused to drag Lyla down that path, down the dark path of my fucked up life.

"Give me a chance, Kace."

Taking a deep breath, I said, "I want to, Lyla. You have no fucking clue how much I want you, but I just... can't."

"Why not?" she asked, growing angry now.

I shook my head and pulled away, chucking the condom and zipping my pants up at the same time. I found Lyla's shorts and handed them to her. She pulled on her shirt and put her shorts back on, as if she hadn't just been fucked against the door.

I grabbed a hold of her neck and placed a kiss on her forehead. She closed her eyes from my touch and leaned into it. I held my lips on her forehead for longer than a couple seconds and then reluctantly pulled away.

"I'm sorry, Lyla. I can't be the man you want."

"How do you know what kind of man I want? You won't even talk to me long enough to find out."

"That's because I know you deserve better."

I had her step aside and unlocked the door for a quick escape. I was stepping out of the room when she called out, "You're not the only one who's fucked up around here, Kace. You're not the only victim."

Without turning around, I said, "That's where you're wrong. I am by no means a victim. I'm actually the furthest thing from it." With a heavy heart, I walked away. "Take care of yourself, Lyla."

CHAPTER EIGHT

My past...

The cold glass of a tumbler full of whiskey cooled my fingers. I huddled in a corner of a lesser-known bar in the Quarter I felt wouldn't be too populated by sports fans. News of my "steroid use" was starting to filter through all news sources, making it almost unbearable to be in my own skin.

My phone wouldn't stop ringing with calls and texts from the press, from friends and adversaries, to the point that I couldn't stomach the contact anymore, so I'd chucked the piece of shit against a wall and gone to the bar.

Five drinks in, and I could start to feel the pain that had been pounding in my chest start to dissipate.

Everything I'd worked for, everything I'd put forward to my career all gone in the matter of seconds because I'd trusted the wrong person, because I'd put my career in someone else's hands.

I had nothing left to live for.

"You see that asshole who thought he could take steroids and get away with it?" a loudmouthed man said, sitting at the bar and talking to anyone who would listen to him. "I don't get it. When are athletes going to realize they can't get away with doing drugs? You would think they would have learned by now."

Grinding my teeth to keep myself from lashing out, I attempted to tune out the man. He was right about athletes taking supplements to enhance their performance, but there were people like me who did everything right and still got fucked in the end.

I downed the rest of my glass, sat it at the end of the bar, and motioned for another. The bartender knew to keep them coming. I wasn't going anywhere soon.

While I waited on my drink, I tugged on the brim of the hood that hid my features from the public. I didn't need anyone recognizing me. I also enjoyed the blinders the hood gave me, like a damn mule in the Quarter, blocked from seeing anything around me, just the mission ahead, and my mission was to continuously bring the glass in front of me to my lips until I couldn't feel anymore. I was almost there.

"Do you really think that's going to help?" someone said behind me.

Jett. Without turning around, I said, "It's been your go-to. Thought I would give it a try."

Jett took the seat next to me without an invitation. He motioned to the bartender to bring him what I was drinking and positioned himself on his stool. He was going to be sorry to see I wasn't drinking his precious bourbon.

"Do you want to talk about it?" he asked, resting his arms on the bar.

"Does it look like I want to fucking talk about it?" I asked, trying to control the anger that wanted to seep out of me.

"For what it's worth, I know you couldn't do anything like that. There has to be an explanation."

There was an explanation, but no one other than Jett Colby was going to believe me. "It doesn't matter," I answered while lowering my head. "It's all over."

Silence fell between us, and we both casually sipped our drinks, not engaging in conversation or any kind of emotional bullshit. That wasn't how we rolled. We sat and we drank. It was the one thing I could count on when it came to my best friend.

Thankfully the bar I chose didn't have any TVs in it. I knew what would be running on them right now.

"Kace Haywood: Positive for Human Growth Hormones."

"Pumping Juice to Get Ahead, the Real Kace Haywood."

"Haywood Hung on Hormones."

Shaking my head, I pressed the glass tightly to my lips and sucked in its contents. I'd never felt so helpless before in my entire life. For once, I wasn't in charge of my destiny. I wasn't able to control my own future. The only control I possessed was how many times I brought a tumbler of pain-lessening liquid to my mouth.

"Want another?" Jett asked as I tossed back the rest of my drink.

"Yup," I responded, directing the glass away from me and pushing myself up, trying to stretch out my back from the tension that was taking over.

I rolled my sleeves up to my elbows and adjusted my hood so it was more secure. The heat of the alcohol started to consume my body, but I wasn't about to take off my sweatshirt. It was the only barrier I had from the real world.

"Can you believe this?" the rowdy guy from earlier said as he held his phone out to Jett. "Did you see this article? Local hero goes and fucks everything up because he's too lazy to put in the real work to be the best."

Jett nodded politely, because that was the way he'd been raised, and then turned away from the man. I sank farther into the corner, trying to separate myself from the loudmouth, trying to drown out his words.

"Fuck, I can take steroids and beat the shit out of people too. What makes a great boxer is talent. Muhammad Ali didn't sit there injecting himself with growth hormones so he could win title after title. No, he spent hours upon hours in the gym, working on his craft."

"Do you mind if we just sit here by ourselves?" Jett asked politely, holding his hand up to stop the man.

From the corner of my eye, I saw the man back off for a second and then nod at me. "Who's that? Your boyfriend? If you fairies want some private time, go to a gay bar."

Raising his voice and projecting his temper, Jett said, "I suggest you learn some decorum and shut your fucking mouth."

"Oh, I get it, you motherfuckers really want some time together. That's fine. Hey, buddy," the guy called to me, but I didn't move, not wanting to engage. "Hey, I'm talking to you," the moron repeated.

"I suggest you drop it," Jett warned.

Getting out of his chair, the man shot back, "You don't fucking tell me what to do." From my view, I could see that he was a broad man, slightly built, still had some fat on his bones, but he was one who could hold his own, and that was why he most likely felt confident enough to confront both of us.

The man brushed past Jett and pushed my shoulder. "Hey, dickhead. I'm talking to you."

Not turning to face the man, I said over my shoulder, "I suggest you leave me the fuck alone."

The bar was empty of witnesses besides the bartender, so the room was silent except for the faint sound of jazz spilling through the speakers. The bartender stood to the side, taking in the whole scene, probably wondering if he was going to have to intervene at some point.

"Oh, you think you're a tough guy? You can't even face me? You're just hiding behind your stupid hood and cowering...."

Rage boiled inside me, and I flipped around, dropped my hood, and stood to my full height.

Immediate shock ran through his eyes as he recognized me. From the look in his eyes, fear passed through him for a brief second before he started laughing, full-on clutching-his-stomach laughing.

"Oh fuck, just my luck. The local hero right in front of me. Did you shoot up before you came here?" he asked, still hunched over and laughing.

"It would be in your best interests if you dropped everything and left this bar," I threatened between clenched teeth.

"And what the fuck are you going to do if I don't?" the man said, standing tall now and puffing his chest out.

I was drunk, I would admit that, but I still knew my left hook from my right uppercut, and the jackass was two seconds away from meeting both of them.

"You're a worthless piece of shit that gives this city a bad name," he said, pushing my shoulder again, making me wobble back into the bar.

The seven or so drinks I had consumed were now testing my balance, but I could still see the man clearly. He had jackass written over his forehead, and soon my fist would be replacing it.

Jett must have seen the way my hands itched at my side because he stood and urged a hand against the man to give us some distance.

"Step down," Jett warned.

"Aw, your boyfriend is coming to your rescue. You know—" the man pressed a finger to his chin "—you actually did the sport a favor by juicing up. Now we don't have to watch a gay fuck like yourself prance around the ring, itching to grab some opponent's balls."

"Watch your fucking mouth," Jett spat, getting angry and in the man's face. Jett didn't take kindly to discrimination and neither did I, for that matter, especially since Jett's assistant was gay and probably one of the most thoughtful and admirable people we knew. The dude would do anything for Jett or me, and we would do the same.

Not wanting Jett to get involved, since he had a reputation to uphold, I stepped in front of him and said, "Get out of here, Jett."

"Kace, do not do something stupid," he warned.

"I'm not going to—" My words were cut off by the blow the man's fist made to my jaw. My head flew back as blood flung from my mouth, splattering on the wall behind me. I fell back onto my stool, my head resting against the wall. It took me a second to register what had just happened, but once I was able to collect my thoughts, the pain in my jaw struck me like a fucking high. I actually enjoyed it.

Jett was seconds from plowing into the man, but I stopped him, shaking my head in response to the impact of the man's punch.

"Fucking fairy, you need those steroids. You're a fucking lightweight."

Jett's fist raised, but I stopped him once again. I knew

Jett could easily take down this guy because I'd taught him everything he knew. Jett wasn't one to mess with, but this was my problem.

"I got this," I said. Jett nodded and stepped away. He knew when I needed to take care of my own business.

I took off my jacket and handed it to Jett. My biceps flexed under the confines of my tight white shirt, and my forearms revved up, ready to do some damage. The same feeling that took me over in the ring took over my body now as adrenaline started to flow through my veins, replacing the alcohol I'd spent the last few hours consuming.

Pure fear flashed through the man's eyes as he observed my stance.

That's right, fuckhead. Don't mess with me.

"Go ahead, take another shot." I egged him on while spitting a mouthful of blood to the side. "I fucking dare you to engage me. You want to know what talent is? I will fucking hand it to you on a silver platter. Go ahead, fucking test me one more time."

"You're not worth it," the man said, waving his hand at me and taking a step back.

"Yeah, who's a fucking pussy now? You're all talk and cheap shots, but when it comes down to it, you know I can fucking destroy you. I made a living dicking people around with my fists. I would be more than happy to show you how it's done."

"What living? You have nothing now because you're the moron who decided to take steroids."

Grinding my teeth, I counted to ten before I exploded. There was no point in defending myself against the steroid allegations. I would just look like a whiney-ass bitch, so I kept my mouth shut and tried to keep my fist from plowing through his face.

He's not worth it, he's not worth it, I kept saying to myself over and over again.

I opened my eyes in time to see his fist fly at me and connect with my gut. I buckled over and coughed up more blood from the first blow he'd made to my face.

Laughter from the idiot filled the small bar. I looked up to see the man holding his stomach and pointing at me.

"Ah fuck, this is the best night of my life. Boxer? Fuck, you're nothing but a piece of trailer trash trying to imitate someone you will never be."

Trailer trash... my fucking hot-button word. I snapped.

Straightening, I quickly stepped forward, cocked my arm back, and blew it through the man's stomach. Not even giving him a chance to think, I threw a right uppercut, sending his head reeling upward, and then to finish him off, in rapid succession I connected my left fist to his temple and then did the same with my right.

It happened in a matter of seconds, white-hot rage flowing through me. For the first time since I'd gotten the call from my agent, I actually felt a little at ease. That was until I saw the man fall backward from my attack and land on the floor, motionless.

Oh fuck.

Time stood still as I waited for the dickhead to move, sit up, and shake his head from the brief knockout. I stood above him, practically begging him to move, but he didn't. Not one twitch, not one breath from his chest.

"Kace, Kace, we have got to fucking move," Jett said, but all I could do was stare down at the lifeless man in front of me, the provoker, the antagonizer.

"The bartender called the fucking cops. We have to

move."

Nothing. I was completely void.

Everything around me faded but the man lying on the floor. "Is he...." I started to ask, but I couldn't even say the words. Just thinking them had my stomach rolling.

"Kace, fucking move!" Jett shouted as he grabbed my arm and pulled me toward the back door.

The bartender blocked our escape. "I can't let you leave," the man said. "And even if you do leave, I will tell them it was Kace Haywood."

Frustrated, Jett pulled out his wallet and grabbed a wad of hundreds from his billfold and shoved it at the man. "This is to keep your mouth shut until the morning. I will be back with more. The man who did this took off toward Royal Street. If you help us, I will help you. If you open your mouth, I will destroy you. Don't forget who owns half this city."

Jett knew when to pull his elite card, and right now, he used it well.

The bartender looked at the cash in his hands, then back at Jett, and nodded. "The man took off toward Royal Street."

"And what did he look like?" Jett asked.

"Blonde, brown eyes I think, six foot with a beard. He was wearing a green shirt." The bartender described the complete opposite of my brown hair, blue eyes, and scruffy jaw.

"Very good," Jett said, patting the bartender on the arm. "I will meet you tomorrow at seven in the morning in front of the steamboat. Don't be late."

He stepped aside as sirens sounded in the small streets of the Quarter.

Jett grabbed my arm and dragged me through the back door where a car was waiting for us. He shoved me in the backseat and climbed in behind me.

Once again, Jett had my back. In the midst of staring at the blood on my hands, Jett constructed a cover-up and getaway.

"Go," Jett said to the driver, who took off immediately, navigating through the one-way streets toward the Garden District where Jett lived.

My mind was numb. I looked down at my fists and realized the impact they really had, the brutal force they possessed.

"He provoked you," Jett said, trying to ease the tension in the car.

"He's dead," I said, looking out the window, saying the words for the first time as realization set in.

"You don't know that. You probably knocked out the fucker. It was well deserved."

It wasn't. No one deserved to be knocked to the floor like that, no matter what kind of dick they were.

"You have to forget about it," Jett said, but I could tell from the way his voice wavered, he was just as concerned as I was.

What if he really did die? A small part of me prayed I was wrong, prayed Jett was right, prayed I hadn't just taken a man's life.

The following morning, I turned on the TV to find a local news station reporting about the bar fight. They'd interviewed the bartender, and he told the story Jett coached had him on without even a slight twitch in his eye. Jett had paid the man off that morning, enough so he wouldn't have to work anymore.

As for the man who'd provoked me, he died from the impact of my fists to his head. There was no chance to save him. I'd killed him. I'd let rage take over, and I'd killed him with my hands.

The worst part was finding out he'd had a family; he was a father of one.

I thought I knew my weaknesses until I realized the trauma a little girl would go through growing up without her father.

CHAPTER NINE

My present...

I stood in front of the community center, taking it all in. The building stood for justice. Justice for those who were wrongfully affected by other's decisions. It was a sanctuary to those seeking second chances in life, new opportunities.

I tried to have a positive outlook on my new job.

Standing outside the majestic building, I felt a twinge of excitement but also nerves, because who was I to help people when I couldn't help myself?

The landscaping still needed to be installed and the sidewalks were missing their cement, but the modern take on the French Quarter wrought iron decorated the façade of the building, making up for what was incomplete on the exterior.

I took a deep breath as I thought about what this building could bring me. This was a fresh start for me. No longer was I under Jett's watchful eye. Enough time had passed where I could walk around the streets of my city and not be sneered at or looked down upon, but I still felt slightly apprehensive.

I wished there was someone in my life I could share this

moment with, someone I could talk to about how I was feeling, someone to be proud of me, but my family was out of my life, and Lyla... fuck.

It'd been a week since I'd taken her up against the wall at the club. Every last inch of me was itching to be inside her, and even though my brain was screaming at me to let her go, to not take advantage of her willing body once again, I couldn't help myself. I was a selfish bastard, I took what I wanted and then left her confused.

That night, she was taunting me, she was testing my limits, and after a few minutes of her rubbing her sweet ass on my lap, I was by no means able to reign in the carnal need that was rushing through my body.

I fucked her...hard and then left. Something I told myself I wouldn't do because she deserved more than that, she deserved the sweet connection every woman deserved. She was a woman who needed someone to caress her, worship her...love her. I wasn't that kind of man. I could never hand over what she needed, not after everything I'd done.

Shaking the negative thoughts out of my head, not wanting them to taint the moment in front of me, I relished in the positive energy coming from the community center. This was my new chapter; this was my chance to give back more than I should have been allowed.

I needed to feel good about myself. I needed to have this change, something to live for, because without it, I didn't know where my life would take me. It was a dark fucking path that tempted me every day. I woke up in the morning and chose to live, chose to move on and continue to suffer with the demons that hung over my head, but fuck if I wasn't tempted to end it all.

I fucking needed this.

"Looks great, doesn't it?" George, Jett's lawyer, asked from behind me.

I turned to see a kind-faced man giving me a gentle smile while he gestured a two-fingered salute. "Kace, good to see you."

"You too, George," I replied. I held out my hand for George. He shook it with a strong grasp and then looked at the center, hope reflecting in his eyes.

"I had my doubts about Justice ever coming to fruition, but damn if it doesn't feel good to see it erected."

I cringed and shook my head in laughter. "Come on, George, don't say erected."

Laughing, he pointed at me and said, "Before you young kids turned that word into something filthy, we used to talk about buildings being erected all over the place. It's not my fault you all have dirty minds."

"We're not in the 1920s anymore, George. It's time to start living in the present day."

"Is that why you have a smile on your face today? You're finally living in the present?"

Caught off-guard for a second, I lowered my head and gave him a quick nod. George didn't know the details of my past, but given the news of the man dying in the bar spreading, the giant deposit Jett had made to an off-shore bank account, and the cover-up George had had to do, I could imagine George connecting the dots. He wasn't dumb.

"Something like that," I said, turning around and facing the center once again.

For some reason, looking at the structure brought me peace, made me forget about the past temporarily, and gave me hope for a new future.

"Do you have the keys?" I asked, holding my hand out to

George.

"I do."

A jingling came from his pocket and he handed them over. The moment the cold metal pressed into my palm, I knew I was going to make the best of the opportunity I'd been given. I was going to try to be the man my parents would have wanted me to be.

I walked toward the building with a renewed sense of life.

The large wooden doors of the community center loomed over me as I worked the keys to find the correct one. We were going to have an electronic security system installed, but that wouldn't be happening for a little bit since Jett couldn't make a decision on the one he wanted. The man was more than distracted these days, and it wasn't from the amount of work on his plate. No, it was because of the gorgeous woman attached to his hip. Couldn't blame him. I would be distracted too.

With the kind of a squeak only a brand new door could offer, it opened and I was instantly hit by new paint smell wafting off the walls. I was pleased to see the walls had been painted a deep purple, the symbol for justice in New Orleans. Even though the walls were dark, skylights and windows brought in enough light to make the space bright and cheery.

In the center was an admin desk where members would check in, and there was a rather expansive wall next to the desk that was covered in corkboard. It was going to be the "To Do" wall where members could see what was happening during the week. I looked right, where classrooms flanked the hallway, offering space for group exercises, educational opportunities, and a daycare. I knew what the rooms looked like already; there were enough to have different classes going on at the same time. Some had desks, some had mirrors and exercise equipment. They were well-built rooms, but they weren't the rooms I was looking forward to seeing the most. It was the room to the left I was itching to explore.

"Take your time, George, and look around. I'm going to head this way. Thanks for bringing the keys."

"Not a problem, Kace," George replied, leaving it at that.

Excitement prickled the back of my neck as I strolled along the left hallway. Pictures of athletes from the past were framed on the walls in black and white. Those athletes were heroes, people to look up to, role models kids should be following, not someone like me.

Apprehension hit me head-on as I thought about what I was getting myself into. These kids were going to look up to me. They were going to look to me for answers to help them with their troubles, to be their mentor and to be honest. I didn't think I was ready for that, nor did I know if I ever would be. I was a destroyed and dishonest man, not mentor material.

I stopped short of the room I'd been eagerly waiting to take a look at. This was supposed to be a fresh start for me, but for some damn reason, I couldn't get over the fact that I wasn't good enough to do this. I shouldn't have been granted this opportunity to influence such young lives. What did I really have to give them?

Slowly, I started to step backward. This wasn't for me. What the hell had I been thinking? Did I really believe I could make a change in someone's life if I couldn't make one in my own?

I was about to turn around when I ran into someone behind me.

"*Oof*," a male voice rang out. "Watch where you're going."

I should have known Jett would be here today, waiting patiently for me to find my room.

"Where do you think you're going there, butch?" Jett

asked, hands on his hips.

"Don't fucking call me that." A smile attempted to split my lips.

"Don't avoid the question."

Shaking my head, I said, "This isn't for me."

"Bullshit," Jett answered. "Don't start this crap again. You're making a change, you're taking over this center, and you're going to help the community."

"Do you really think I'm the perfect citizen to run this place? Kids are going to look up to me. They're going to compare me to all these other athletes on the walls. What does it say about your community center if you allow some steroid-raging ex-boxer to teach kids how to improve their lives?"

"Because you're the prime example that second chances happen. Do you realize the kids who will be coming here will be looking for an escape? They'll need someone like you to show them life isn't fucking perfect, it isn't easy, but with perseverance, they can make something of themselves."

I fell against the wall and slid to the ground, gripping the ends of my hair with my fingers. "The only problem with that, Jett, is I haven't made something of myself. I've sat around, dictating to the girls what to do at the Lafayette Club, but what have I really done?"

"You work your ass off to give money to—"

"Don't." I glared at him. "Do not fucking talk about that and make it sound like it's something of value. That is my job, my responsibility. That is not making something of myself."

I didn't choose to give money to the family I'd ruined. It was a duty, to make sure they were taken care of.

Frustration poured out of Jett. He wasn't very good at hiding it, especially around me. I knew it wasn't easy for him to understand the way I felt, and I knew he wanted me to move on, but he couldn't control everything like he wanted to.

"When are you going to stop wallowing in self-pity?"

"Self-pity?" I roared as I stood up and got right in his face. "You think this is self-pity?"

"What else is it? A better man would try to make a positive change rather than mope around like a damn fool, feeling sorry for himself."

I knew he was egging me on, trying to push my buttons, but I couldn't help but let it affect me. He knew how to get in my head, and he was doing it on purpose right now.

"I don't feel sorry for myself," I gritted out, my hands clenching at my sides. "I know what I did. I destroyed—"

"Hey, guys." Goldie bounced down the hall with a huge smile on her face, her hair piled on top of her head and a green sundress gracing her petite body. "Whoa, looks like you two are discussing something serious." Not getting a clue, she cuddled up next to us and rubbed her hands together. "What are we talking about?"

"We are not talking about anything," I responded, turning away.

"Jeez, is he having man cramps again? I have some tampons in my purse if you need one," Goldie said, making Jett snort. "Kace, this is a fantastic day. Can't you try to be happy?"

"Yeah, whatever," I said with my hands on my hips.

"That was convincing," Goldie sarcastically said to Jett. "He won't be getting a movie deal anytime soon for his acting skills but then again, he does have the body for stardom. Hmm, I mean a few acting lessons could make some improvement, but does he have the dedication to make it work? Is he too committed to making his body perfect? Would he be willing to spend time on his craft? If he took a few classes, I would be willing to represent him. What do you think?" she asked Jett, wrapping an arm around his waist.

"I think you would be a great agent for Kace," Jett replied, kissing the tip of her nose. Ever since they started dating, Jett supported every little random thought Goldie had.

"Me too," she squealed. "Then it's settled, Kace. I am now representing you."

Rolling my eyes at a classic Goldie ramble of nonsense, I said, "I'll pass, but thanks for the consideration."

"You're passing up a pretty fantastic opportunity. You might want to rethink it."

"I'm good."

"Fine, but I was only going to take thirty percent."

"Nice," Jett said, smiling down at her. "Look at my little one, being a businesswoman."

"Thirty percent is outrageous." I gave in to her stupid way of cheering me up. Fuck, I hated that she had an effect on me.

"I'm worth it."

I looked her up and down. "Unless you would be delivering me scripts naked, thirty percent isn't worth it."

"Watch it," Jett warned, making me laugh from his jealousies. I had just been in a bad mood. Damn them.

"I can do naked for thirty percent." Goldie held out her hand to shake on it.

Quickly grabbing her arm and shoving it back down to her side, Jett said, "The fuck you will. I swear I can't let you out of the house."

"Is that a threat to tie me up?" Her eyes lit up.

"Don't tempt me, little one."

Leaning past Jett so she was looking me in the eyes, she said, "I will do naked for twenty."

"You're done," Jett responded.

With one big swoop, Jett wrapped his arms around Goldie

and turned to me. He pointed to the room on the right at the very back. "That is your new sanctuary. Learn to deal with it. You deserve this, and you owe it to yourself to at least give it a shot."

Jett took a squealing Goldie down the hall and into the other corridor of the community center, leaving me to my thoughts. Sometimes I wanted to punch the cocky motherfucker for his "saving" ways. His attitude to those in need of second chances was commendable, but I didn't want to be one of the people he saved. I didn't believe I deserved it.

I turned toward the room in back and observed the black door that had a small window just big enough so someone could peek in to see if the room was occupied. Since the doors were new, there was paper still on the window, covering up my view of the inside.

Next to the room was a plaque that displayed the name of the space. As I drew closer, a knot in my throat started to grow tight from what was written in raised metal. I ran my fingers across the plaque as I read what it said.

"The Haze Room," I read out loud, lowering my head.

I was instantly pitched back to the day I'd earned the nickname Kace "The Haze" Haywood. It had been my first ever fight. I was still an amateur, but I was someone to be watched on the circuit, someone to look out for. I'd been so fucking young and full of life and goals.

My opponent had been young too, not as well trained or as talented as me, and with one swift punch to the jaw, he was down. Total knockout. That evening, the announcer said I'd cast a haze over the arena, putting out a warning to all future opponents I wasn't one to be messed with. I was going to take the sport of boxing to a new level.

Anger set in and I itched to rip the plaque off. I didn't want the reminder of who I used to be. That man was dead.

I grabbed the edge of the plaque and tugged on it but knew there was no hope in pulling it down. Knowing Jett, he'd told the construction workers to embed the damn thing so I wouldn't be able to remove it. Little did Jett know, I wasn't opposed to tearing down walls.

Standing in front of the door, I played with the idea of walking in, of seeing what was inside, but the hammering of my heart prevented me from entering. The moment I walked inside that room, the memories were going to come flooding back, and I wasn't sure if I was ready for that.

Fuck!

I dropped to the floor and ran my hands through my hair. I was distraught, confused, conflicted.

I wanted this new change. Standing outside the building, I had told myself this was a good change, this was a fresh start. So how come it was so hard to accept?

The guilt I'd lived with for the past several years had weighed down on me in a way that was hard to explain, to the point that living my everyday life had become almost unbearable.

Growing up, my parents had told me my actions had consequences and that night, the night I'd taken a man's life, I'd found out how right my parents had been.

Pain erupted in my chest from knowing how much I'd let my family down, how much I'd let my friends down, how much I'd let myself down, all because I'd trusted the wrong person.

No, I couldn't blame someone else for my bad decisions. I decided what I put in my body. I should have done the research. I should have known better.

I was a sorry motherfucker with no future.

Pressing a hand against my chest, I wondered when the

pain was going to stop, when I was going to finally just live a numb life without feelings, without the possibility of being happy.

That was what was killing me the most. I flirted with chances to be happy. Small opportunities gave me a peek into what my life could possibly be like if I gave into the temptation, and it was torture because every time I thought I could live a different life, it was snatched away from me.

I looked at the door and thought this could be one of those moments where I had the chance to find some peace within myself, but I was too fucking nervous to go after it, to accept it, because like everything else in my life, it could be taken away from me, right from under my feet. It had happened with my boxing career, it had happened with my future, it had happened the moment I met Lyla. It was the reason I couldn't get close to her. I couldn't chance it.

This could be different, right?

Standing up, I played with the knob. This all could be different. Who would take this away from me? Jett couldn't; he was the one who gave me this opportunity. What about my reputation? Would that tarnish the center? Would people not want to come inside because they wouldn't want to associate with me?

Jett's voice rang through my head about how this center was for those who needed second chances, those who wanted to be free and learn. Maybe I could possibly show others that second chances were possible even though deep down, I didn't believe in them.

Nutting up, I took a deep breath and entered the Haze Room.

The smell of fresh wrestling mats and leather hit me dead-on as I pushed the door fully open. I wiped my mouth in shock and took in my surroundings.

In the center of a room was a state-of-the-art boxing ring with black and purple ropes circling the mini square. To the right, an exposed brick wall flanked the side with punching bags dangling from the ceiling. I counted at least five from where I stood. Next to the hanging bags were speed bags, and off to the side there were two body bags and two double end bags. There were brand new boxing gloves piled in the corner, and on the wall opposite the bags was a variety of TRX bands, weights, jump ropes, medicine balls, and even a trampoline.

The room was state of the art, and I itched to take advantage of the training facility. Combinations of punches ran through my mind as I stepped up to the punching bags and gave them a light push.

Fuck, this place was amazing.

I walked along the ring and glided my hands over the ropes, testing their strength. The smooth texture brought back distant memories of leaning up against the ropes while trying to catch my breath during a brutal practice. When I was in the ring, it felt like I was home. I busted my ass whenever I set foot on the canvas because I respected sacred ground. That was what I'd been taught. That was what was ingrained in my brain.

Behind the ring were mini bleachers that could probably hold ten people. It was a small viewing section, but it was strategically placed so viewers could watch all the hardworking aspiring athletes in the room.

I shook my head in disbelief that Jett had put this together with me in mind, knowing full well once I saw this room, there was no way in hell I would be able to say no to his offer. The fucker had known what he was doing all along.

Needing to sit down, I sat on the top bleacher and surveyed the room. Visions of kids training, learning self-defense and discipline, flooded the space. I could smell the sweat, I could hear the smack of gloves on the punching bags, and I could see the comradery that would form among them.

Like a tidal wave, ideas for classes flooded my brain as I assessed the equipment. Excitement started to boil in the pit of my stomach, and I tried to tamp it down, but looking around this room, taking everything in, it was damn hard not to get passionate.

Maybe Jett was right. Maybe I could show everyone second chances were possible. Maybe I could have a positive influence on the kids who walked through the doors of this facility. I could only hope my demons didn't eat me alive while I tried to find a new place in this world.

CHAPTER TEN

My past...

Rain pounded on my windshield while I tried to decipher who was in the row of black standing about one hundred feet away. I wasn't ready to step out of my car yet. I wasn't ready to see who I'd ruined.

I hadn't been able to sleep the past four nights, not since blinding rage had taken over my body and I'd found myself leaning over a bloody and breathless Marshall Duncan. The image of his lifeless body had yet to escape my memory. There were many times I'd decided to turn myself in, but Jett had stopped me. His need to keep me in his life, to help him with his club and be the one solid person in his life, had me reneging on my idea, but fuck if the decision didn't make me feel guilty as hell.

I had yet to face the family, to see what they looked like, who they were, to see the grief-stricken looks on their faces. Seeing them was the last thing I wanted to do, but I felt like it was a punishment I deserved. I had to see whose life I'd destroyed by taking a loved one away from them. I needed to see their pain, feel their pain. I wanted to be tortured.

The day after the bar fight, I'd started collecting every article about Marshall's death and read them to myself on repeat at night as I burned the words into my memory. To someone on the outside, my collection of articles might have seemed like a psychopathic action, but to me, it was the act of a broken man. I made sure to remind myself every chance I got what a horrible person I was. I wanted to make sure it was quite clear in my brain I was a murderer, a machine who didn't think but reacted on emotion. I thought losing my boxing license had been difficult, but I hadn't known what difficult was because right here and now, sitting in my car and watching over the crowd dressed in black surrounding one single person was the hardest fucking thing I'd ever done.

The rain let up slightly, making it easier to see out my front windshield. Above-ground gravestones scattered the land in front of me and surrounded the group of friends and family who'd shown up to bid their soulful farewells to Marshall Duncan.

"Are you going out there?" Jett interrupted my thoughts.

"Yes," I replied, my voice completely devoid of emotion.

"You don't have to do this."

"I do. I need to see them."

"Why?" Jett asked, frustration lacing his voice. "You can barely hold yourself together right now. Why do you think this is going to make it better?"

"I don't think it's going to make it better. It's going to show me everything I took away. I need to see his family, see how I affected their lives. I can't be a selfish bastard who hides in your club. I need to know exactly what the ramifications were that came from my decision."

"He is just as much to blame for what happened as you

are," Jett replied.

"No. Don't go fucking blaming him."

"Kace, he punched you twice. He was asking for a right hook. You can't take the blame for all this."

"Yes I can," I practically spat back at him. "I'm a trained fighter. I know my limits. I know how to handle the adrenaline surge that runs through me when I'm provoked, and that night, I chose to ignore it. I should have walked away. I should have turned my back, but instead I chose to engage. I chose to let my anger loose on a man who was in the wrong place at the wrong time."

"How can you say that?" Jett argued. "He went out of his way to approach you, to aggravate you, to make it impossible for you not to get upset. It's his fucking fault!"

"Enough!" I shouted. "I'm not going to go through this with you again. If you want me to stick around, you need to just accept the fact that when Marshall Duncan died, I died with him. I will be here for you, Jett, and I will help you with your club, but I refuse to hide behind excuses to make myself feel better. I killed a man. I ran away from his dead body, and I'm living a life I don't deserve. From this day moving forward, I have no life. I don't deserve to be happy, and I will go out of my way to make sure I keep it that way."

Without allowing Jett to utter another word, I got out of the car, pulled the hood of my black leather jacket over my head, and headed toward the huddled mourners.

A priest was speaking solemnly when I walked up to the group, sticking to the back so I wasn't noticed. I didn't want any trouble. I just wanted the soul-crushing punishment of looking in the eyes of the woman I had ruined.

"Marshall was a well-respected businessman, a beloved husband, and a cherished father. He left us too early in this world, but we will cherish the moments we had with him and hold them in our hearts for eternity."

My gut twisted from the priest's words.

Cherished father... fuck.

I looked at the wet grass, watching the drops of rain fall off my nose and onto the ground. How did a man move on from something like this? How did he face life every day, knowing he'd taken the breath away from another man? Was such a feat even possible?

"The family will now place a rose on the casket while Marshall's sister plays 'Remember Me' on the guitar."

The light strum of a guitar filled the air, overlaying from the sad sound of rain pelting the wood of the casket. I stepped to the side for a better view and trained my eyes on the casket, waiting to see Marshall's family.

A hand gripped my shoulder, and I didn't have to turn to know it was Jett. He might not have agreed with what I was doing or approved my choices concerning this matter, but I knew he supported me. He always would.

"Kace...."

I shook my head and pulled away slightly. He wanted me to leave, but I couldn't. I needed to see his family.

Just as Jett tried to pull at my shoulder again, I tugged free and saw someone I could only assume was Marshall's wife step up to the casket, holding a single rose in her hand. She was holding the hand of a little girl with bright blonde curls poking out from her hood.

Everything in my body went numb as realization hit me. She would grow up without a father. She wouldn't have someone to take to the daddy/daughter dances. She wouldn't have a man to watch over her when she started dating. She wouldn't have someone to walk her down the aisle on her wedding day.

I'd taken that away from her. I'd taken away her father.

The wife turned toward me after she placed the flower on the casket and held on to her daughter. For a brief instant, her eyes met mine, and I was able to see the hole in her heart I'd put there. I was able to see the pain I'd caused, the uprooting I'd forced upon her.

It was too much.

My heart beat out of my chest and my breathing became erratic. Without turning to Jett, I said, "Get me out of here."

His strong hand took hold of my shoulder, and he guided me back to the car, not saying a word. There was nothing to say. I was an animal.

I would never forgive myself.

CHAPTER ELEVEN

My present...

"Where do you want these thongs?" Tootse called, drawing me from my thoughts. I looked up at the blondest women I'd ever met, carrying an abnormally large box and about ready to tip over from its size.

I rushed over to help and grabbed the box from her so she didn't end up face-first into the wall.

"Thanks." She shook her arms out. "Thongs are heavy." She huffed and held on to the wall.

I set the box on the floor in front of the counter at the community center just as the contents of the box registered in my head. "Thongs?"

"Tootse, make sure Kace doesn't see the box...." Goldie stopped in her tracks when she saw me standing over Tootse with my hands on my hips. "Oh shit...."

"Yeah, 'oh shit' is right," I said. "Care to explain why there is a box of—" I bent over and looked at the number of thongs on the shipping label and then glanced at Goldie. "Why is there a box of a one thousand silk thongs being delivered to the community center?"

Goldie stepped up to me and pushed her pen against my forehead. "Before that little vein pops, stop worrying. They are just parting gifts."

"Parting gifts for what?" I questioned.

"Nothing you need to concern yourself with," Goldie said while trying to grab the box off the ground. She struggled from the weird size of it. Jett called her 'little one' for a reason.

Instead of helping her, I stood back and watched her struggle. She tried holding the box in different positions. She even pushed it with her toe to scoot it along the floor, but in the end, she just gave up.

With a huff, she looked up at me and said, "Do you mind helping?"

"I do, actually."

She stomped her foot on the ground. "Kace! Don't be an ass and help me."

"What are the thongs for?" I said between clenched teeth. "I'm in charge of the center, so I am privy to whatever information I want to know. Now tell me why you have one thousand thongs in a box in the community center."

"You're so frustrating," she whined.

"Well...?" I waited.

She gave in, like I knew she would. "Fine. We're going to offer pole-dancing classes, and we thought a little gift bag for the attendees would be nice."

"No," I said, going back to the front desk and checking on my paperwork. The center opened in a few days. It was a soft opening but an opening nonetheless, and I wanted to be prepared. We would only be offering a few classes to start, but once everything was complete, we would be expanding our schedule.

"No?" Goldie said, coming up next to the counter. "How

can you just say no?"

I glanced up at her. "Because I can."

"Ahh! I want to strangle you," she complained. "Did you know pole dancing is actually a really good form of exercise?"

"Goldie, we are not going—"

"She's right, you know," Lyla said, interrupting me as she sidled up next to Goldie and put her arm around Goldie's waist. "I already have a full list of names of people who want to participate in Friday's class." With obnoxious confidence, Lyla tossed a clipboard full of names on the counter and looked at me with quirked lips.

"See!" Goldie cheered. "A full class! It's popular already, and we haven't even started."

Of course in a city like New Orleans, spots in a pole dancing class would fill. That didn't mean I wanted to have a class like that at the center. Justice was supposed to have a wholesome, family-type environment, not a night club atmosphere, which was what I was getting from the girls with their box of thongs.

With my hands on my hips, I looked at Goldie. "All right, smart-ass, how do you expect to teach a pole dancing class without poles?"

She looked away for a second and then said, "We have poles."

"What are you talking about?"

Biting her finger, she stepped back from the counter. "I had Jett put them in for me."

"What!" I roared. "Why the fuck would he do that when I'm in charge of this place?"

Goldie cringed and stepped back again, Lyla enjoying the interaction between us the whole time. "Maybe because I told him you approved it."

"Fucking hell," I breathed out as I scrubbed a hand over my

face. Gathering all my will not to fly off the deep end, I pointed at her and said, "Go behind my back again, and you will not fucking like the results."

"I'm sorry, Kace," she apologized.

I took off to the boxing room. I could tell she wasn't that sorry, because as I retreated, I heard her cheer with Lyla and Tootse about the new class Justice would be offering.

Even though I hated it, I smiled and shook my head. Leave it to Goldie to get her way.

Once in the Haze Room, I took in the rich smell of fresh leather and brand new wood floors. It had taken me a couple of days, but I'd finally accepted the gesture from Jett, the gesture to reconnect with something that had been so unfairly taken away from me. It felt odd to be surrounded by something I loved so much once again, but I started to take advantage of the new room. I couldn't help it. It was my new play yard.

I walked over to the stereo that was situated against one of the walls and hit the play button. Classic rock blasted through the speakers, putting me in the mood to do some damage. I stripped off my shirt, grabbed a jump rope, and bounced up and down to warm up. I started at a slow pace, letting my heart gradually warm to the rhythm running through me, but once I felt comfortable, I whipped the rope faster, enjoying the challenge of keeping up with the intense pace. It only took a few minutes for sweat to form on my brow and drip down my back.

Pleased with my warm-up, I quickly wrapped my hands, grabbed a pair of gloves, and secured them around my hands and wrists. It was time to attack the bag.

Freddy Mercury's voice boomed through the speakers as I circled the bag. Finding the right position, I threw right hooks and left uppercuts. Alternating punches, I rapidly took all my pent-up aggression out on the bag, focusing on one thing and one thing alone: the feel of my fist connecting with the sand-filled bag.

The impact was hard, it was intoxicating, and it was exactly what I needed.

The nightmares were getting worse, they were haunting me every night, and I wasn't sure if it was because of this new venture I was embarking on or the fact that I boxed on a daily basis now so I was releasing the demons I'd stowed away for so long, but whatever it was, I was reliving my worst sins at night. I woke up every morning, sweating and feeling ill with beads of sweat at my brow. It took me at least one boxing session and the morning to get over the raw and unsettling feeling I woke up to now on an almost daily basis.

Right hook, right hook, right hook.

I gripped the bag with my left arm and kneed it while throwing punches at it with my right hand. The pain gripping my chest eased with my full-on attack, and I could feel the weight resting on my shoulders start to fade.

"Take it easy there," someone shouted over the music, stilling my workout.

Lyla turned down the music so it wasn't blasting through the walls. When she first arrived, I didn't get a good look at her since it had been my mission to avoid the woman, but now that I was alone in the Haze room with her, I had no other option than to soak in her appearance. Her hair was curled loosely over her shoulders. She was wearing a cream-colored tank top that was very flowy—flowy enough I could see the turquoise bra she had on underneath, which was propping her breasts up to mouthwatering standards. And to top it all off, she was in a pair of short shorts with pockets that hung a little past the hem. I wouldn't expect anything less from Lyla than to find the shortest pair of shorts in the store. It was a casual look for her with sandals and her hair down, but it had my blood starting to pump through my veins again, reminding me I was alive. She was absolutely fucking gorgeous and unfortunately, I couldn't do a damn thing about it.

"What are you doing here?" I asked, taking my gloves off with my teeth.

She shrugged and looked around the room. "Just wanted to check it out in here. You know, maybe take some lessons."

Smiling, she grabbed a pair of boxing gloves and walked toward me. Her breasts swayed with each step, enticing me to the point that I had to look away or else I would be throwing her up against the wall in a matter of seconds.

"Lessons?" I asked with a quirk of my brow. I leaned against the wall with my arms crossed over my bare chest, waiting for her to answer.

"Yeah, I heard there is a pro here, teaching lessons."

I went rigid and stood up straight from the mention of my past. "Lyla…"

"Funny thing about the internet, Kace. You can find out anything about people, especially if they've been in the limelight."

Fury blazed through me, and I tried to tamp down my anger, but it was too much, there was too much pent-up aggression. I didn't want her searching me on the internet. Who knew what she would find.

I got in her face and said, "You had no fucking right looking up my shit."

"Public knowledge," she shrugged, not startled one bit by my proximity. "If you're not going to open your mouth, then I'll look things up myself. You know what's funny, though? When I was doing my research, I saw you lost your license for shooting up steroids."

"We're done here," I said, blowing past her, knocking into her shoulder so she was thrown off balance for a second.

As I walked away, my past came flooding back to me in full force. That morning I received a call from Dale hit me hard and all the painful memories from that night came to the forefront of my mind. I didn't want to relive it. I knew I deserved to live with my past sins, but I didn't want to, not now. Not with Lyla in the room.

Keeping my back toward her, I held on to the wall and hung my head, trying to shake the sickening feeling that was trying to bubble to the surface of my emotional state.

Coming up behind me and placing her hand on my back, she said, "Let's talk about it."

I whirled around. "I don't want to fucking talk about it. You're not my shrink, so do us both a favor and leave."

My booming voice echoed through the room, but it didn't affect her. She continued her pursuit of trying to "help" me.

"I don't believe what everyone said to be true," she stated softly. "I don't believe you would do such a thing to your body, not after seeing the strong work ethic you have. It doesn't match up."

I ran my hands down my face, trying to wipe away the moment. They stopped mid stroke from her confession. "What?" I asked, almost shocked by her statement.

"I don't believe the accusations." She pulled a paper from her back pocket and unfolded it. "Your trainer did it. See?" She pointed to the paper as if she'd solved the world's greatest mystery.

"I know he did," I responded, relaxing only slightly.

"Oh," she replied, a little shocked by my knowledge.

"Well, if you knew he did it, then why didn't you clear your name?"

I shook my head and looked at the ground. "Too late."

"It's never too late—"

"It's too fucking late, Lyla, so just drop it."

I leaned against the wall and crossed my legs at my ankles and my arms over my chest. Her gaze landed on my bare chest, and she lightly licked her lips, like I was her lunch, waiting to be consumed.

"Don't look at me like that," I told her.

"I can look at you however I want. You're not the boss of me," she replied defiantly.

"Mature." I nodded.

"It's the truth, but if you ever let me into that closed-off world of yours, I might let you be the boss of me."

The proposition was incredibly tempting. To be able to control the mouthy yet sexy woman standing in front of me would be something I would enjoy immensely, but that would mean letting her into my world, letting her know who I really was, and that was something I just couldn't do.

"Tempting, but I'll pass," I answered, hating the betrayal I was playing on my true feelings.

She shrugged as if my rejection was no big deal and started putting on the boxing gloves she held in her hands. The first one went on smoothly, but the second glove she struggled with because she didn't have the use of her right hand anymore. A seasoned boxer had no problem slipping on gloves, but she was a newbie, and it was painfully obvious she had no clue what she was doing.

Instinctively, I went up to her and grabbed the glove from her struggling hand. Her green eyes searched mine as I held the glove open for her to slip her hand inside. A small smile crossed her lips as she slipped her hand into the glove. Once the gloves were on, I helped secure the straps. She punched her fists together to test them. Clearly she was happy with their fit from the light in her eyes.

Lightly, she tapped me on the shoulder with the gloves and said, "Thank you." Then she knocked her gloves together once again and bounced on her toes. "All right, how does this work?"

Shaking my head, I grabbed her hand and led her over to the row of punching bags. "Go ahead." I nodded at the first one in the row.

"Just punch it?" she asked, looking hotter than hell in her skimpy outfit and boxing gloves. Visions of her only wearing the gloves and possibly tied to my headboard ran through my mind. That was a sight I wouldn't mind seeing.

"Punch it," I confirmed.

She cocked her arm back and geared up for what seemed like was going to be the whammy of all punches. Before she could do serious damage to herself, I grasped her arms and stopped her.

"Hey, I was about to gut this bastard." She nodded at the bag.

"Yeah, and you were about to most likely snap your wrist while doing it." Standing behind her, I wrapped my arms around her upper half and held her wrist. "See this?" I breathed into her ear. "This is a weak little wrist that can break if you're not careful. You don't have any wrist stability on, and by the way you were about to hammer out a punch on this bad boy, you were going to snap something."

She leaned into me, her hair brushing my shoulder and her face turned toward mine. "Okay, so teach me how to knock things out."

Her voice was breathless, and a faint flowery scent wafted from her hair, practically bringing me to my knees.

I wanted her.

I ran my hand from her wrist up her arms, feeling the effect I had on her from the goosebumps that instantly rose on her skin. With my hand on her elbow, I pulled her arm back and showed her the proper technique for punching, all the while holding tightly to her hip.

"So just pull back like this and let go?" she asked, her face turned toward mine, slaying me with those green eyes of hers. I nodded to confirm, not able to open my mouth in case I said something stupid.

"All right, look out."

With the biggest wallop she could muster, she cocked her arm back and let it fly, making contact with the punching bag. An immediate cry escaped her as she bent and gripped her wrist. She sat on the floor and started to rock back and forth, holding her arm.

"Are you okay?" I asked, sitting on the ground next to her and pulling her onto my lap so I could take a closer look at her hand.

"Remove these," she said, referring to the gloves.

Quickly, I took off the left glove and chucked it aside. Then I went to her right one and held it steady as I took off the strap and pulled it, fearing I was going to find a bone popping out of her skin. To my surprise, everything was fine. There was no bruising or swelling. I looked at her to see where she was hurting only to find her smiling at me with an evil grin.

Before I could even move, she straddled my lap and pushed me back on the floor so she hovered over me.

"What the hell do you think you're doing?"

"Getting you into a position I know we both enjoy."

"Are you hurt?" I asked, trying to keep my eyes away from the obvious cleavage shot Lyla was handing me on a silver platter.

"No." She lowered herself so her face was mere inches from mine. "I just wanted to get you in a position where I could entice you."

"Not going to happen, Lyla," I gritted out, annoyed she'd faked an injury to top me and annoyed I'd fallen for it.

"Oh, really?" Her hand seductively found its way down to my crotch, where with one stroke over my workout shorts, she had me growing in seconds. It was impossible not to when I was presented with such a gorgeous and enticing woman. "Looks like your dick is singing a different song," she teased.

"What do you expect when your shirt is hanging open like that?" I nodded toward her shirt. She looked down and smiled right before she pulled on the hem of her shirt and took it off, revealing her perfectly toned body.

"Is that better? I don't want my shirt distracting you."

"It was the contents inside, not the shirt itself."

"Mm, I love it when you get all moody." She ran her hands up my bare chest, gradually running her fingernails over my skin.

"Lyla," I warned, starting to lose control.

"Take me out to dinner tonight," she demanded.

I wouldn't have been more surprised by her demand if she'd kicked me in the dick. "What?" I asked, confused from the change of subject, from her change in attitude.

"Take me to dinner, Kace. Take me out on a date. It's the least you can do."

She was now lying flat against me with her elbows propped up on my chest, looking down on me. If I paid close attention, I could feel the weight of her breasts on my chest, which was turning me on even more.

"It's the least I can do? How do you see that?"

"You can't just fuck a girl and leave her throbbing up against a wall, wondering what the hell just happened—at least not a girl like me. You owe me a date if you're going to toss me aside like that."

"Isn't that a little backward?" I asked.

"Yeah, but you owe me. We've fucked, but now you owe me a date. It's protocol."

I gripped her hips and tried to move her off me, but she planted her hands on the floor and hovered her mouth right above mine.

"You know you want to," she teased.

There was a whole lot more that I wanted to do to this woman, but fucking her against the mirror in the Haze Room seemed like a bad idea.

"Please," she said, batting her eyelashes. She cupped my face and very slowly lowered her mouth to mine. I gripped her hips tightly, bracing myself.

A low growl escaped me as I grabbed the back of her head and pressed her down to my lips so she couldn't move. Like it was second nature, her mouth opened to mine and gave me access. Warmth spread through me from her touch, from the way her tongue matched mine, and the heat that poured off her and into my very core.

My hand that had once been on her hip found the back of her bra and without even thinking, I snapped the clasp and let the straps fall down her shoulders.

I thought I'd known what perfection was. I had been so fucking wrong. How I'd missed the fact that Lyla embodied everything I ever looked for in a woman was beyond me. Her skin was a beautiful mocha color, her eyes penetrated me every time I looked into them, and her attitude matched mine perfectly. She didn't put up with my crap, hence why I was inches from stripping her naked in the new community center.

"Am I interrupting something?" Goldie asked from the doorway of the Haze room.

"Shit." I fumbled, trying to get Lyla off of me, but she was no help because she just giggled and clung on to me, making no attempt to get out of the way. "Lyla," I warned.

"Looks like you're about to christen the new mats," Goldie said, walking toward us.

"It's not what it looks like," I replied even though I was still lying on the ground with Lyla's half-exposed body stretched out against mine.

"Not what it looks like, huh?" Goldie asked, moving over to sit next to us with her legs crossed. She pointed at our connection and said, "Looks like you two are making out on the floor and about to hit second base, judging from the way Lyla's bra is undone."

"Kace undid it," Lyla said proudly.

"I bet he did. He's always had a thing for your boobs."

"No I haven't," I lied.

"Oh look, he's blushing," Lyla said, patting my face. "How adorable. It's all right, Kace. My boobs are pretty hot." She bent and kissed my lips one last time before sitting up on my lap.

I watched in fascination as her bra slipped down, exposing her breasts for a few seconds before she readjusted it, taking away one of the sexiest views I'd ever seen.

I knew she could feel my arousal because the minute she shifted her seat on my lap, she winked, letting me know she knew exactly what she was doing to me.

She turned to Goldie, who was smiling like a dork, and said, "Kace is taking me out on a date tonight."

"Ahhh! Yay!" Goldie clapped her hands in excitement.

"No, I'm not," I replied, getting annoyed by these two, who should never be left alone together.

"It's all right, big guy. No need to be shy about it." Lyla turned to Goldie. "He can be so tender and sweet at times, but he doesn't want to let people think he's going soft."

"You damn well know there is nothing soft about me," I gritted out.

"Oh my," Goldie cooed, glancing down at me. "Looks like you've poked the bear."

Lyla shrugged. "I've dealt with it before. A quick tap to the nut sack, and all will be right with the world. Isn't that right, Kace?"

"Touch my nut sack and get your hand cut off."

"Damn," Goldie replied. "Be nice to the girl, Kace."

"What did you want?" I asked Goldie, hating that she'd interrupted my make-out session with Lyla.

"Just got a shipment in of towels, wanted to know if you want me to divide them up in the locker rooms?"

Running my hands over my face, I let out a long breath. "That couldn't have waited?"

"Sorry. I didn't know it was sex-o'clock in the Haze Room. Next time leave a tie on the door or a condom hanging off the knob so I know not to enter."

"Run the towels through the wash first, then divide them," I ordered, ignoring her sarcasm.

"Thanks, boss man," Goldie replied, getting up and taking off. "Want me to hang a condom on the door?"

"Get out," I shouted, making her squeal and laugh at the same time.

Once the door was closed, I looked at Lyla, who was still sitting on my lap.

"Are you going to sit there all fucking day, or are you going to let me get up?"

Without a word, Lyla got up and grabbed her shirt. She quickly put it on and didn't look at me as she headed for the door.

I should have let her go, let her walk away, because that was what would be good for me, but fuck if I still didn't feel the heat of her body on mine. I didn't want to lose that feeling.

Groaning, I chased after her and pulled on her arm before she could open the door to leave. When I spun her around, a giant smile spread across her face.

Motherfucker. She'd played me. "Shit," I mumbled.

"I knew you cared." She poked my chest with her pink painted finger.

"I don't," I lied once again.

"Lie all you want, Kace, but I can see it in your eyes, the longing you have for me. Strap on your balls, because you're taking me out tonight. We're going to spend an evening living in the present and forgetting the past for at least a couple of hours."

I bowed my head and gripped her hips, wishing she would just give up on me, wishing she would leave me alone, but the determination in her eyes told me that wasn't going to happen anytime soon. So I gave in. "What time should I pick you up?"

"Seven." She leaned in, pressing her chest against mine and placing a soft kiss on my jaw. "Don't shave. I like you all scruffy."

Before she took off, I couldn't help but ask, "Why, Lyla? Why now?"

From over her shoulder, she answered, "Because everyone deserves a second chance in life, Kace. It's about damn time you take yours."

Fucking hell.

CHAPTER TWELVE

My past...

Everything I had ever cared about, ever worked for completely vanished in the matter of a day. I was stripped bare. I was left with nothing but an old pair of boxing gloves, my worn out guitar, and a picture of me and Jett from when we were young. Those were my items, my valuables, the only things besides clothes that I moved into my new dwellings with.

The first room Jett tried to give me in the Lafayette Club was unacceptable. It was lavish, it was expensive looking, it had amenities I didn't want. I wanted simple, I wanted plain, I wanted something that resembled the four cell walls I was supposed to be in.

Luckily there was a room on the first floor of the old servants' wing that was suitable. New construction made that part of the house more modern, but it wasn't as lavish as the rest of the house. There was a double bed against a wall, a nightstand, and a single chair in the room. To the left, there was an attached bathroom that would do the job. There was minimal light coming through the one window on the largest wall, and the room seemed almost cold, sterile. It was as close to a jail cell as I was going to get.

It was surprising how much a person's life could change in a matter of minutes. One moment, I'd been on the verge of a breakout career and the next, I was hiding in my best friend's mansion, helping him start a gentleman's club for the city elites.

This wasn't how I'd envisioned my life ending up.

No, I'd spent hours upon hours training and making the right decisions in my life to help accomplish my goals, to help me become the boxer I'd always wanted to be, but one wrong move, one lapse of judgement and I lost everything. I lost my house, my job, but most importantly, I lost the respect of everyone not only in my life but everyone who had ever believed in me, especially the city that I loved.

My father passed away shortly after his reprimanding, leaving behind debt and a spiteful diary of how much of a disappointment I was. Using the money from selling my house and belongings, I paid off his debt, leaving me with nothing left from my past besides guilt.

The only person who had even given me the time of day was Jett, and that was because he knew the truth, he knew who I truly was. He knew the kind of hard work and passion I had for the sport I loved. He knew I would never do anything to compromise my future, but only one person believing in me could only get me so far, even if Jett had some pull in the city we called home.

I hung my boxing gloves on a nail that was already in the wall and stared at them solemnly. It was a symbolic and gut-wrenching move for me. I was hanging up my career. I was done and painfully moving on.

The next chapter in my life was starting, and to my demise, I wasn't fucking ready to move on, but stopping life wasn't an option, so I swallowed my pride and let the changes overtake me, starting my new job as a glorified babysitter. That's how I saw it, even though Jett said it was a lot more than that. Apparently there were plentiful activities the club was offering, but with my faded outlook on life, I couldn't quite see the big picture.

A light knock came at my door, and Jett entered with a neutral look on his face.

"I don't like you down here," he said, looking around and taking in my bleak surroundings.

"You can't control everything in the world, so fucking deal with it," I replied. I tossed my duffel bag on the bed. "What do you want?"

"Our first girl is about to arrive soon. Thought it would be appropriate if we both greeted her."

"I thought you wanted to be elusive with these women."

"I do," Jett replied. "But Barbara is different. She needs a lot of help, and the state you're in right now, it doesn't seem you'd be the best welcoming committee."

"You got that fucking right," I replied. "Why are you doing this, Jett? Why are you taking these women in? Trying to change them?"

Jett blew out a long breath and ran a hand over his face, clearly not wanting to engage in this conversation right now, but I didn't care. Anything to take the all-encompassing ache off my chest for a short period of time was all I cared about.

"Why?" I asked again. "Does this have to do with Natasha leaving? You just want to be a man who doesn't get close to another woman, so you bring them to your mansion, fuck them, and give them a place to stay?"

"It's not like that," Jett cut in, angry.

"It's not? Because it damn well looks like that. So tell me, if it's not Natasha, then what is it?"

"I'm over Natasha. She can have a grand fucking time with Rex for all I care," Jett replied, clearly not at all cool with the turn of events in his life.

"Yeah, you're real convincing."

"It has to do with my mom, asshole," Jett shot back.

Taken back, I asked, "Your mom? Why?"

Jett leaned against the doorframe of my room and placed his hands in his pockets. His black dress pants were a stark contrast to his white dress shirt, and his hair looked like he'd been running his hands through it again. I'd known Jett for a very long time, and seeing him almost disheveled, key word being almost, was a change for me. He was always confident in everything he did. He never second-guessed himself, but because of the new venture, he was a little uneasy.

"I feel like I need to do something to honor her, to give back due to the short life she had. I've been thinking about it for a while, and the only thing I could come up with to honor my mom was helping out these women who have gone down the same path as her. I couldn't help her, but I sure as hell can help them, starting with Barbara."

I nodded and thought about all of the rules and the system Jett had put together for these women. It was complicated. There was a lot for me to absorb, but I could see how utilizing what they knew best to earn them a lot of cash while being able to control their environment was smart. In addition to the girls dancing and making money off the city elites, they were required to earn an education, which meant they couldn't stay a Jett Girl forever, a very smart idea on Jett's part. If they were going to be a part of the club, then they were going to work at developing a future outside of what they already knew.

The idea was crazy, possibly weird to accept looking in

from the outside world, but it might just work. If Jett wanted to honor his mother, who was I to stop him? Hell, when the man set to accomplish something, he didn't allow anything to stand in his way. I wasn't about to test his limits.

"Well, we should go greet her, then," I said, motioning for Jett to leave my room.

He took one last glance at the bare walls and tight space and shook his head. "I wish you would allow me to give you a better room."

"Not happening, end of discussion. Let's move."

Jett quirked an eyebrow at me. He didn't take kindly to direction but let it slip as he led the way through the servants' quarters of the aged plantation house in the middle of the Garden District. The house screamed of old money, but everyone in the city knew differently. Jett wasn't a man from old money. He'd developed his own fortune, strategically investing, developing several contacts throughout the city, and conducting business in a respectful manner, which was more than what his father, Leo, could account for.

Just as we walked up to the front door, Jett's driver pulled up in front of the gates and walked around to open the door for a very timid-looking woman.

Barbara.

Her ratty hair was a dirty blonde color, and I wasn't sure if it was unwashed or the true color of her hair. Her clothes swallowed her whole, she was so thin. Her eyes widened in surprise at the extravagance of the house in front of her.

Between her arms, clutched to her chest, was a garbage bag that seemed to have some of her possessions in it. I scanned her up and down, and a light stab took place in my chest. This woman needed help, she needed a second chance in life, and Jett was willing to offer her that chance.

Jett stepped forward. "Welcome, Barbara. Please, come in."

She walked toward us suspiciously, clutching her bag and eyeing us up and down. She wet her lips and said, "How much?"

"Excuse me?" Jett asked.

"How much am I going to owe you for this? I don't have any cash, but I can suck you off every night if you want. I pretty much will do anything sexual. Just name it, I've probably done it at least five times for cash."

My stomach flipped from her candidness. I'd thought my life was a pile of shit, but looking at Barbara, seeing the desperation in her eyes, I knew I didn't have it half as bad.

"Barbara, you don't owe me anything. I want to help."

A shrill laugh escaped her as she set her hand on her hip and prepared for battle.

"You want to help?" she asked, using air quotes. She stepped forward and poked Jett in the chest. "I don't know what it is with you rich fucks and denying what you want until you make us spell it out for you. It's like some kind of shame factor for you. Let's just get this out in the open. I've got holes. Use them how you please while I crash here for a while."

She blew past us and walked in the house. Jett turned his wide eyes to me, and I almost laughed from the comical look on his face.

"She's got holes, Jett, use them how you please," I repeated with a slight grin.

"Christ," Jett mumbled, walking into the house.

For some reason, I knew I was going to get along with Barbara very well.

"Nice digs. Homeboy's got swag," Barbara said, taking in the house. "I mean, chrome and leather, nice touch." She turned toward Jett and looked him up and down. "What's your worth?"

"That's none of your concern," Jett responded, looking almost offended. What did he expect from a girl like Barbara? She was rough around the edges and had zero tact.

"Hmm, are you going to have that stick up your ass the entire time I'm here?" Barbara asked. "Because honestly, I don't prefer to work around it, but I can do it. It wouldn't be my first time fucking a rich boy like you. At least you have the decency to put me up in your dubs. So where am I sleeping?"

"Barbara, you're here to better yourself, to earn an education, and make something of your life," Jett offered, trying to help her realize his intentions.

A pop of gum echoed in the room from Barbara as she crossed her arms over her chest and analyzed us with a suspicious look.

She pointed to us and asked, "You two an item?"

"Fuck no," I said quickly, making Jett turn toward me with a half-smile.

"Too good for me?" he asked.

"We're not doing this," I replied. "Barbara, I will show you to your room."

"Oh, my own butler. How fancy," she sassed me.

I turned quickly on my heel and got in her face. "I'm not your fucking butler, and I'm not your friend. I'm here to make sure you do what you're supposed to do and follow the rules. Understand?"

The grit in my voice made Barbara gulp slightly before she nodded. I was walking her up the stairs when Jett called.

"Before you leave, Barbara, you will no longer go by your born name. Now that you're a Jett Girl, you are to be elusive. You are an ambiguous human being now. The only people who will know who you actually are, are Kace and myself. From now on, you will be known as Babs. Your past is just that—your past. This is the first step to a new beginning. After you leave the Lafayette Club, you will have an education and a purpose in life. Your days on the streets are done. That life is behind you. It's time to move on."

"Ehhh, okay," Barbara answered skeptically as she followed me up the stairs, clearly not motivated by Jett's speech.

Even though Jett was talking directly to Barbara, I couldn't help but think he was also trying to get through to me as well. A new beginning? There were no new beginnings where I was concerned.

I led Barbara, or Babs, to her room and opened the door for her. The space was exceedingly nicer than mine. A wall of windows flanked the right side, bringing in a great deal of sunlight. Deep orange curtains framed the windows, while sepia-toned pictures of New Orleans graced the walls. The bedding was white, and the walls were light orange, making the room almost look like a Creamsicle. It was a room that would bring happiness and solace, a room I didn't need to be in.

"This is your room. Inside the closet—"

"This is my room?" Babs asked, cutting me off. She walked around the space in awe, taking in the small touches and pops of color.

"Yes, this is your room," I answered, not wanting to hang around for her to clearly cry. I could see it happening in the way she walked around her new space, taking everything in. Her eyes beautifully glistened in awe. Nope, I didn't do crying women. "Like I was saying, there are clothes in the closet, a bathroom to the side with makeup—"

"This is all for me?" she interrupted again. "What's the catch?"

"There is no catch. Jett wants to help you."

"Why? Why me?"

If I'd known this was going to be a twenty-questions kind of thing, I wouldn't have signed up for it. I didn't do social interactions, either. "I don't know," I responded, trying to end the conversation.

"You're lying. You know why he chose me, so tell me."

Running a hand over my face, I took a deep breath. "I don't know, Babs. Maybe you remind him of someone from his past, but that's not a story for me to tell. I'm here to make sure the club runs properly, that you're minding your business and doing what you're supposed to do."

Suspiciously she eyed me and then said, "What happened to you?"

"Excuse me?"

She looked into my eyes, her face relaxed, and some kind of realization hit her. "You're Kace Haywood, the boxer."

"We're done here," I said, walking away. "I will be around tomorrow morning with a contract for you to sign. Don't get into any fucking trouble tonight."

My chest had constricted around my heart when she recognized me. It was still very raw. The scandal still swallowed me whole at night, making it hard to sleep. I didn't need to relive it with this woman whom I'd just met and who frankly needed a shower, because she smelled like piss, and her hair looked like it had been knotted for days.

"I can understand the need to hide," Babs said as I reached the door. "For what it's worth, I don't believe a word of it. I've watched your career, and from what I've seen, you've been nothing but a hard and honest worker. You got fucked, just like me. You might not want to be my friend, Kace, but just so you know, we are very much alike. If you need someone to talk to, you can always come to me."

Without turning around and acknowledging her, I left. What I needed was to get the hell out of her room before I broke down in front of her. I was prideful, like Jett, and never showed weakness, but the lump in my throat was growing at an alarming rate, making it impossible to breathe. I needed to find some alone time, away from the entire world.

CHAPTER THIRTEEN

My present...

Everything in my body was telling me to turn around, to forget the little agreement I'd made with Lyla and walk away, but for some godforsaken reason, I found myself standing outside Lyla's shitty apartment, about to knock on her door.

I'd spent zero time getting ready for this. I didn't want her thinking I was attempting to make something of this date, so I'd thrown on a pair of black jeans, a *V*-necked gray shirt with the front sloppily tucked in the waistband of my jeans, which showed off my worn out black belt, and then to top it all off, I put on my old Vans that had seen better days. I was the epitome of casual.

Running my hands through my hair, I took a deep breath and knocked on her door.

While I waited for her to answer, I looked around the dump she was living in with disapproval. I was surprised the building was still standing, it looked so dilapidated. There was some definitely illegal business being conducted on the first floor, and her neighbor on the second floor apparently didn't care about the blood splatters on his door.

I didn't want Lyla living here. I fucking hated everything about it, actually. Why she had to be so stubborn and not accept Jett's offer for her to help out at the community center drove me mad. She could have such a better life if she just accepted the help.

Fumbling of locks brought me out of my thoughts, and I tried to remove the crease in my brow that had formed from taking in her dwelling.

Lyla whipped open the door and smiled brightly at me. She was wearing a pair of skinny jeans, brown ankle boots, and a cream tank top that was short in the front and long in the back so her midriff was peeking out. Her breasts were most likely pushed up by her bra because they crested at the neckline of her shirt, making me quite aware of their size. Her hair was pulled back in a tight ponytail, exposing her gorgeous neck. My mouth watered just thinking about running my tongue up and down it.

"Mmm, you look good," she said, grabbing her purse and shutting the door to her apartment. Before she turned and locked her door, she stepped into me, pressed her hand on my chest, and lightly kissed my lips. A waft of feminine perfume hit me hard, causing me to yearn more than I ever wanted.

She turned quickly to lock her doors before I could even consider deepening her kiss. I stuffed my hands in my pockets to keep myself from touching her as I observed the perfect curve of her ass. There were only so many ways I could control myself.

Turning around, she had a big smile on her face that almost cracked the neutral look I was trying to portray. Why did she have to be so damn beautiful?

"Ready?" she asked.

"Where are we going?" I responded, not sure what she had planned.

"What?" she asked in an offended tone. "You didn't plan a date? You're supposed to take me out."

I scratched my head and thought about it for a second. *Shit, was I really supposed to plan something?* I couldn't remember the last time I actually went on a date. I had no clue where to even begin. "I'm going to be honest with you, Lyla. I don't do dates, so I have no clue where to fucking start."

"Well, this is a lost cause. Have a good night," she said, disappointment in her voice.

"Wait," I said, pulling on her arm. "Help me out. Where do I start?"

Why had I just said that? Her turning around on me was my out. Did I really want to go on this date? The realization was too much to even think about, so I blocked those thoughts out of my mind and brought her closer to me. Once again, that 'gotchya' smile greeted me, and I knew she'd played me, just like she had in the Haze Room.

"You're the devil, you know that?"

She laughed and linked her arm into mine. "Take me to dinner first, Kace. Anywhere you want to go."

"Anywhere?" I asked as I led her down the stairs.

"If you take me to Kitten's Castle, I will castrate you," she said with humor in her voice.

"Shit, now you took all the surprise out of it."

"Kace...," she warned.

I chuckled, a foreign concept to me. It almost felt good, I almost felt light. For a short period of time, I actually felt like the weight of the world wasn't sitting on my shoulders.

I led her out onto Bourbon Street, guided her past the already drunk people enjoying the raunchiness of the French

Quarter, and walked her down Toulouse Street to one of my favorite restaurants.

"How was your day?" she asked, striking up conversation, something I wasn't good at, at all.

"Fine," I replied, not really knowing how to elaborate.

"Okay, want to tell me more?"

"Not really," I replied, opening the door to The Chartres House that was tucked away in a salmon-colored building. I ushered her in, not letting her respond to my inability to discuss my day like a normal person.

"Will it be just the two of you?" the hostess asked.

"Yes. Can we have the table over there in the corner?" I nodded at my favorite seat. The restaurant was small and had a bar that took up most of the space, not allowing for too many diners at once. There were small cabaret tables with either two or four seats each, and when the weather was nice, the doors that faced the street were open. But the wind was a bitch today, and the doors were closed, blocking out the bustle of the street, which I was grateful for.

"Sure thing. Right this way." The hostess led us to our seats, and I took the one in the back corner, where I was able to look out over the restaurant. I never liked having my back turned to a room so I couldn't see what was behind me. The hostess handed us menus. "Enjoy."

Feeling uncomfortable, since this whole dating scene felt like foreign territory to me, I shifted in my chair and asked, "Have you ever been here before?"

Lyla's light green eyes looked at me. "They have the best boudin. Good pick, Kace."

"You like boudin?" I asked, a little shocked. I wouldn't have picked Lyla for a sausage lover.

"What's not to like? Meat stuffed in a little roll you have to suck on. It all works for me."

Shaking my head, I was about to respond when the waitress appeared. "Hello. My name is Ana. I will be serving you. We have a special today on crawfish with two sides if you're interested. Can I get you something to drink to start off with?"

"Water," I said briskly.

"I'll take water as well, thank you." Once the waitress left, Lyla turned her gaze on me and said, "Can you lighten up just a bit? You nearly barked at that poor waitress."

"I did not bark," I defended myself.

"Kace, you could have at least smiled."

"I don't really smile."

"That's not true. I've seen you smile."

"You caught me in a weak moment when you saw that," I countered, a grin trying to peek past my strong façade.

"You're frustrating," Lyla huffed, putting her menu in front of her and blocking her beautiful face from my view.

This was going just as well as I thought it would. My awkwardness and inability to relax was shining brightly as silence fell between us. I thought about saying something to break the tension that quickly fell upon our table, but I had no clue what to talk about.

There were so many things I wanted to tell her. A part of me wanted to open up to her because I felt like she would understand where I was coming from. A part of me wished she would understand, but I couldn't take the risk. Right now, she at least wanted to be in my presence. If I told her what kind of a monster I was, would she ever want to see me again?

Did I want to see her again? I didn't want a relationship—it would be too complicated—but the short walk from her apartment to the restaurant with her arm in mine had been one of the best couple of minutes I'd experienced in a long time. Her body had been soft against mine, and I'd enjoyed how her ponytail brushed against me when she turned to point at something, or the way little whiffs of her perfume fluttered into my nose. She was so incredibly feminine and so incredibly fuckable.

"Here you are," the waitress said, placing two waters on our table. "Have you decided what you're having?"

"I have," Lyla said while glancing at me from over her menu. I motioned for Lyla to go first. "I'll take the special with red beans and rice."

"Very good, and for you, sir?"

"I'll have the same," I replied. "And can we get an appetizer of the boudin, please?"

"Yes, certainly."

The waitress wrote down our order and took off.

"Wow," Lyla said while leaning back in her chair.

"What?"

"You know the word 'please.' I'm actually kind of shocked."

"Don't be a smartass," I replied, not liking the snarky look on her face.

She smiled sincerely at me and then grabbed my hand. She entwined her fingers with mine and for some odd reason, I liked it and didn't pull away. Normally in a situation like this, I would tighten up and bail, but Lyla made it seem so easy. A light touch felt good.

I allowed her thumb to glide across the back of my hand while she spoke to me, and I let myself, for this brief moment in time, enjoy it.

"Thank you for taking me out tonight, Kace."

"You're welcome," I said uncomfortably. "It's the least I could do after taking you in the back of Kitten's Castle," I tried to tease.

"It's the least." She smiled brightly.

"Speaking of Kitten's Castle, how much longer are you going to work there?"

"Kace...," she warned. "We're not going to talk about that unless you want me to ask you questions about your past."

"Nope," I said. "Fair enough."

I wanted Lyla out of Kitten's Castle, but it looked like she wasn't going to budge, at least not right now. I still had plans to try to convince her otherwise.

"So tell me, are you excited about Justice opening soon?"

I nodded and took a sip of my water. "I think it's come along nicely other than some of the classes the girls have come up with."

"I think the classes will be well received. Pole dancing is all about fitness."

"Is that right?" I asked with a raised eyebrow.

"It is. Do you think it's easy hanging upside down with only your legs to keep you in place while your boobs flop around?"

"Well, I've never tried it with my boobs flopping around, but I can't imagine it being easy."

"Was that a joke?" she asked, tightening her grip on my hand.

"Last one you will hear tonight, promise."

"That's a promise I hope you plan on breaking." She smiled. "I'm happy for you and the girls. You've worked so hard putting together the center. I know it will do great."

"I'll be excited when everything is done. The housing portion will take the longest since Jett decided to offer miniature apartments for those seeking refuge. But for now, having the classes and gym open will be sufficient. It's a work in progress."

"Are you getting yourself ready to teach some boxing lessons?"

I shrugged. I still wasn't sure how I felt about the whole thing. I didn't want to teach adults how to box, at least not right away, because they would be the ones who knew who I'd been, so I decided to hold classes for kids at first and some self-defense classes too.

"You seem apprehensive," Lyla pushed. Just like Goldie, she never let anything just go.

"Not sure how I feel about it all," I said, gripping her hand a little tighter. I never brought up my past profession, ever, so talking about giving boxing lessons was bordering on uncomfortable since it was so close to what I used to do.

"Self-defense lessons seems like an interesting class. I might join in on the fun."

Grateful for the change in subject, I smirked. "Is that right?"

"Yeah, and I might need a practice dummy. You would be the perfect match."

"Watch what you ask for, sweetheart. If I was your practice dummy, I wouldn't take it easy on you."

"You know I like it hard, so no worries."

Fuck if I didn't just grow stiff from the way she bit her lip and looked at me seductively. Her thumb continued to graze my skin as heat poured off her. No matter how far I tried to push her away, she always managed to work her way back into my life somehow.

Our waitress brought over our plate of boudin, smiled, and left.

"Did you see that?" Layla asked as she grabbed one of the small plates on the table and put it in front of her.

"See what?" I asked.

"She was totally checking you out, right in front of me."

"Do you blame her?" I said in an egotistical tone, holding my arms out so she got a good view of my chest.

Lyla crossed her arms. "The man doesn't have manners but can be a cocky son-of-a-bitch when he wants to be."

"What can I say? I'm a man of many talents."

She shook her head and looked down at the boudin. "Well, this is not what I was expecting. They changed things on me."

"Yeah, these are fried balls, huh. Never seen boudin like this." I grabbed one and popped it in my mouth, not worried about the heat coming off them since I practically had a metal mouth. I swallowed and said, "Not bad."

"Well, that was a disgusting display of macho eating."

"Macho eating?" I asked. I watched her take a ball and use her fork to cut into it. Steam evaporated in the air.

"Did you even chew it?"

"Yeah, of course I did. Only need a couple of chews to get it down the gullet."

I grabbed another and tossed it in my mouth, quickly making that one go down as well. There were four on the plate, so the last one was for Lyla. Pleased, I sat back and watched her eat.

In disbelief, she shook her head at me and then put the rest of the boudin in her mouth. She struggled significantly with its size and heat, and her eyes watered while she tried to cool the boudin down by breathing out of her mouth and taking swallows of water. After some fancy mouth maneuvering, she was able to break the ball down and swallow. She held her mouth open for me and said, "Ta-da!"

I looked around and then leaned forward. "Should I clap?"

"You better fucking clap. That was torture."

Chuckling, I gave her a slow clap while she bowed and

waved her hand in appreciation.

"The best boudin is the kind in the sausage casing that you suck out, and after you've got it all, it looks like a used condom, all shriveled up and gross."

"Yes, I love it when my food ends up looking like a used condom. Rather appetizing," I replied as she stuck the remaining boudin with a fork.

"Who doesn't?" she smirked.

Our main entrees showed up shortly after that, and we talked about trivial things while we sucked on the heads of our crawfish and enjoyed the traditional rice and beans. It was obvious Lyla used her meal to entice me by the way she sucked on the crawfish and moaned about their Cajun flavors. To say I didn't let it affect me was a lie. With each lick of her fingers and devilish look in her eyes, I grew harder by the second. Her pink lips glistened, and her cheeks hollowed as she sucked, reminding me what her lips were capable of.

I'd never been this turned on during a meal.

"You're quiet," she said, licking her fingers once again.

Clearing my throat and adjusting in my seat, I said, "Never saw someone turn eating crawfish into a sexual experience."

"Oh good, you noticed." She grinned. "I was afraid you weren't paying attention."

"Is that why you dropped sauce on your breasts?" I asked, remembering the way she'd made it seem like an accident, but knowing damn well it wasn't.

"Of course. Did it work?"

I wiped my hands on my napkin and then leaned back in my chair. "What do you think?"

"I think if I ran my hands up your jeans, I would be very happy with what I found."

She pushed her chest toward me, displaying her breasts

next to her plate and gripping my thigh under the table. The feel of her hand was like an electric shock, kick-starting my body. It felt fucking good.

"Don't start something you can't finish," I warned.

"I always finish." She winked, pulling away.

After I paid and finished my water, I stood up and waited for Lyla to stand as well, but she just sat in her chair and looked up at me.

"What's going on?" I asked, wondering why she didn't move. "Did you want dessert or something?"

"So romantic," she teased and held out her hand.

"What?" I asked, looking down at it.

"Part of going on a date is holding hands, Kace. Go on, take my hand. It won't hurt."

Little did she know the hand-holding we'd done earlier had done a number on my soul. Walking around the French Quarter with her hand in mine was most definitely going to hurt because I knew damn well I was going to want more of it after tonight.

"Go on," she encouraged.

Taking a deep breath, I grasped her hand, giving in to her little demand. Her hand fit perfectly in mine and once again, our fingers intertwined. Our palms connected and the warmth of her hand ran up my arm and straight to my heart, slowly melting a little part of the black soul I'd developed.

"Where to now?" I asked, leading her out the door and onto the cobblestone streets of the Quarter. "Do I take you home?"

"What kind of date would that be?" she asked, insulted that I'd even suggested the idea. "Let's go shopping."

I groaned. "Shopping?"

"Haven't you ever gone into the touristy shops around here? They have the best items."

"I try to avoid any place crawling with tourists," I replied as she pressed her side against mine. I felt comforted. It was an odd sensation.

"It'll be fun. Come on."

Her enthusiasm and light spirit was contagious, so I allowed for her to pull me down the crowded streets and into the heart of the Quarter, where drinking in public was encouraged and street entertainers performed for the masses.

"I love it here," Lyla said, looking around. "Where else would you find such eccentric people?"

"Eccentric is a nice way of putting it," I said as I eyed a lady who was wearing a dress made of bottle caps, her nips barely covered.

"You've lived here your whole life. You can't tell me you don't love it."

I did love living in New Orleans. Growing up here had been a teenage boy's dream. There was always something to do, something to see, somewhere to get into trouble. I'd learned how to fight here, learned about the French culture, about jazz and zydeco music. I'd made friendships here, but my love for the city had died a little the day it turned its back on me.

I'd been a hometown hero, the guy who got free drinks at bars when I walked in, the guy who was stopped on the street for a handshake for representing New Orleans, but that all changed the minute the media found out about my alleged steroid use.

Steroid use. Just the term made me cringe. Never in my life had I taken the easy way out. I'd worked my ass off to get everything I'd earned, and one lapse in judgment had put a black mark on my name.

Tension started to roll through me, and Lyla instantly picked up on it.

"I'm sorry. I'm sure you probably have some sour feelings about this city after everything that happened."

"You could say that," I responded, gripping her hand tighter, trying to find solace in her touch.

"Have you ever thought about clearing your name?"

"Let's not ruin the night by talking about that."

Lyla's shoulders deflated from my rejection. I knew she wanted to know more, that she wanted to help, but it was pointless opening that wound. That was in the past. It was over. No use trying to relive it. I'd moved on, or at least I'd convinced myself I had.

"Let's go in here," Lyla said, dragging me toward Toulouse Royale, a typical souvenir shop.

The shop was well maintained and had a large variety of shirts, Cajun hot sauces, beads, and of course, make-your-own-beignet kits stocked on multiple shelves. There were stuffed alligators everywhere, and the back wall was covered with burlesque masks.

"Oh, let's look at the masks."

The masks were on display at the back. They weren't as nice as the Jett Girl masks I used to order for the girls, but they came close. They were intricate and nicely made, considering we were in a souvenir shop. I was impressed.

"What do you think?" Lyla said, putting on a grey and yellow lace mask.

"I think you look hot," I admitted, loving the mask on her.

"Is that flattery?"

"Take it how you want it." I smirked, leaning against a pillar with my arms crossed. "Try on that green one with the feathers." I nodded toward one that had caught my attention. I knew the color was going to make her eyes stand out.

"This one?" she asked, pulling it off the wall.

"Yes, that one."

A large smile lit up her beautiful face right before she put the mask on, taking her time to make sure it was in place before she showed me.

With all the drama and flair I would expect her to use, she turned slowly and showed me what she looked like in the mask. My heart beat faster as her green eyes lit up behind the mask. She looked beyond sexy.

"Come here," I said, looping fingers through her belt loop and pulling her into my personal space.

My heart wavered with my mind as I tried to decide what to do with this woman who'd made it her mission to constantly stay present in my life. I wanted her more than anyone before, but the dark part of me knew I didn't deserve her, knew if she actually understood who I was, the real man, she would want nothing to do with me.

But I was a selfish prick, and even though I knew we wouldn't work out, maybe just for tonight I could give in, I could have another small taste of Lyla.

I pulled her in close and rested my hands on her hips. She looked up at me, searching my eyes, wondering what I was doing by pulling her in, in such an intimate way. I had no clue what I had planned with her being this close, but what I did know was that the way she rested her hands on my chest and the way she lightly nibbled lips when she looked up at me was my undoing.

Slowly, I lifted her chin and brought her perfect lips to mine. I kissed her lightly, then pulled away quicker than she wanted and touched the mask, letting the feathers run between my fingers.

"You look fucking sexy in this. It will be taken home tonight."

"Are you getting it for me?" she asked, a little shocked.

"Yeah. Isn't that what guys do for girls on dates? They buy them things."

"My, my, my, Kace Haywood, you're a regular charmer."

"What can I say?" I said, shrugging.

I started toward the register, but she stopped me. "Wait, I need to get you something."

"I don't need anything," I answered honestly.

"But I want to. How about some hot sauce?"

"Nah, that's just novelty crap."

"Beignet kit?"

"Rather go to Café du Monde," I replied, liking this little game.

"Magnet?"

"No fridge to put it on, and to hell if I'll be sharing my magnet with Diego and Blane."

She looked around the store and then her eyes lit up. "Oh, I know."

I cringed when she walked over to the graphic T-shirts. I was very much a plain T-shirt kind of guy. I didn't think much about my style, and I never wore novelty shirts, especially of the city I was born and raised in, but by the way Lyla's face lit up, I knew that rule would be changing quickly.

"Lyla, not a T-shirt," I said, hoping to avoid the thoughts that were running through her mind.

"Yes, a T-shirt. Oh, these are great. Let's see, shall I get you a classic NOLA shirt? Maybe a fleur-de-lis? Maybe an alligator rowing a… wait." She squatted to reach a stack of shirts on a lower shelf. "You're a medium, right?"

"Large, sweetheart. Man's got muscles," I replied, making her snort.

"How could I forget," she said sarcastically. "All right, this is perfect. I'm getting it."

"Let me see it." I reached for her arm, but she snuck past me and practically ran to the register. She pulled money out of her wallet and asked about the return policy, telling the cashier she needed to write "no return allowed" on the receipt.

I shook my head at her ridiculousness and thought about how, in one short evening, Lyla had been able to lift the dark cloud that'd been hanging over my life temporarily. She had a way of making me forget everything that had happened to me in the past and possibly look forward to the future. It was confusing, but damn if I didn't like it.

"I don't need a bag, but thank you." She turned to me. "Once you purchase the mask, we can get you changed into your new shirt."

"Why do I feel like taking you out is going to come back and bite me in the ass?"

"Don't worry," she whispered in my ear. "What I have planned for you next will make up for it."

My pulse skipped a beat as she rubbed her soft body against mine. Was the date over? I wouldn't mind too much if that meant I was able to go back to her place and slip under her covers with her, and possibly worship that perfect body of hers.

I paid for her mask, all the while the cashier giggled about the shirt I was about to put on, making me wonder what kind of shirts they sold in this shop that could be that bad.

Taking my bag, I took Lyla's hand in mine, and we left the store. Outside, I turned her so she was facing me and pressed her up against the side of the building.

"Do I get my shirt now?" I asked, eye-fucking her to my best ability.

"Are you going to wear it?" she asked, fluttering her eyelashes at me.

"You think your pretty eyes are going to convince me?"

"I was hoping they would," she said, running her hand up my stomach, making my nerve endings jump in anticipation of what was to come.

"I think that might just work."

"Yay!" She stood on her toes and kissed my jaw. Warmth spread over me from her touch, something I was starting to grow fond of. "You're going to love it."

From the bag, she pulled a folded black shirt and shook it out. On it were two animated nipple tassels perfectly placed for a man of my size.

"You're kidding, right?" I asked, tickled.

"Nope, this is just for you, big guy. Now put it on."

She yanked on the hem of my shirt and started pulling it over my head.

"Whoa, hold up," I said while I tried to slow her down, but she had the thing almost over my head, ready to come off.

Not being able to fight her off, I removed my shirt, and I was standing in the middle of the French Quarter bare-chested. Weirdly, it wasn't a strange occurrence at all.

Standing there, I watched Lyla take in the contours and caves of my chest with heat in her eyes, heat that immediately started to turn me on. She was taking her sweet-ass time perusing my body and honestly, I didn't give two fucks that she did. *Stare all you want*, I thought.

Clearing my throat to gather her attention, I held out my hand. "Are you going to give me that?"

"Uh, yeah." She handed it over. She held my other shirt as I put on the nipple-tasseled garb. The sleeves were a little tight and the bottom was slightly loose because of my narrow waist, but that was a given with regular shirts like these. They always fit me in a weird way.

After staring down at the tassels, I looked up to see Lyla covering her mouth and laughing. The sound of it was intoxicating. It melted my cold, dark heart on the spot.

"This funny to you?" I asked, holding out my arms.

She nodded and pulled a bonus item from the bag.

"Buy a shirt, get a free hat," she said. She popped the back of the hat out so she could place it on my head. It was a black trucker's hat, and on the front was an animated crawfish holding up its claw. To one side, it said, "Suck this."

Novelty to the extreme.

She adjusted the size of the hat and placed it on my head, cocking it to the side just slightly.

"Can't have you looking like a total dweeb." She winked. She stepped back and took a look at me. "Even with that ridiculous hat and shirt on, you're still hot as fuck."

"That's good to know." I grinned, enjoying the candid compliment. "Are we headed back to your place now?" I asked, a little too eager.

"No, I have something else in mind."

"Kitten's Castle?" I teased as she linked my hand with hers and led me down the street.

She glared at me. "No, not Kitten's Castle."

We walked hand-in-hand, enjoying the blustery night and the sounds of zydeco music being played on the corner of Toulouse and Royale.

"Hey, suck this!" a drunk man said while grabbing his crotch and walking by us, referring to the stupid crawfish on my hat.

I gave him a thumbs-up and kept walking. Fucking idiots.

"Got to love the atmosphere," Lyla said.

"And the tacky hats you get for free."

"It's a very nice-looking crawfish, plus it has meaning,

Kace."

"How do you figure?" I asked, adjusting the hat.

"Uh, hello. Our first date was eating crawfish."

It didn't escape me that she'd used the term "first date." Instead of correcting her that this would be our only date, I let the comment slide because frankly, I was having a good time, and I didn't want to spoil that, even if this night was a onetime thing for me. If I was only going to be with her in a "boyfriend" capacity for one night, I wanted to remember it as a good time.

"Here we are," Lyla said, stopping and letting the awkward moment slide away.

I scanned the street and saw we were standing outside a building that was smartly lit up on the inside. A sign hanging over it said Trashy Diva.

"Where are we?" I asked, wondering what Lyla was up to.

"You'll see." She smiled, pulling me inside.

I didn't have to walk too far into the store to realize Lyla had brought me to a lingerie store. Chandeliers lit up the small space. Light bounced off the white walls and racks of dresses were lined up in the front of the store, but that wasn't what caught my attention. What had a light sheen of sweat breaking out over my skin were the small pieces of fabric in the back.

"Help me pick something out," Lyla suggested with an evil glint.

"Hey, Lyla," a clerk called to her. "Looking for anything in particular?"

"Hey, Tammy. I am. I'm looking for something green or something that would look pretty with green."

Tammy tapped her chin with a pen and then said, "I've got a couple of ideas. Shall I set you up in a room?"

"Please. Can I have a corner room, please? I want this guy to be able to sit comfortably while I try things on."

Tammy gave me the once-over and hid a snicker the minute her eyes landed on my shirt.

Rolling my eyes, I said, "It's the only kind of lingerie I will wear."

Tammy out-right laughed. "Well, it's very becoming on you."

I liked Tammy.

While she and Lyla talked, I went to the back, where a gold chair was tucked in the corner. I took a seat and waited patiently as Tammy pulled a couple of items for Lyla. I wasn't going to lie; I was actually pretty damn thrilled about this portion of the date.

Once Lyla was behind a curtain, I stared down at the tassels on my shirt, wondering who the hell had printed such a thing. Apparently there were zero standards when it came to shirt-making.

"Are you ready?" Lyla called from behind the curtain.

I looked around to see if anyone else was in the store. In the midst of looking at my shirt, I missed the fact that Tammy had put up a sign in the store front that had a clock on it, making me assume she'd taken off for a quick break, leaving Lyla and I alone.

Excitement boiled inside of me. "Yeah," I answered.

Lyla whipped open the curtain and strutted toward me, taking my fucking breath right from my lungs.

Standing before me, she was wearing the mask I'd just bought her with a piece of lingerie that should have been illegal. It was a green top that came to just below her hips, it was skin tight, and it was fucking see-through. She'd neglected to wear a bra, displaying her hardened nipples to perfection. A black thong was wrapped around her hips, making me silently beg for her to turn around.

She stood in front of me with zero shame. "If only I had on some strappy heels, it would be the perfect the outfit."

"Fuck the heels," I rasped, taking her entire body in. I shifted in my seat, but it did nothing for the raging hard-on I was sporting.

"Do you like?" she asked, as if she couldn't tell.

Linking our hands together, I pulled her down on my lap so she was straddling me and said in a husky tone, "You tell me. Do you think I like it?"

"Hmm, not sure. Let me see." Her hips started to rock back and forth on my lap, creating a mind-numbing friction. "It seems you might like it."

"Don't start something you can't finish," I reminded her as my hands fell to her hips, forcing her to press down harder.

"I thought we went over this at dinner. I always finish, Kace."

Her hands ran up my chest and wrapped around my neck. She pulled her body in closer to mine and nipped at my jaw. I felt the feathers of her mask run along my face, turning me on even more.

I slowly moved up to her rib cage, where I rested for a short period of time, allowing for her heart rate to pick up from my touch. She became breathless as my hands moved up even farther until the pads of my thumbs just barely grazed the underside of her breasts.

A light moan escaped her, and her hips started to move faster across my lap.

I whispered in her ear, "Are you dry-humping me right now?"

"Yes, I have no shame when it comes to you," she answered breathlessly.

And I had no control when it came to this gorgeous woman

sitting on my lap. "Get your clothes, we're leaving," I commanded her gruffly.

"I have a robe I can borrow. No time for clothes," she answered.

Reluctantly, she retreated to the dressing room as I rested my elbows on my knees. I ran my hands through my hair, wondering what the hell I was thinking. This woman was tearing me apart and all in one night.

I kept reminding myself this was going to be a onetime thing. Once I fucked her out of my system, I would go back to the dark hole where I belonged, but just this night I would live without worry, without self-hatred, without the thought of the kind of monster I was. For one night, I was going to be the free-spirited man I'd once been.

The man I'd been before taking someone's life.

CHAPTER FOURTEEN

My present...

The trip from the lingerie store to Lyla's apartment seemed to take forever when in fact I knew it had only been a short few minutes. But with the way she was rubbing up against me, nibbling on my ear, sticking her hand down the back of my pants, she had me panting and wishing I could just take her down one of the dark alleys of the Quarter.

The rickety steps of Lyla's building creaked in distress as we ran up them to get to her apartment. I watched with impatience as she fumbled for her keys.

"Need help?" I asked, desperation in my voice.

"I got it." She winked.

I pressed my front against her back as she worked the locks on her door, tasting the skin below her ear. She was intoxicating; her smell, the velvet texture of her skin, everything about her was like a dream, and I was getting so fucking lost in it.

The creak of her door broke my lips from her neck, and without giving her a chance to move, I picked her up and took her inside.

I had time for one quick glance around. The walls were made of cracked plaster, her floors were wood that dipped with every step you took, and the temperature of her apartment was stifling from the warm but windy night we were having.

"Bedroom?" I asked, looking into her beautiful green eyes, not quite remembering my way around.

"Second door down the hall."

I found the room easily. I pushed her door open and was greeted with a large bed that took up all the space in the room. There was a small dresser to one side that I wasn't sure if she could actually open the drawers to. Even though her bed took up all the space in her room, she had the softest looking sheets, and a thick comforter invited me to lay down.

I placed Lyla on the bed and looked down at her as I grabbed the back of my T-shirt and pulled, giving her a little show. Her eyes lit up with elation as she pushed her robe to the side and tossed her clothes to the limited amount of floor space between her wall and the bed.

Laid out on her bed, Lyla showed off her delectable body as she leaned back on her elbows and waited for me to make the next move. Her nipples were puckered from excitement. Her breasts were prominently on display from the lingerie, and her flat, toned stomach showed me just how much she trained for her job at Kitten's Castle.

The thought of other men seeing what I got to see made an animalistic and possessive thought pass through me. I didn't want anyone seeing her like this. No one besides me should have the pleasure of seeing her naked.

"Are you just going to stand there?" Lyla asked, taking in my physique.

I gripped the back of my neck and contemplated my next

move. If I did this, if I spent the night worshipping every inch of her, I would be setting myself up for sheer disappointment when it was over, because I knew what Lyla and I had was never going anywhere beyond tonight. But could I really walk away? Could I honestly grab my shirt and walk out her front door with her looking so damned sexy and tempting?

Looking at her glistening pink lips and such yearning in her eyes, I knew then and there I was going to be screwed. I needed her.

"Scoot back." I motioned for her to move deeper on the bed.

She obliged, giving me room to lean down on one knee and stretch out over her. I placed both of my hands on either side of her head, and her eyes flickered across my chest, watching my muscles flex with my motions. She acted tough most of the time, but I saw the weakness I brought out of her, and like the sick fuck I was, I enjoyed it. I liked seeing I could bring such a strong woman down a peg, that I had an effect on her.

Carefully, I lowered my head until I was mere inches from her face and spoke softly to her, revealing a little part of my soul. "What are you doing to me?" I asked, wondering why I was voicing my worries.

Her hand ran up my chest, then to my neck, and finally cupped my cheek. Her thumb brushed the scruff on my jaw and her eyes softened as she pulled my head down to hers. Very lightly, she nipped at my lips, and I slowly let her open my mouth with her tongue, igniting a flame inside me that'd been burned out for a while.

I went down on my elbows so my body weight was more evenly distributed on top of her and gripped her face while I kissed her back with the same kind of passion she was giving me. Her lips glided perfectly across mine. Slowly, I felt her fingertips work their way under the back of my jeans, looking to tease me.

The heat of her touch sent a blaze of fire through my veins, igniting my desire for her, my need for more, my need to be deep inside her.

I dipped my tongue farther into her mouth, matching her thrusts. A moan escaped her throat. Her hips pressed against mine, begging for more, wanting me to move lower, to pay attention to the rest of her body, but I was too lost in her kiss. I was enjoying her mouth way too damn much to move away.

"Kace...," she said breathlessly. "Touch me."

"I am," I said gruffly as my mouth went back to hers. There was something to say about making out with a gorgeous woman. Yes, fucking was the end result, but getting their way of mouth was how I fucking rolled.

Wanting to keep her satisfied, I lightly stroked her hair, then moved down her side, where I played with the side of her breast by lightly stroking it with my thumb. Through the sheer fabric of her lingerie, I could feel the heat pouring off her, a light sheen of sweat starting to cover her delectable body. That's when I realized I needed her naked, completely and utterly naked.

Reluctantly, I tore my lips away from hers, causing an unpleasant protest to erupt. I chuckled from the look of displeasure on her face but then grabbed the bottom of her lingerie as I straddled her lap and started to bring it up and over her head. She sat up and raised her arms, making it easier for me to take it off. I tossed it aside. To my shock, she still wore a sheer bra underneath the lingerie set. At the lingerie store, I never would have guessed she was wearing one.

I rolled off her lap, hooked her thong with my fingers, and easily took it off.

I kneeled to the side, observing Lyla as she rested on the bed with her hair fanned out and her legs slightly bent and crossed at the ankles. If she was trying to seduce me, she didn't have to give it much thought because I was hard as a fucking rock.

While staring at her, I undid my belt slowly, tossed it to the side, and then undid my jeans. I didn't take them off because I wanted her to do that for me, but I did leave them open, showing off just enough of my happy trail to entice her.

She licked her lips and reached out to me. I accepted her gesture and entwined our fingers. I lay down next to her, putting our clasped hands above her head. I stroked her stomach, reveling in the feel of her skin. Her muscles twitched under my touch, and her breathing picked up while I explored every inch of her.

I swirled my finger around her belly button and danced low on her pelvic bone but pulled away quickly, torturing her. My hand then went up to her chest where I moved my fingers very slowly through the prominent cleavage on display.

She twisted under me, begging for me to touch her more, to touch her where she wanted, but I was taking my sweet-ass time. Tonight was going to be on my terms.

I lowered my head to her neck and she leaned to the side so I had better access to run my tongue along her pulse. I would never get enough of how she tasted. It was sweet like honey and maybe a little bit of spice. It was unique—everything about her was fucking unique—and that was why she'd captured me so quickly.

Instead of using my fingers, I spread the palm of my hand against her and ran it up the front of her stomach, stopping below her breasts. She rolled to one end, trying to force me to go higher, but I didn't let her win. I kept myself still and continued to nibble on her neck, all the while knowing I was driving her crazy.

"Please, Kace," she moaned, her legs now moving, her hips lifting in the air. If she was as turned on as I was, I knew she had to be soaking wet. I wanted to see if she was, but I knew if I ventured down to her pussy, I was never going to be able to leave.

I pressed the side of my finger against the underside of her breast, causing her to push down enough that her breast fully rested on my finger. If I hadn't been so lost in the moment, I might have laughed from the desperation she was displaying.

"Touch me, Kace. Don't make me ask again," she demanded, trying to top me from the bottom. Little did she know she wasn't getting anywhere with her little commands.

"Every time you ask for something, you will have to wait even longer." I nuzzled her ear.

"You can't do that," she complained.

"I can do whatever the fuck I want," I replied. "I could fucking leave right now if I wanted," I threatened, knowing damn well there was no way in hell I was going to follow through. I was almost positive I wanted this more than she did.

"Don't go," she said with a touch of sadness.

I rubbed my hand up against her breast, cupped her face, and said, "I'm not going anywhere, baby." Even though it was a lie, it eased the worried look on her face. "Why me?" I asked, needing to know what the draw was, what she saw in me. If anything, I needed to know that maybe someone saw me for who I wished I could be—a strong, confident man—not who I actually was.

Sadly though, I wasn't that man. Instead, I was eaten alive every day by a set of demons that wouldn't leave me alone, no matter how hard I tried to ignore them.

Lyla's patience was wearing thin. I saw the tension that was starting to coil inside of her ease a fraction. She shifted underneath me and placed one hand on my chest, right above my heart. The other caressed my jaw gently.

"There is so much about you that attracts me, Kace. It's hard not to be drawn to you. It's not just because you're devastatingly handsome, but it's the heart I see in you. You might not think you show it, but you have a giant heart. You care about the girls, you care about Jett, and you care about this community even though they turned their back on you during the lowest point in your life. You're strong, you're sure of yourself, and you know what you want. You're sexy as hell, and even though you're fighting an inner battle, you still have a spark in your eye that I see occasionally when you get excited about things like the community center or helping others. You're a good person, and you've made it incredibly hard on me, not giving me a chance."

My breath escaped my lungs from her words. How could she see me so differently? When I looked in the mirror every morning, I saw a murderer, a coward, a detached and broken man. How could she think such positive things about me? How could she see me in such a shining light when I knew the way she described me was so off-base?

I shook my head and started to retreat from her, but she gripped my shoulders before I could pull away.

"Stay with me, Kace. Please don't leave. Live this moment with me. Even if it's just this moment, live it with me. Be with me for this piece of time."

Her eyes watered as she stared up at me, begging me to stay. I'd told myself I would give her this night, and even though her words shook me to my core, I knew I had to stay, if not for her than for myself. I wanted to be selfish one more time.

I pressed my hand against her cheek and wiped away a stray tear. Leaning down, I brushed a soft kiss against her forehead, lingering my lips while I breathed in her sweet scent, a scent that immediately calmed my raging heart and eased my soul.

Slowly, I moved my lips down her cheeks to her jaw, kissing her all along the way, taking my time as I relished in the soft feel of her skin against my mouth.

Her fingers found the belt loop of my jeans and gripped tightly, pulling my hips closer to hers. I pressed my erection against undulating hips that were begging for more, making me inwardly smile from her neediness. Even though I was a corrupt bastard, I still enjoyed the feeling of being needed, the feeling of being able to take care of a woman, to own her, at least for one night.

I continued my descent until I got to her breasts, which were aching to be released from the confines of the lingerie she had picked out at the store. Thankful for the flimsy fabric, I tore it, exposing her bare breasts to the warm night air. Her gasp made her chest rise and fall, moving her breasts at a rapid rate that had the crotch of my jeans throbbing.

"You're better naked," I said, moving my lips to the swell of her breasts.

Her legs wrapped around my hips, pulling me in even closer. Like a desperate man, I rubbed the crotch of my jeans against her heat, soaking in every mew that escaped her mouth.

My tongue darted out to her skin and made deliberate circles around one nipple, causing a frustrated cry to escape her lips. Carefully, my teeth nipped at her puckered nipple, making her fingers to claw into my back. I welcomed the new pain and in return pushed my tongue against her nipple and lapped at her skin. I rounded her nipple, flicked it, and then finally sucked it into my mouth while biting down with little pressure.

"Yes," she screamed as she arched under me.

Pleased with her reaction, I moved to her other breast and gave it the same treatment. As she writhed under me and ground into my hips, I moved my hand down to the juncture of her thighs, letting her know what my next move was going to be.

Pulling away from her now red nipples, I looked at her and was rewarded with the vision of a picture perfect woman lying naked under me. Her eyes were glazed with passion, her skin was slick with sweat, and her hair was messy from my hands. She was a woman in need, and fuck if I wasn't about to fulfill that need.

I stood up and found the button of my jeans. A gorgeous smile caressed her face as she scooted forward on the bed and pulled me between her spread legs. From my view, I could see how turned on she was for me, which in return turned me on even further.

She ran her hands around my waist, to my back, where she pressed them down into my pants and briefs, dragging them over my ass and down to the floor. My heavy shaft sprang free.

I stepped out of my clothes and faced her, my cock at her eye level. With greed in her eyes, she gripped the root of my dick and pulled on it hard, milking me in one smooth stroke.

A sharp hiss escaped my lips as I dropped my hands to her shoulders to gain some balance. Her tongue darted to lick the tip of my cock. The little teasing motion didn't escape me; I knew she was trying to torture me just like I'd done moments ago, but the difference between my torture and hers was that mine had been short-lived.

I pressed against her shoulders, making her fall to the bed. I fell on top of her, our skin meeting, the warmth of our bodies igniting a flame I knew would burn until the early morning light.

I gripped her hands in mine, threading our fingers together, and brought them above her head as I straddled her body. My cock lay heavily on top of her pubic bone, and I lowered my head to her mouth where I greedily nipped, sucked, and kissed her full lips.

"God, Kace. I need you so fucking bad. Fuck me, please just fuck me."

A part of me wanted to do as she asked, to plow into her and take what I wanted, but I couldn't do that, not with the way she'd spoken to me earlier, not after the kind words she'd expressed to me. She deserved more, she deserved to be made love to, and that's what I set out to do.

I dug my fingers into hers, and my muscles rippled above her as I continued the slow, arduous process of worshipping her body, of slowly rolling my hips just enough where she gasped, where I could barely feel the wet seeping from her.

The feeling of having Lyla underneath me, completely at my mercy, was addicting. It was mind-altering. It had me thinking I could possibly give her more, that I could stuff away my demons and try to live a normal life with this woman. She gave me hope for a future, a future I knew wasn't for me.

Releasing one of my hands from hers, I ran it down the length of her body to the juncture of her thighs, where I pressed a finger against her clit. Immediately I was welcomed by a warm liquid that was all Lyla.

"Fuck," I groaned from realizing just how wet she was. "Lyla, you're so fucking wet."

"For you, for only you," she replied, kissing lightly against my jaw.

Growling, I pressed two fingers inside her and watched as her entire body reacted to the invasion. She moaned, squeezed her eyes shut, and covered her forehead with an arm.

Needing a small taste, I made a trail of kisses down the front of her body until I hovered right above her pussy. I took the opportunity to spread her legs wide enough so I could fit between them and then lowered myself.

Her breath hitched, she squirmed, her skin glistened from sweat as my fingers spread her apart, and my tongue struck her with force, causing her hips to hitch upward.

"Yes," she breathed, pulling on one of the pillows resting near her. I watched in fascination as I worked my tongue in and out of her as she gripped the sheets, begging for more.

While I ran my tongue up and down her pussy, I kept my eyes on her the entire time. I watched as her lips parted slightly, soft cries escaping her plump lips. I relished in the taste of her, in every reaction and every movement she made. She was addicting.

This was what a little breath of heaven must feel like. Right here, watching the woman of your dreams crumble to pieces from the touch of your tongue. I was in a fucking dream.

From under my lashes, I stared at her stomach muscles contracting with each swipe of my tongue. Her mouth gasped for air with each inhale of her heady scent, and her control slowly slipped. I showed no mercy.

"I'm going to come, Kace," she announced just as I pressed two fingers inside of her. She arched off the bed as a shrill cry escaped her. "Yes! Fuck, fuck! Yes, more, please more."

Her hips undulated against my tongue, taking her orgasm to a new level. I allowed her to ride me just the way she wanted and watched in fascination while she dissolved into a puddle of content pleasure under me.

My cock painfully throbbed between my legs, begging to enter her, to take what it wanted. I itched to feel what it was like to be inside her again. I wanted to be sheathed by her warmth, to get lost in her body, so I reached down to my jeans while she recovered and grabbed a condom from my wallet.

Quickly sheathing myself, I hovered back over her and waited for her to open her eyes. The moment her pools of meadow green stared at me, my heart swelled and I smiled. There was something different about Lyla, something that made me think for only a moment that maybe, just maybe, she would understand my drunken sin.

She cupped my cheek. The unspoken emotion we were both feeling settled in the pit of my stomach just as she spread her legs open for me and pressed her hand deeper into my cheek, urging me to move forward.

My eyes instantly closed from the warmth pouring from her.

"Take me, Kace. Take me to a place far away from here. Make us forget the past and the present." Her voice was soft, encouraging.

Taking a deep breath, I lowered my mouth down to hers and passionately kissed her while my arms fell to the sides of her head, framing her in my heat. My hips settled between her legs, and the tip of my needy cock rubbed against her slick core. Her hips moved against mine, allowing my cock to play with her entrance, but that's all I allowed while I fucked her mouth with my tongue.

I was greedy, I was selfish, I took everything I wanted, not letting her have a say in any of it, but she didn't complain. Instead, she matched every stroke of my tongue, every thrust of my hips, and every tightening of my body.

She was just as greedy as me if not more. It was a battle

of wills. Who was going to crack first? Who was going to give in and start begging for more?

My cock pounded with need, with yearning, and even though I wanted the upper hand, I wanted her to beg just one more time. I didn't think I could take the wait any longer, so I grabbed her hands and pulled away.

Linking our hands together again, I brought them above her and lowered my forehead to hers. Looking into her eyes, I pressed my hips forward and felt my cock slowly slide inside her tight canal. Her eyes squeezed shut, and her breath hitched.

Kissing her forehead, I said, "Look at me, baby. Let me see those beautiful eyes."

Immediately her eyes flew open, and my fucking gut twisted in my stomach from the loving kindness radiating off of her. Her eyes glistened, and the strong walls I'd erected around my soul started to fade.

Instead of focusing on her eyes that were tearing me apart, I tried to bring my attention down to our most intimate connection. I focused on the feel of her tight pussy, the way her hips moved with mine, and the building of pressure inside my cock with each stroke.

I'd had sex with Lyla before. We'd fucked but never shared an intimate moment like this before. We'd never looked into each other's eyes, trying to understand one another. This was different from fucking. This was making love, and why I was letting it happen, I would never understand.

Maybe I was a masochist. I enjoyed inflicting pain on myself, well-deserved pain. Maybe I knew that after tonight nothing could transpire between us, so I'd gone all in. I gave her everything I had, knowing in return my heart was going to be ripped out of my chest when I left.

But what about Lyla? Could I really do that to her?

"Kace, yes, harder." Lyla writhed under me, seeking more from me, and even though I knew I was going to destroy both of us when we were done, I couldn't fucking stop. I wanted to give her everything she wanted, so I did.

With brutal force, I slammed into her and then pressed my lips against hers. Her fingers gripped mine tightly, showing me how forceful I was being, how much pleasure I was able to deliver.

The weight in my cock was undeniable. I was on the precipice of orgasm, waiting, prolonging the inevitable, wishing she would come with me, needing her to come with me.

I was about to release my hand from hers to push against her clit when her chest arched up into mine and she gasped.

Like a fucking vice, her pussy clenched around me and an indescribable sound departed from her enticing lips. She rocketed against me, screaming my name as tears fell from her eyes.

That was all it took. I felt from the rumble of my stomach to the base of my cock the explosion of my pleasure inside of her.

"Fuck...!" I roared as I pounded into her until she milked me dry.

I slowed my hips down as my cock continued to throb inside her. Her breathing evened out, and that's when I realized I'd buried my head in her shoulder. Slowly, I picked my head up and smiled at her.

"You're so fucking sexy when you come," she said as her erect nipples teased my chest.

"I can say the same about you, baby."

CHAPTER FIFTEEN

My present...

Hundreds of cracks covered the plaster ceiling of Lyla's apartment, just another feature that bothered me about where Lyla lived. I stroked her back as she pressed against me, resting her head on my shoulder and running the tips of her fingers along the ridge of my abdomen.

No words were spoken as we lay in her twisted sheets, the moonlight shining through her window and on our slightly sweaty bodies.

The silence was welcome. It was necessary for my beating heart, my uneasy thoughts of what was to come next. I didn't want to talk about the future—whether I was staying the night, whether I would be able to get out of her bed and leave.

With my spare hand, I rubbed the top of my head, agonizing over my feelings for her, my desire to keep her near but my urgency to push her as far away from me as possible.

"Are you thirsty?" she asked.

"I'm all right," I replied, feeling awkward.

"I need a drink." She pushed off my chest and crawled

across the bed butt naked and then walked out of the room, wiggling her ass for me in the most delicious way.

Once she was gone, I groaned and pulled on the strands of my hair. What the fuck was I thinking? Inner turmoil churned as I weighed my options. One part of me kept telling me to leave, get the fuck out of her apartment while I still had a shred of protection around my black soul. The other part of me yearned to hold her all night long.

With a racing heart, I threw the sheets aside and was getting out of the bed when Lyla reappeared. Her hair was mussed from my fingers, her lips swollen from my unyielding kisses, and her eyes sated from my lovemaking. She was a completely satisfied woman with a kind understanding coming from her eyes.

"Leaving?" she asked, leaning against the wall of her room and sipping a glass of water. She didn't look upset or mad, almost like she'd expected me to want to go.

"I don't know," I answered honestly. I wasn't sure what the fuck I wanted. I'd never been so unsure about something in my life.

Staring at her fucking amazing body and beautiful personality, I knew I didn't deserve her. The moment I'd taken a man's life, I'd sworn I would never be happy again, that I would serve my repentance and then die on this earth alone, so why was I half kneeling on Lyla's bed, considering doing something I had no right to?

"What does it say?" Lyla asked, nodding at the tattoo on my ribs.

"Nothing of importance," I answered, turning so it wasn't so visible.

Indignation passed over Lyla's features as she placed her cup of water on the floor near the window and walked toward me. My gaze fell to the floor to avoid the beautiful sway of her hips and the way her plump breasts tried to capture my attention. If I didn't look down, I was going to be swept up in her body again, a mistake I so desperately wanted to entertain.

She grabbed hold of my shoulders and pushed me down on the bed. Like a fucking leaf in the breeze, I floated to the mattress, not putting up a fight. I was too damn weak, too damn desperate for human contact to fend her off.

I was a desolate man, broken and battered and clinging to the one thing I knew would ruin me.

Lyla straddled my hips, keeping her heated core away from my growing erection, torturing me by not giving my cock what it wanted. I was too engrossed in what she was doing to notice her hands running up the side of my ribcage.

"Seeking Repentance," Lyla read, softly trailing her fingers over the black ink that branded my body. Her soft gaze found mine and her head tilted to the side in question. "What are you seeking repentance for, Kace?"

My eyes quickly shut as I tried to block out the question, tried to ignore the fact that she was digging further and further into my fucking soul.

I didn't talk about my past to anyone. I barely spoke to Jett, the man who knew the whole story, about it. It was a general understanding that we didn't talk about it. The only time we ever reflected on my actions was on the anniversary of the day my soul had died, no other time.

"Kace, it will help to talk about it."

"It won't," I gritted out. I pushed Lyla to the side and sat up. My elbows rested on my legs while I bent my head down and gripped my hair. The once euphoric yet confusing feeling vanished at the mention of my tattoo, and in its place was a cold, dark void, the emptiness I counted on to help me through my days.

My pain was much easier to forget than relive.

Small hands rested on my back while the bed dipped behind me. Lyla gripped me from behind and wrapped her arms around my waist.

"I'm sorry," she mumbled as she ran kisses up my back.

I went stiff from her tender touch. I didn't deserve this, this warm, caring woman. What did she even see in me? "Don't. Don't fucking apologize," I swore, hating myself.

She gripped me tighter and her warmth started to penetrate my cold exterior, melting me in her arms.

She encouraged me to lie down. I told myself to get up instead, to grab my clothes and get the fuck out of her place, but my body betrayed me and rested on one of her pillows. Lyla settled into my side and wrapped an arm around my waist. I moved my hand to her hair and ran my fingers through it.

A lump settled in my throat as I studied the cracks of her ceilings again and our breathing evened out. Why couldn't I let this woman go?

"You're not alone, Kace," Lyla said, breaking the silence between us. "You're not the only one with demons."

This wasn't the first time Lyla had mentioned something from her past. I knew there had to be something that happened in her life, that had her turning to the life she held now. A part of me wanted to know her story, wanted to help fix her problems, protect her and give her everything she needed, but how could I help her when I couldn't help myself? She wanted a whole man, someone to stand by her side, to fight and walk through this dark world with her.

I wasn't that man.

"You don't have to talk," Lyla said, rubbing my side. "You don't even have to ask any questions. I just need you to know where I'm coming from. I wanted you to know you're not alone, Kace."

There was no way in hell our stories were even close to being similar, but it was hard to resist what she was offering. Even though I knew I had to distance myself, I still wanted to know about her.

Instead of answering her, I pulled her closer, savoring the way her breasts felt against me, the way her nipples were puckered even though I wasn't trying to turn her on.

"I didn't always live in poverty, scraping for every last cent," she said. I tensed, wondering if I really wanted to hear this. "It was me and my dad my entire life. My mom wasn't interested in being a mom, which was fine because I would rather have no mom than a mom who lived with me but never gave me an ounce of attention. My dad gave me all the attention I needed."

I could feel her smile against my chest as she talked about her him. It was endearing.

"He was the best man I ever knew. He worked hard, provided for me, and made it to every dance recital I had. He was the perfect father."

"Sounds like it," I responded, surprising myself since the lump in my throat grew. I didn't understand what a close relationship with a father was like. Like my dad had said, I was a disappointment. He was probably laughing in his grave at me right now, watching me struggle with my day-to-day life. I knew in his eyes, I was a complete fuck-up, not worth the air I breathed.

Carefully dropping all thoughts of my father, I listened to Lyla continue her story. "After each recital, he would take me to get ice cream. We'd sit on a bench overlooking the Mississippi River and talk about our day. He would praise me for my pirouettes and tell me how pretty I was."

I kissed the top of her head. "You talk as if he is no longer in your life."

She gripped me tighter and sighed. "He's not." She took a deep breath. "He had a temper."

"Did he fucking touch you?" I growled, instantly ready to snap.

"No!" she practically shouted. "He'd never do anything like that to me. I was his entire life, Kace. His temper was never directed at me. He loved me dearly."

The tension in me eased. I didn't think I would have been able to handle hearing she was abused by her father.

"How did he die?" I asked, hating how invested I was getting in her story.

"My dad used to work at the Domino Sugar Refinery."

"In Chalmette?" I asked, referring to its location.

"Yup, he was a line supervisor."

I was impressed. That refinery was one of the oldest and biggest in the country. It brought a lot of needed jobs to the city of New Orleans.

"He worked hard to get to where he was," Lyla continued. "He was driven, determined to give me everything he thought I wanted when in fact all I wanted was him. He was my hero."

"What happened?" I asked, my heart splintering for Lyla.

"When he first got a job there, he started with a bunch of his friends. It was my dad and three other guys who entered the system together. They were inseparable and were like uncles to me. When I would visit my dad, they had a little pink hard hat for me."

Fuck my heart.

"My dance lessons got more expensive each year, and my dad insisted upon me taking them since I had talent and it was an after-school activity that kept me occupied while he was at work. Because expenses were high, he buckled down and worked harder, pushing his limits, pushing his friends' limits."

"He wanted to make more money. There is nothing wrong with that," I said.

"There is when you have a trigger-happy temper that goes off at the slightest disturbance. I don't really know the details, because no one would tell me, but I guess my dad got in an altercation with someone at work. It was quickly broken up, but it put a target on my dad's back. Later that night, when he was walking to the dance studio to pick me up, he was murdered in the back of an alley, brutally beaten to death."

Someone took her dad's life?

Sweat started to skate across my body, and my chest began to seize. "Someone murdered your dad?" I asked, barely able to squeak out the words.

"At first they thought he was kidnapped since they couldn't find him. I waited for hours in the dance studio for him to pick me up. Once I realized he wasn't coming, I went to my dance teacher, who called the cops for help. I was put into protective custody. They found his body in a dumpster in the alley."

My throat closed on me. I was being swallowed whole by the Lyla's grief and the thought of her father being taken away from her...just like Madeline.

"Shortly after, I was thrown into the foster care system since I didn't have any family, and I was quickly introduced into a different world where dance lessons didn't exist and a loving father no longer lived. I was tortured by the other girls, called nicknames like 'princess' and 'spoiled' because my stuff far exceeded what the other girls had."

"How old were you?" I choked out.

"Fourteen. I endured four years of torture until I was able

to get out of the home and survive on my own. My lack of education and my jaded outlook on the world landed me in the hands of Marv, the owner of Kitten's Castle. He took me in and showed me the ropes. Slowly, I worked my way up to the pole, where I am now."

Fuck, I couldn't breathe, I couldn't focus. The room was spinning, causing a kaleidoscope of cracks to appear on Lyla's ceiling. A black fog entered my brain as one sole thought appeared in my head.

Madeline, the daughter of the man I'd killed. She could end up just like Lyla, jaded and living in poverty with no future.

The urge to throw up had me springing up from the bed. Sweat trickled down my back and saliva flooded my mouth. I quickly grabbed my clothes and ran to the bathroom, making sure to close the door.

I fell to my knees in front of the toilet and retched violently, purging the contents of my stomach, along with the horrible pain that overtook my body from hearing Lyla's story. My throat burned from stomach acid, my muscles shook violently, and I clutched the cool porcelain until I didn't think I had anything left in me.

A light knock sounded at the door, and I prayed she didn't let herself in. I couldn't possibly recover from her seeing me like this. I was already gutted. I didn't need the humiliation as well.

"Kace, can I come in?"

Taking a deep breath, I replied, "No."

I could hear her sigh on the other end of the door, but I didn't give in to the temptation this time. I kept the barrier of the door between us.

Pulling myself off the floor, I put my jeans on and looked in the mirror.

An ugly version of the man I'd once known stared back at

me. Instead of the youthful face of someone full of potential and stardom, a broken, battered, and bruised man stared back at me. A man with age showing in his eyes, a man full of absolutely nothing, a man who only knew the feeling of remorse.

I gripped the counter and lowered my head, not able to look into my vacant blue eyes anymore. A lonesome tear left my eye and trailed down my face, surprising me with the heavy emotion I was feeling, knowing everything Lyla had been through had the potential to be what I put Madeline through or what she would be going through.

A piercing pain shot through my stomach, crippling me into the bathroom counter for support. My legs wobbled beneath me as I tried to regain control of my body. I was better than this. I was stronger than this. I didn't let such feelings enter my body.

With a need to extract myself from Lyla's apartment, I turned on the faucet and doused my face with water. I dried off with a little pink towel that was resting on a hook, reveling in the smell of Lyla on it. She was everywhere, making the need to leave that much stronger.

I flushed the toilet, pulled my tasseled shirt over my head, and took a deep breath before I opened the bathroom door. I half expected to see Lyla waiting for me, naked with her arms crossed, but she wasn't there.

Grateful, I went to her door, forgetting anything else I might have left behind. I was about to leave when a flash of purple caught my eye. Lyla was lounging on her couch, wearing a short purple silk robe, holding a glass of wine in her hand, and staring at the wall.

She didn't look at me, didn't even acknowledge my presence as I grabbed the doorknob. Without saying goodbye, I slipped out and walked the few blocks to Diego's apartment, where I grabbed a liter of whiskey and brought it up to my room.

It was time to forget.

CHAPTER SIXTEEN

My past...

Cheers erupted in the distance as I stepped out into the bright, stifling weather of New Orleans. The sun was brutal, bouncing off every surface in the park, making it almost unbearable to open my eyes. I put on my sunglasses, providing a protective layer not just from the sun, but from the truth I was about to face.

Several months had passed since the death, and I thought maybe the crippling feeling I experienced every day would have eased slightly with time, but that was the furthest thing from the truth. It only felt like the pain grew deeper.

Jett tried to distract me with the Lafayette Club, giving me more responsibilities and adding three more girls to the roster. He had me training them in the state-of-the-art gym, but it was just a minor distraction, nothing more.

A typical day of mine began with a long workout, beating a sand-filled bag until my knuckles felt raw in the boxing gloves, then I would shower, meet the girls in the gym, and train them with simple plyometrics. Afterwards, we would spend hours in the Toulouse Room, where I watched the girls practice their routines until I was satisfied with their performance. Food fell in there somewhere, but it was never anything I enjoyed because frankly, I couldn't taste anything anymore. It was all bland nourishment required to help me endure my arduous self-hatred. My nights were filled with getting lost in a bottle of hard liquor that was kept well stocked in the Lafayette Club. The next morning, I would repeat my day, never allowing myself to enjoy any aspect of my life.

I was a dead man walking the streets of New Orleans, a lifeless soul with no future, a fragmented and beaten down human with a passion to live a miserable life, serving a lifetime of repentance.

The crack of a ball against an aluminum bat shifted my thoughts to the tee-ball game. There was no baseball field, just a grass lot mapped with cones and bases, and lined with chairs of parents, cheering on their children. There were at least four fields in the park with the same setup, maximizing the park's space for the growing little league the city offered the community.

A snack table flanked one side of the fields, where a group of moms took money in exchange for sports drinks and sunflower seeds.

Children's laughter echoed through the park, owners walked their dogs, and parents tried to confine their littles ones who were supposed to be watching their older siblings play the simple game of baseball.

The park reeked of family, making me itch all over.

This was welcome torture.

The masochistic pain buried itself deep into my bones and radiated through my veins, reminding me once again that I was alive to feel such pain.

"Got you!" a little boy screamed in front of me, tagging his friend.

"No you didn't. You got my shirt. That doesn't count," his friend replied.

"Your shirt is on you, so I got you."

"Doesn't count," the boy who was not making a valid statement said.

"Does too," the tagger fought.

"No it doesn't," the cheater replied.

"Fine," the little boy said, stepping forward and punching his friend in the arm. "Got you now!"

Hell, a small smirk crossed my face from the genius move.

The other boy fell backward for a second and then regained his balance while holding on to his arm. His face raged and in an instant, they both took off running, yelling at each other the whole time.

The interaction made me think of all the times Jett and I had chased each other around during recess. We'd been from different classes in society, but that hadn't stopped Jett from meeting me out on the playground and forming a bond that could never be broken.

We'd been through everything together, and even though we'd had our fights, our disagreements, there was always an underlining understanding that whatever happened, we would always have each other's backs.

That pact had been prevalent in the last year. Jett had never left my side at the beginning of my boxing career. He'd been the driving force behind me, making sure I stayed true to myself. When I'd lost everything, been stripped of my career, he'd stood by me, believed in my innocence. When I had taken the life of another man, he'd covered up my guilt. He'd taken me in and provided shelter, a refuge for my contrition.

He stood by my side on days like today, when the urge to persecute myself weighed heavy on my shoulders.

"Do you know which field it's on?" Jett asked, pulling up next to me and putting on his sunglasses.

"No," I replied, looking around.

"Are you sure you want to do this?" Jett asked, placing a hand on my shoulder.

"I have to. This isn't an option."

"Why are you torturing yourself?"

I spoke as softly as I could over the uproarious cheers of the parents edging the fields' sidelines.

"You can either walk with me to the field and stand with me, or you can leave. Questions are not welcome. I fucking do this because I want to. Deal with it."

Without a word, Jett gave me a curt nod and followed me as I took off toward the fields, looking for the woman ingrained in my brain.

She had long brown hair that floated around her shoulders. Her skinny frame was not hard to see since she was tall for a woman. Her pointed shoulders and knobby knees were also easy to find, but it was the dark circles under her eyes I could never forget.

Linda Duncan, mother of one, wife of none.

I scanned the parents sitting in their camping chairs, lounging over coolers, and talking to each other while watching their children attempt to play baseball.

The first field was occupied by two teams wearing a hodge-podge of clothes, but you could tell one team was supposed to be yellow and the other orange. I didn't see anyone who resembled Linda Duncan, so I turned my attention to the second field, where teams of gray and purple played against each other. There was a huddle of parents on one side, drinking from their water bottles and laughing, but I didn't see Linda there either. I was about to turn to the third field when I heard a bunch of parents clap and start cheering for Madeline.

"Knock them in, Madeline!" a stout man called while he fist-pumped the air.

I spotted the little girl who'd been haunting my dreams. She wore a pair of jean shorts that were entirely too big on her and hoisted up around her waist with a pink belt. Her large purple jersey was tucked in, and the white shoes with pink laces she was wearing were marked with dirt.

She grabbed a bat from the ground and pushed up a helmet so she could see where she was going. She was tiny, too fucking tiny. It broke my heart in half.

"Come on, Madeline. You got this, baby," said a woman behind me.

Just before I looked behind me, Linda Duncan brushed past me on her way to the field, holding a bag of orange slices. My heart seized in my chest as the widow of the man whose life I'd taken passed me, her brown hair lifting in the light breeze. She was still too thin, but from the brief glance I got of her face, the dark circles were gone and she wore a bright smile.

Confusion hit me hard as I wondered why she looked so free, so happy. I glanced over at Madeline, who held the aluminum bat in one hand and pushed on her helmet again with the other. Freckles graced her cheeks and a tiny smile spread across her face when she saw her mom walking toward the field. Madeline raised her hand and waved at her mom with excitement. Linda gave her a thumbs-up and pointed at the field.

With determination, Madeline nodded and lifted the bat, barely able to hold the metal tube with her little arms.

"Is that them?" Jett asked.

Not able to speak over the knot in my throat, I nodded and stepped closer as Madeline waited for a ball to be placed on the tee in front of her.

Runners loaded the bases, waiting for Madeline to take her chance at a swing.

"Play ball," one of the coaches yelled.

Loading up, she swung, making direct contact with the tee and missing the ball completely.

"Strike one," the umpire called, putting the ball back on the tee.

Madeline ducked her head as she realized she'd zeroed in on the wrong target.

My stomach pitched at the look of defeat in her stance.

Linda went closer on the sidelines and bent so Madeline could see her. "Baby, you got this. Keep your eyes on the ball and swing hard, just like we practiced. You can do this, baby."

Madeline lifted her gaze to her mom, adjusted her helmet again, and nodded. She lifted the bat that was entirely too large for her and got in her stance.

"Play ball," the umpire called again.

Madeline took a deep breath and swung again, this time making contact with the ball just as her helmet fell forward.

"Run, Madeline, run!" Linda cried.

Comically, Madeline lifted her helmet and looked around, finally spotting the ball she'd hit toward the shortstop. Like a baby giraffe running for the first time, she took off toward third base, colliding with her teammate in the base path. The crowd laughed as the coaches and Linda told Madeline to run the other way.

Madeline scrambled to her feet and cut across the diamond to the other side of the field, where she touched first base before the other team was able to toss the ball in the right direction.

The whole attempt had been a clusterfuck of "what the hell do I do with this ball."

"That was funny," Jett said to me. I could hear the smile in his voice, and fuck if my lips didn't twitch to the side in amusement.

This was not what I'd wanted to see. I didn't want to see Linda leaping up and down, cheering for her daughter with a carefree attitude. I didn't want to see little Madeline prevail and do well. It was like they still had their husband/father, as if I hadn't robbed them of one of the most important people in their lives.

"This isn't right," I mumbled to Jett, turning away.

"What do you mean?" Jett asked, walking next to me.

"They're... happy." I gestured toward them. "They're fucking happy."

"And that is a problem because...?"

I ran my hand over the nape of my neck and looked up at the sky while I tried to find the right words to express my feelings. "I don't know. I just thought...they should be mourning the loss of Marshal."

"Maybe they are trying to move on, Kace. Something you should be doing. What you just saw were two souls trying to get on with their lives. Humans move on after traumatic incidences. The strong move on, Kace. You should be doing the same. If they're happy, if they're enjoying life, you should do the same."

"I'm not going to fucking learn from them," I snapped at Jett. "So they're having a good day. That doesn't mean they still aren't reeling from their loss. Appearances aren't everything." Not wanting to hear Jett's retort, I took off toward the car.

There was a bottle of whiskey waiting for me in my room, and it wasn't going to drink itself.

CHAPTER SEVENTEEN

My present...

Numb.

My entire body was numb, and it wasn't from sitting on the hardwood floors of my bedroom for hours on end. No, it was from the realization that Lyla was the grown-up version of Madeline.

It had been a week since I'd last spoken to Lyla, a week of living in my room, not moving from the confines of the four small walls unless I had to go to the bathroom or reload on liquor.

Diego and Blane had given up trying to get me to come out of my room after day four, especially after I threw my mattress at them.

My room was torn apart, my bed flipped upside down, my dresser tossed to the ground, and my bedding up against the door, blocking off any invaders. What used to be a safe haven was now a place of desolation.

A case of Maker's Mark rested next to me, as well as multiple empty bottles. Booze seeped from my pores, and every time I went to the bathroom, I peed out a little piece of my liver, but I was unfazed. I welcomed the destruction of my body. It was almost a high for me.

My brain was in a fog as I looked around my room, taking in the torn curtains, the broken cellphone that rested at the baseboard of my floor from when I'd smashed it into the wall. Then there were the multiple holes in the wall from where my fists had plowed through it, searching for a little relief from the misery I was feeling.

My hands were swollen, bruised, and battered. Multiple lacerations lined them, and dried blood crusted my knuckles.

The last time I had taken a shower was about a week ago, and even though I smelled like a rotting body, I didn't give one fuck. The only thing I cared about was the bottle in my hand and how quickly it was able to reach my lips.

I took pride in my ability to hold my alcohol, live a liquid diet, and waste my life away one amber droplet at a time.

I welcomed the challenge.

I rested my forehead against my arm that was propped against my knee while my hand gripped onto the neck of my bottle. I stared down at the ground, the cold, hard floor, wishing for the miserable life of mine to end. There was too much pain in my body, too much regret. I promised myself I would live this life out in torment, to pay back my sins through the agony of remorse but right about now, I would give anything to have it end.

Lyla had lost her dad, taken from her by the hands of another man. She'd grown up in the foster care system, fending for herself, praying day in and day out to be removed from her situation, to be extracted from the hell she was living in.

Now, she lived in a crumbling apartment, spending her nights stripping for horny and creepy men, wishing they could bone her in the back, wasting her life away just so she could earn a living.

Because of everything that had happened to her, she relied on no one, which was the main reason she wouldn't take Jett's help. She believed in the idea of being able to provide for herself, which was commendable, but she deserved so much better.

The telltale creak of the stairs gave away the approach of someone coming to my room. I kept my eyes on the ground, not letting the room spin on me from the amount of alcohol blazing through me, instead of trying to search out the intruder.

In a matter of seconds, there was a knock on my door. "Kace?"

Jett fucking Colby. I should have bet a million dollars on him showing up today. I'd felt it in my bones he would be making an appearance soon.

"Go the fuck away," I grumbled, feeling the effects of the alcohol in my system.

Not listening to my demand, not that I thought he would, he pushed the bedroom door but was stopped by my mattress on the floor. I smiled inwardly at my attempt at a barrier.

"What the fuck," Jett said behind the door, still pushing forward.

"I can squeeze through," Goldie said, making me groan.

What the fuck was she doing here? "Don't fucking come in here, Goldie," I shouted, lifting my head and toppling to the side, spilling my liquor on the floor. With great panic, I swiped the bottle upright and tipped it toward my mouth while my cheek rested on the hard wood.

My taste buds were completely anesthetized from the alcohol, allowing the liquor to burn down my throat at an easier and faster rate.

"Shut up, Kace," Goldie said. She wiggled in through the crack between the door and jamb, letting herself in.

From where I could see her, she was a blur of black cotton-covered legs and long golden hair.

"Holy shit," she said. "What the hell did you do?"

"Let me in, Goldie," Jett said from the other side of the door.

"Hold on. The dresser is blocking the mattress propped up against the door."

In a fog, I watched Goldie struggle with moving the mattress to the side, trying to make room for the door to open. Her heels clicked on the floor, and she grunted as she worked.

Even if I'd wanted to fucking help her, I couldn't. I could barely focus on what she was doing, let alone get up.

She must have made enough room for Jett to get in because from my perch on the ground, I saw two pairs of suit-covered legs walk into the room.

"Shit," Jett mumbled as he entered and took in the devastation I'd created. Bending down to my level, Jett tried to grab the bottle from my hand, but I cradled it closer to my chest. "Kace, give me the bottle," Jett warned in his domineering voice.

"Fuck you," I spat, bringing the opening of the bottle to my lips.

The lid of the bottle clattered against my teeth before I was able to place my lips over the opening. In one smooth motion, I dipped my head back and waited for the liquid to burn down my throat, but I wasn't awarded with the sweet smolder of whiskey. Instead, the bottle was ripped from my grasp, and I was pushed to the side.

My head fell forward, my neck muscles no longer working in accordance with my brain.

"Goddamn it," Jett said. "Goldie, go get me some water and bread. I need to get something in him."

"Don't listen to him," I replied, falling forward.

"Go, little one," Jett said softly.

"Jett, I'm scared." Goldie's voice sounded weak. For the first time in my life, I could tell she was frightened.

"I got this, little one. Please go get some water and bread, okay?"

"Okay." She sniffed and then left.

I felt relief at her departure. I welcomed my drunken state—I relished it, actually—but I hadn't wanted Goldie to see me like this. I didn't want her to see me wearing my demons like a fucking scarlet letter.

Jett pushed me back against my bed frame so my head was at eye level with his. My vision was blurry, but from what I could see, Jett wasn't happy.

"What the fuck happened?" Jett asked, holding my head still so he could look at me straight.

"Aw, you look upset," I taunted him.

"Of course I'm fucking upset. I haven't seen you in a week and come to find you're drinking your life away. What the fuck, Kace?"

I reached out to the cloudy vision of his head and made contact with his cheek. "Don't cry, baby."

"You're a dick," Jett said, grabbing hold of my arm.

"Whoa, fucking slow down," I demanded when the room started to spin.

My world tilted on its end as Jett guided me to the bathroom, me stumbling the entire time. My stomach twisted, and I knew the quick movements were going to result in me purging every last drop of alcohol I'd stocked up on.

"Slow the fuck down," I demanded again.

Jett didn't listen and continued to drag me into the bathroom. "You smell like shit," he said, pushing me toward the toilet.

The cool porcelain called to me. I grabbed hold of the round bowl, moving my head forward just in time as my stomach convulsed and I threw up.

Sitting in my own filth, not moving, just drinking, was an almost serene position, but the minute you moved me, the minute you made me focus on something other than the grain in the hardwood floors, all the alcohol I had consumed over a week threatened to come back up, and that was what happened to me now.

Jett pushed my head into the hole of the toilet, making sure everything coming up made it into the right area.

A cold chill ran over me as sweat slicked my skin from the convulsions of my stomach. Retching, I gripped the toilet, praying for it to finally be over.

Slowly, my stomach stopped rolling, and in its place was a scorching headache, throbbing through my brain.

I collapsed on the floor and placed a forearm over my eyes, blocking out the florescent lighting of the bathroom. My shirt stuck to my sweat-slicked skin and my head pounded while it rested against the tile of the floor, begging for relief.

"You done?" Jett asked, showing no mercy.

"Yeah," I croaked. My throat burned raw from the mixture of stomach acid and alcohol. Talking was currently an alien concept to me.

"Good." Jett picked me up again, impressing me since I had a couple more pounds of muscle than him. He dragged me into the shower, placed me on the floor, and turned on the cold water.

An arctic rainfall fell down upon me, erasing the fog in

my brain.

I didn't squirm, I didn't even move. I welcomed the frigid water, turning my once hazy outlook into a more crisp view.

Jett stood outside the shower with his arms crossed and a disapproving look on his face. Hell, it wouldn't be the first time I'd disappointed him.

"When was the last time you took a shower?" Jett asked.

"The last time you sucked my dick," I retorted, pleased with my smartass comment.

"Glad you think this is funny."

"The only thing funny in this whole world is the unrelenting bad luck I was fucking blessed with."

"That's cryptic," Jett replied.

"But is it, really? You know everything about me. You should know exactly what I'm talking about."

"All I know is you've taken a perfectly good life and wasted it, living in the shadows of your past and never moving forward."

"You don't fucking know anything," I spat back. "You don't know what it's like to be me, to live with the guilt of what I did."

"Have you even talked to them?" Jett asked, referring to Linda and Madeline. "Have you even tried to see how they've been? Last time you made an attempt was watching them at the tee-ball game. Now you just sneak around, being an elusive fuck and never facing them. They could be doing just fine, Kace, and you would have no clue."

"They're not fine. How could someone ever recover from losing a parent? Fuck, you lost your mom several years ago, and you're still affected by it today."

Jett went to respond but then shut his mouth.

That's what I fucking thought.

I reached up and turned off the water. I sat on the bottom

of the shower and shucked my shirts and pants as Jett tossed me a towel. I ran it over my face and then slowly stood, letting my legs adjust to the weight of my body. I wrapped the towel around my waist, grabbed the side of the shower, and exited.

Jett stood in front of me with his hands in his pockets and the cuffs of his long-sleeved business shirt rolled up to his elbows. He exuded wealth and power, but I knew differently. The man was hurting as much as anyone else who'd lost a parent. I knew the toll it had taken on him when his mom passed away from AIDS. I knew the grief he'd experienced. I knew because I was the one person who'd stood by him during those dark days, and even though he'd been blinded by pain, he'd continued to move forward with his life, just like Linda and Madeline. He couldn't tell me he still didn't think of his mom.

"It was different," Jett said. "My loss was different from theirs."

"A loss is a loss, Jett."

"It was different." Jett cleared his throat. "I didn't even get a chance to be with my mom. I had a little glimpse of what it was like to have a mother in my life at a late age. I saw what my life could have been. Madeline is young. She can move on not knowing the regret I experienced."

"I know you like control, Jett, but you can't dictate people's feelings."

"I know that, but it was different."

Jett's dad had been a dick of epic proportions, using Jett's mom for providing a kin and then ditching her to the streets after she gave birth, leaving her homeless with nothing but the clothes on her back to fend for herself. It wasn't until Jett was able to leave the raft of his father and have his own life that he was able to welcome his mom back into his life, but it was too late. He'd only had a short while with her before she died of

AIDS in the comfort of his house.

I could see the difference Jett was talking about, but I stood by my statement. A loss was a loss, and who were we to judge how someone reacted? It wasn't our place as humans to judge; it was our place to love and support or mourn and grieve with them.

I'd chosen the route of grievance, but instead of slowly coming out of my place of darkness, I felt it reasonable to stay there, to mourn for a lifetime.

"I got the water!" Goldie shouted from the bedroom, breaking the tension between Jett and myself. "Where are you?"

"In here," Jett called, still looking at me.

Her little heels clacked against the floor, but she halted when she saw Jett and me staring each other down. I glanced at her and saw her heated gaze peruse my body. Even though I was still half drunk, I appreciated her appraisal of my body.

"Get a good look?" I asked, swaying a little.

"You look like a turd nugget," she responded.

"Hottest turd nugget in town," I replied, stretching my arms above my head, knowing fully well that my towel hung low. Too bad I still had my briefs on, or else I could have possibly put on a very good show for both Jett and Goldie.

Shit, I really was still drunk.

"I will take those," Jett said to Goldie. "Go hang out with Diego. I won't be much longer."

"No," she said defiantly. "I want an explanation."

"An explanation of what?" I asked. I walked past them and back into my room. Normally, I would have flopped on my bed, but since that was deconstructed, I sat on the edge of the dresser that was lying flat on the ground.

Goldie and Jett followed and stood in front of me, waiting

for me to say something.

"What?" I asked, rubbing my face, wishing I had a bottle of valium at my disposal.

"What the fuck did you do to Lyla?" Goldie asked, her temper rising.

"What are you talking about?" I asked, my pulse picking up from the mention of Lyla's name.

"She is walking around like someone sucked the life out of her," Goldie responded, hands on her hips and ready to fight.

She was five foot nothing, hence Jett's nickname for her, and had zero meat on her bones, but I didn't doubt her ability to put up a good fight.

"I bet she's fine," I responded, feeling more gutted than ever from hearing about Lyla. The person who'd sucked the life out of her was me. Another soul I was able to damage.

"She's not fine, Kace. She won't talk to me about what happened, so you better start speaking."

"We fucked. Then I left," I breathed out, skipping over all the intimate details and moments we'd shared.

"I don't believe you," Goldie responded.

"You don't?" I grabbed the back of my neck. "Check my wallet. You will find one less condom."

Stomping her foot like a child, she said, "No, I don't believe that's all that happened."

"Come on, it's not worth it," Jett said to Goldie, pulling her into him.

"I'm so sick of dealing with his evasiveness. It's about time you got over yourself, Kace. It's tiresome being friends with someone who thinks the world is going to end any day."

"Glad you finally realized we shouldn't be friends," I replied, really wishing she would leave me alone.

"You're an asshole."

"Yup," I said, resting my head on the wall.

"Let's go," Jett encouraged her.

"This is so stupid. Why do we have to walk on eggshells around him? What the fuck does summer have to do with anything?"

Like a fucking semi careening into a wall, realization slammed into my chest. "Holy fuck, what's today?" I asked, looking up at Jett.

The sad look on Jett's face confirmed my thoughts.

It was Madeline's birthday, and I'd fucking forgotten. I'd been so caught up in drowning my sorrows I'd forgotten it was her birthday.

"What's today?" Goldie asked, looking at both of us. "What the hell is going on?"

"I need to leave," I replied, grabbing jeans and a T-shirt off the floor.

"Sober up first," Jett said, tossing the water and bread at me. "Then you can go. Being half drunk won't help."

Even though I wanted nothing more than to leave, Jett was right. In order for me to take care of business, I needed to be sober, so I grabbed the water and bread and forced it down.

CHAPTER EIGHTEEN

My past...

"It's about time," I said to Jett as he met me at the base of the stairs nestled in the servants' quarters at the Lafayette Club.

"I had some business to attend to," he said, buttoning the front of his suit jacket. He gripped my shoulder and looked me in the eye. "You don't have to do this, Kace."

It was the conversation we had every time I wanted to do something that dealt with the loss of Marshall Duncan. Jett always gripped my shoulder and told me I didn't have to do what I had planned, and I always countered him. I didn't foresee the interaction changing in the near future.

"I do," I said, leading him out the back door.

We were headed to the garage when we were stopped by a whistle from one of the girls. I turned to see the Jett Girls tanning in the backyard, topless of course, drinking margaritas and gossiping. It was their day off and they were taking advantage of it. I averted my eyes from their breasts and continued forward.

There were four Jett Girls now: Babs, Pepper, Tootse,

and Francy. They'd all been found by Jett and invited to the club to change their current way of living. Tootse and Francy were a couple—annoyingly cute to see together, actually. Jett had found them at a local X-rated club, where they used to make out topless in front of a bunch of horny men. Francy was a fucking fantastic bartender and Tootse had been taking fashion classes and was a pretty good seamstress. Once Jett had found out about Tootse's talents, he'd put her to work on some costumes for the girls. I was pretty impressed with her hidden talent.

Pepper, on the other hand, was a tough one. She had a serious dark side that rivaled mine at times. I could see it in her eyes, the damage that had been done. The only information I'd gotten from Jett about Pepper was he was able to pay off her pimp to help her come to the Lafayette Club. I didn't want to know how much Jett had paid. All I knew was Jett had saved her from an atrocious position she hadn't put herself in.

Surprisingly, all the girls got along. That had been one of my biggest fears when stepping into my position at the club— that there was going to be a lot of catty bullshit from the girls— but it was an unspoken rule they didn't fight with each other. Instead, they supported one another. They all came from a rough background and with that knowledge, they formed an unbreakable bond.

On occasion they gave me sass. They most definitely pushed my buttons, but then again, I think they found pleasure in such interaction. But they knew my boundaries and never crossed the line. They didn't ask about my personal life. They knew I had demons and they left me alone.

At first, I thought Jett's plan to help save these girls was a little far-fetched, maybe a little disturbed, but I got it now. I saw what the club was able to provide them: a safe sanctuary from the sins that once clung to their skin every day. Now they were able to thrive, to make something of themselves. It was refreshing to see their change in demeanor, to see hope in their eyes. If only the club had had the same effect on me.

"Where you going, boss man?" Babs called out, directing her comment to me, even though I wasn't technically their boss, just their manager.

"None of your business," I shot back. They knew better than to ask about my daily routine. Unless we were in the Toulouse Room practicing or in the gym working out, they didn't talk to me. This wasn't because I was a dick. It was because I had nothing to say to them.

The girls giggled from my short answer and made scary noises, making fun of me.

"How do you deal with his moodiness?" Francy asked Jett, who was trailing behind me.

"Bourbon," Jett answered. "Lots of fucking bourbon."

"Fuck you." I chuckled.

"We'll miss you," Tootse said. She wiggled her fingers at us. I shook my head at the biggest blonde in the house. She could be really dense at times. Thank God she was pretty.

I slipped into Jett's black Range Rover and settled behind the wheel. Jett quickly sat in the passenger side and shut his door, silencing the catcalls the girls were giving both of us.

I pressed my fingers to my eyebrows. "Why you thought outnumbering us with women was a good idea, I don't know."

"Not one of my better decisions." Jett smirked, buckling up.

"You have no idea what it's like to try to wrangle them together and get them to focus."

"I do know. I watch you do it." Jett laughed, referring to the cameras he had in the room. "I'm glad I'm not doing it."

"Yeah, you just make me do the dirty work."

"Isn't that how it's always been?" he asked. "I'm the mastermind, you do the grunt work."

His comment was said with humor, but it was very true. Ever since I'd known Jett, he had come up with schemes for the trouble we loved getting in, and I always followed through with the deed. We were never caught. It was a small high we'd lived on when we were young. Now that we were older, our schemes were heavier in weight. Instead of covering up misadventures, we covered up sins and helped people escape them.

"Where are we going?" Jett asked, breaking my thought.

"I don't really know." I shrugged. "I was thinking about going to Target." I really had no idea where to shop.

"Target? Seriously?" Jett asked with disapproval.

"Shit, I don't know." I rubbed the back of my neck, trying to think. "I don't know what to get a little girl."

"You don't have to get her anything," Jett replied. "You give them money already."

"It's the least I can do," I said, feeling the weight of responsibility on my shoulders.

Madeline didn't have a father in her life because of me, so I'd taken it upon myself to make sure she was well taken care of from a distance. The checks I earned at the Lafayette Club went straight to her every month. I dropped a pile of cash in her mailbox every month with a note of sorrow and regret. It was her birthday, and I'd decided it was a day I would help celebrate, so I was out to get her a gift but had no fucking clue what a little girl wanted.

"Why am I coming?" Jett asked. "You should have brought one of the Jett Girls."

"That would have warranted too many questions. I

don't want questions. I don't need them."

"I can understand that. So instead it's going to be us shopping for a little girl?"

"Yup," I responded, holding back a smirk. "Should be a good time."

"Or a major clusterfuck," Jett shot back. "We're not going to Target though. Head to the French Market. You can at least get her something with meaning of the city she lives in."

"Are you getting sentimental on me?" I teased.

"Do you want my help or not?"

"I do. I just didn't expect you to get into this."

"I'm not," Jett said. "I'm just making sure you don't look like an idiot."

"She's not going to know it's from me," I replied. I turned onto St. Charles Street and headed toward the Quarter.

"Explain how that's going to work," Jett said.

I felt Jett's questioning eyes on me. He always had to know every aspect of a plan he was a part of, and it drove me crazy sometimes. I just wanted to execute my plans without talking about them. But with Jett, you had to make sure you checked all your boxes and took every possible precaution. He wouldn't be the brilliant business man he was today if he didn't have that kind of mindset. Too bad it irked me every fucking time.

Blowing out a frustrated breath and gripping tightly on the steering wheel so I didn't lash out, I said, "I'm just going to drop it off at her front door. Do you think I personally hand them money every month?"

Jett knew my monthly paycheck went to Madeline and Linda, and he'd never said one word about it. He was a silent partner when it came to my drunken sin, and it was an uncommunicated rule we were both in this together, that I was the one who'd killed a man but Jett had covered it up. And for that, we were both at fault. So Jett accepted the fact that my money went to Madeline; he had no qualms about the exchange.

"You're really going to leave the present on her doorstep? You don't think that's creepy in any way?"

"Fuck, you know it's creepy, me sneaking around and delivering things to them, but what other choice do I have? Show my face? You know I can't fucking do that."

"It might help you get past the pent-up emotions you have," Jett suggested.

I guffawed. "Oh, okay, so I go up to them and hand her a present? A complete stranger? Or should I introduce myself as the man who ruined their lives?"

"You haven't ruined their lives," Jett countered.

"Bullshit—"

Jett cut me off. "They could be completely fine, and you wouldn't know that because you sneak around, hiding and living under a cloud, hoping for your death to come along quicker. Get your fucking head on straight and go see if they are truly hurting."

It was the same rage Jett went on every few months once he couldn't stand seeing me hurt anymore. I knew what my sulking did to him. I knew the position I put him in, and I felt bad he had to deal with my past.

"Drop it," I warned. He was pushing my buttons, and I was about done with it.

Shaking his head, Jett leaned back in his seat. "I don't get you, man. Why do you keep punishing yourself?"

"Why do you keep asking?"

"I have no clue," Jett said softly, ending our conversation.

Silence rang as I found my way through the Quarter to the open market where vendors from around the city gathered to sell their homemade souvenirs and crafts. It was a tourist destination, but also, when you looked closely, past the knock-off sunglasses and corny T-shirts, you could find real treasure.

Once I found a parking spot, I cut the engine and studied the bottom of the steering wheel as I contemplated what I wanted to say to Jett.

"I know what happened that night was my fault, and I know you've done everything in your power to protect me, Jett, and I appreciate that."

"It was for selfish reasons," Jett cut in. I knew fully well Jett had protected me because he couldn't lose me, not after he'd lost his mom.

"I know," I responded. "When it comes to my life, you can protect me from the law, but you can't protect me from my state of mind. The day my fist connected with Marshall Duncan, my life was taken from me, and it's about time you accept that. The man you once knew no longer exists."

With that, I got out of the car and headed toward the market, not turning to see if Jett was following me because I knew he would be. He never left my side.

The market buzzed with midday excitement, but there was nothing exciting about the task at hand. All it did was open me up to another kind of darkness that I welcomed with open arms.

***

"This is stupid," I said, judging the present I tried to wrap. "It looks like a kindergartner wrapped this."

"Then maybe she will think it's from a friend." Jett chuckled next to me.

"Why did you make me wrap it?" I asked, looking at the birthday candle-covered wrapping paper that was crunched together and held down by a long piece of tape.

"Because it was too comical to pass up," he answered.

"You're a dick," I replied, fumbling with the wrapping paper. "If it was in the shape of a box, it would have been easier."

"It's a flat handbag," Jett pointed out. "You just had to tuck the corners in nicely."

"What are you, the fucking wrapping police?" I asked, trying to smooth out a wrinkle in the paper.

"No. I also don't have time to sit around in the dark with you while you wait to drop off the present. Just do it already. I'm ready to eat dinner."

"Missing a meal won't kill you. You're starting to look pudgy."

It was the furthest thing from the truth. Jett was as toned as I was, thanks to our sparring sessions in the gym and the rigorous workouts I put him through.

"Pushing your luck, Haywood," Jett grunted, answering emails on his phone.

I looked at the gift again, nervous. Was I doing the right thing? I thought of it as an act of kindness, the least I could do for Madeline, but how would she take it? How about her mother?

Jett and I had wandered the market for hours, examining every table until we found a gift we thought she would enjoy. I'd purchased a handmade bag that was pink and purple and made out of a fun printed fabric. It was very juvenile looking but perfect for a little girl. I didn't know what she would do with a handbag, but I thought it would be a nice, bright gesture. Before

I'd wrapped it, I slipped a note in the bag, a note of encouragement.

Love is unyielding, loss is undeniable, and love will help you move forward, which will show your true courage in life. Keep moving forward, Madeline.

Words of wisdom I should have followed myself. I was too far gone to recover. I'd accepted my sentence, but Madeline still had a bright future ahead of her.

"Drop it off, Kace. I'm not going to let you skip out on this part."

He knew me too well.

With reluctance, I opened the car door and got out, not letting the slam of a door echo through the silent night. I waited until the streets of the city emptied to drop off my gift.

I'd parked around the corner to go unseen. Silently, I made my way to the front of their house, stopping behind a tree to see if their lights were out. The streetlamp was ready to go out. I made a mental note to tell Jett about it so he could get someone from the city to replace the bulb. Jett had connections and could make things happen quickly, even if it was as simple as changing a light bulb.

The house Madeline and Linda lived in was small and quaint with green shutters and peach walls. Potted plants hung in front of the windows, and a cobblestone walkway let me to the front door.

Silently, with very little breath, I eased toward the door and placed the present on the welcome mat. Before I retreated, I observed the bright white door with wrought iron fixtures. The cottage-type house was a classic in New Orleans, warm and inviting.

I started to walk away but felt a pair of eyes on me. I stopped and looked around to see if anyone was eyeing me from their windows. All the houses were dark with curtains closed over the windows, blocking the view of any onlookers. It was dark enough I knew no one would be able to see who I was, but the feeling of eyes on me still felt eerie. I headed back to the idling car.

Once I got in, Jett said, "Did you drop it off?"

I nodded and buckled up. I took one last look at the neighborhood and inhaled a deep breath of relief. One birthday down, an eternity left to go.

CHAPTER NINETEEN

My present...

Pound after pound, pain shot through my head, making my eye twitch and my brain seize. My stomach rolled with each step, but the pain was welcome. After a week of an alcohol-induced coma, I was feeling the effects.

I brought a water bottle to my mouth and relished the cool water that slipped past my dry lips and down my scratchy throat. Jett forced me to eat something, but I was regretting my intake of food as nausea once again embraced me.

I hated that I'd scared Goldie, that she'd feared for me. Jett knew my limits and knew I could slip into a much darker hole than where he found me, but Goldie hadn't seen that side of me before. She tried to be tough most of the time, but I'd seen fear in her eyes when she'd looked at me today, an expression I never again wanted to see on her pretty face.

Goldie still affected me. From the moment I'd first met her, I'd known she was someone who would be a part of my life. There was no denying it.

The ache I'd had for her died though. The urge to claim her

as mine, to tear her away from my best friend, was gone, and a true friendship was developing.

She had latched on to me, and now I had to deal with her worrying about what was going to happen with Lyla and me.

The minute she'd noticed I was coherent, she'd made it her mission to find out what had happened between me and Lyla. I'd spared her the details and said things hadn't worked out. According to Goldie, that wasn't a good enough explanation.

The badgering I'd received was the reason for my second wave of nausea and headaches. The little honey-haired girl was relentless when it came to her best friend. It wasn't until Jett saw I'd suffered enough that he took Goldie away and shoved more food in my direction.

Feeling half human, I sat on the hood of Jett's black Porsche Cayenne, nursing my water and waiting for Pepper to meet me in front of the hotel. I had one foot propped on the bumper of the SUV and the other on the ground, testing my half-drunken balance. The sun beat down on my back, and the Louisiana humidity made the alcohol seep from every pore in my body. Detoxing was a real bitch.

"God, could you look any sexier?" Pepper asked as she walked up to me, snapping gum in her mouth and sporting a pair of short denim shorts and a low-cut tank top. The girl was looking damn fine. She stood next to me and ruffled my hair. "You really nail that whole brooding man look." She scanned my easy outfit of worn jeans and a white T-shirt. "Why is it so simple for a man?"

I took off my sunglasses and eyed Pepper up and down. "Why is it so simple for a woman?" I asked in return.

Pepper and I had had our on and off moments, especially after Jett and Goldie had finally started a relationship. We both had demons to fight off, and we found losing ourselves in each other's bodies was an easy way to forget. It wasn't until Lyla walked into my life that I had stopped all interaction with Pepper. It had been abrupt, but she'd known going into the arrangement it was just sex, nothing else.

Still, by the way she was eye-fucking me, I knew she wanted to go back to our old agreement. A part of me had thought about it during my drunken stupor. I'd thought about calling her, but I was too twisted to even lift my phone to text her, let alone fuck her senseless. Plus, in the back of my mind, I knew I would be hurting Lyla, and I didn't want to do that.

Lyla and Pepper got along, but there had always been an underlying tension between the two girls when they were both working at the Lafayette Club. It was noticeable when they were in a room together. It made dealing with both of them that much harder.

"Where we off to?" Pepper asked, blowing a bubble with her gum.

"I need your help picking out a present," I said, standing and catching my balance. I still felt like I had sea legs. "Want to drive?" I asked, unsure how sober I really was.

"Fuck yes." She fist-pumped the air.

Instantly I regretted my decision to let Pepper drive. If she drove anything like Goldie, I would be needing a barf bag. According to Jett, Goldie was by far the scariest driver he'd ever been in a car with. Apparently she liked riding on the sidewalks, treating pedestrians like bumper cars, and defying any and all speed limits. With Pepper's "fuck off" way of life and her free spirit, I could imagine what I was in for.

"Where to?" she asked after we got in, and she started the engine. She gripped the steering wheel tightly and pumped the gas a few times while we were still in park.

Jesus.

"Easy there, Mario Andretti. We're just driving to the French Market."

"Let's see how fast we can get there," she said, pulling into traffic and slamming on the gas. I flew back into my seat and my hand instinctively went to the "oh shit" handle above the door.

"Unless you want me puking in your lap, slow the fuck down, Pepper."

Pepper laughed and dropped to the speed limit. "Jett was right. This is going to be fun."

I should have known Jett had spoken with Pepper. He'd probably told all the girls about my drinking binge and asked them to be extra annoying around me. I wouldn't put it past him. It would be his way of teaching me a lesson.

"Just fucking drive," I replied, relaxing into my seat and pressing my throbbing head against the propped up hand that rested on the window.

"What kind of present are we getting?"

The girls didn't know about Madeline. Only Jett knew, but he wasn't able to come with me this year, so he'd sent the next best thing. She would understand my need not to talk about it, unlike Goldie, who would be asking a million questions. Babs was pre-occupied with helping out at Justice, and Francy and Tootse were no use because they were either too occupied with each other or Francy was trying to explain everything to little blonde Tootse. I would rather take Goldie over Tootse and Francy, and that was saying a lot.

Answering Pepper, I said, "A present for a little girl."

"Um, that's an odd thing for you to be getting. Care to explain?"

"Nope," I replied, resting my head against my window.

And that was that. We sat in silence as Pepper drove to the

French Market. We could have easily walked from the hotel, but I wanted to go straight to Madeline's house afterward, and with the bitch of a hangover I was nursing, walking up and down the vendors row at the Market was going to be hard enough.

Since it was a Saturday, the Market was full when we pulled up, but we were lucky enough to find parking on a side street. With my sunglasses covering my bloodshot eyes, we walked through the Market, dodging tourists and avoiding the cheesy souvenir stands. I was looking for something handcrafted and original to New Orleans. Ever since the first time I'd bought Madeline a gift, it had been a tradition of mine.

I had no clue if she actually liked what I got her, or if she even opened the box. Her mom could have flagged the boxes as something from a psychotic and not even given them to her. If that was the case, I would continue to bring her presents on her birthday and Christmas because she deserved them, even though they might not be given to her.

"What about a voodoo doll?" Pepper suggested, grabbing a creepy-looking one off a table.

"Probably not the most appropriate gift," I replied, trying to avoid eye contact with the doll's wandering eyes.

"I had them when I was young. They never worked though. I asked for my teacher's hair to burn every day, and every day she walked in with a full head of hair. Damn thing was a hoax."

"That is so disturbing on so many levels, I'm not even going to ask."

"Best you don't." Pepper smiled at me and continued to walk down the aisles of vendors.

We passed a vendor selling knock-off sunglasses and looked at each pair, examining the color and size.

"You know we're not shopping for you, right?" I placed my hand on her back and leaned close so she could hear me over the bustling crowd.

"Can't stop a girl from shopping." She smiled back at me. "Hey, what about a necklace?"

Pepper led me over to one of many jewelers in the Market, but there was something about this vendor that was a little different. Her necklaces had more of a French feel to them rather than the typical beading. Silver pendants, dangling on delicate strands, were displayed on black velvet stands, catching my eye.

"These are kind of nice," I said, looking at a circular pendant with a purple gem stone in the center. "But are they too old for a little girl?"

"Maybe," Pepper said, eyeing a chunky turquoise necklace. I didn't like it, but who was I kidding. I knew nothing about jewelry, so who was I to judge?

"Fancy meeting you two here."

I froze and my hand instantly retreated from Pepper's back as if she'd burned me. Not taking my aviators off, I looked up to see Lyla standing in front of us with a fake smile on her face. Even though I told myself not to check her out, my eyes betrayed me as I took in white shorts that showcased her gorgeous legs and a mint green T-shirt that dipped too fucking low in the front. She wore a pair of brown sandals that matched the belt she was wearing. Her hair was up in a ponytail, exposing her neck, her silky, caramel-colored neck, which enticed the fuck out of me.

She was breathtaking.

"Hey, Lyla," Pepper said with a little too much cheer in her voice. She gave Lyla a hug. While Lyla wrapped her arms around Pepper, she maintained eye contact with me, searing me with her green eyes. From the way her jaw twitched and the hard set of her brow, I saw she was not happy. I didn't blame her.

"Hey, Pepper," Lyla practically whispered. "What are you two doing here?"

"Shopping," Pepper answered innocently, not knowing the history between Lyle and me. "What are you up to, girl? We haven't seen you in a while. Are you not working out with us anymore?"

Interesting. Lyla had stopped working out with the other girls, even though she still had access to all the amenities. Was that because of me?

Of course it was because of me. She was best friends with Goldie. The only reason Lyla wouldn't be working out was because she was worried I would be in the vicinity.

Lyla shrugged. "I like to do my own thing."

As Lyla and Pepper continued their small talk, I left their conversation and considered Lyla's pink glossed lips glistening in the sun. Images of them sliding over my cock, over my rock hard body, over my own lips, ran through my mind. Yearning took up a place inside the pit of my stomach, and I itched to reach out to her. I not only wanted this woman, but I needed her.

Standing a few feet away from her, I felt the pull of our souls, the heady urge to claim her as mine. It was undeniable. Lyla was my other half. I'd known it from the moment I met her. I'd known she was supposed to challenge me, understand me, and give me everything I ever wanted. That was why I couldn't love her, why I couldn't be with her. There was no place on this earth for my happiness.

"How are you, Kace," Lyla asked, taking me out of my thoughts.

"Fine," I responded, not elaborating.

"Doing some shopping?"

"Looking for a present," I answered.

She nodded. "Well, I guess I will leave you two to your

date."

Date? Oh hell.

"Not a date," Pepper and I said at the same time.

Lyla smiled. "Could have fooled me."

And then she walked away. I watched her retreat, her short shorts dancing dangerously with her ass cheeks. I wanted to rip her out of the crowd and block her from view of all the other men in the vicinity. I hated that she flaunted her body for the whole world to see. I hated that she worked at a fucking strip club, where men could see what belonged to me.

Fuck, what should belong to me. A tidal wave of torment attacked me as I tried to steady my beating heart.

"Hey, you okay?" Pepper asked, gripping my hand.

"No," I replied, looking after Lyla.

Before I could stop myself, I moved forward until I stood right behind Lyla. "Lyla...."

She turned slowly, gripping her purse with one hand and putting the other in her pocket, striking a casual pose even though the tension between us was palpable.

"Can I help you?" she asked.

Fuck, what did I want to say? Many thoughts ran through my mind.

Forgive me.

Be with me.

Fucking save me.

But I couldn't speak any of those truths.

"I don't have time for this," she said, not giving me much time to gather my thoughts. Before she could entirely shut me out, I grasped her arm and made her face me. I slid my hand down her arm until our fingers linked together.

Her shoulders visibly deflated and the strong façade she'd erected around her heart came tumbling down with one squeeze from my hand.

"I'm sorry, Lyla."

"For what?" she asked, searing me with her green eyes. "For treating me like a whore the other night, taking what you wanted, exposing me, and then leaving? Or are you sorry for not being man enough to be with me?"

My heart twisted in my chest. The last thing I wanted was to hurt Lyla. I needed more than anything to hold her in my arms, brand her as mine, live in her beauty. I'd never wanted to cause her pain, but that's exactly what I'd done. I'd let her into my world temporarily and wound up hurting her because I wasn't strong enough to say no.

"I didn't mean to treat you like that," I stated. "You're the furthest thing from a whore, Lyla, so don't ever call yourself that."

"I'm just telling you how you made me feel, Kace. Did you think I would be okay with how you treated me? Do you think I enjoyed telling you my secrets and having you be repulsed?"

A lone tear ran down her cheek, but she pulled her hand out of my grasp and quickly wiped it away.

I gripped the back of my neck, a nervous tick of mine, as I tried to figure out how to fix this. No easy solution struck me, and that made me nervous. Even though I knew I couldn't give her what she wanted, I still didn't want to lose her.

There'd been a time in my life when I would have taken a woman like Lyla and never let her go. I would have instantly claimed her as mine and made sure every fucking penis in the locality knew it. It was a time in my life I would do anything to go back to. To just have a moment in time where I wasn't wearing the weight of the world on my shoulders, where I could be the Kace I once was, the Kace who knew what it was like to live, to enjoy life.

I wasn't that man anymore.

Taking a deep breath, I gave a little piece of my heart to her. "I wasn't repulsed by you, Lyla. I was repulsed by myself."

"Because you had sex with me?" she asked, getting in my face and ignoring the passing crowd.

I was about to answer when someone bumped my shoulder, sending my weight into Lyla. We both stumbled backward for a second before I was able to right our balance. I turned to see who'd bumped us and was greeted by an apologetic-looking man.

"Dude, sorry about that. This 'gator jerky line is out of control."

"No problem," I said gruffly.

"Hey, you're Kace Haywood."

I prayed he would just move on, forget he'd ever seen me. I didn't need this right now.

"Dude, you were the shit. You had the sickest uppercuts I've ever seen." The man threw a couple of fake punches my way. Little did he know, I had an uppercut that could end a life.

"Thanks," I said, trying to give the guy a hint that I wasn't interested in talking about my boxing career.

"Did you hear the trainer you were using—Jono—was nailed for slipping his athletes supplements? You should look into that because honestly, I didn't think you would ever do steroids. This just proves that."

"Yup, I'll check into that. Thanks, man." I shook the guy's hand and pulled Lyla behind a pillar so we could have an ounce of privacy.

"That was kind of rude," Lyla said. "That guy was being nice to you."

"I don't want to talk about my boxing career."

"But he was clearly a fan—"

"Of a has-been," I interrupted her. "There is no need for me to save face with fans. That career is long gone."

"Still, you could have been a little nicer. You walk around on this earth like people owe you something."

"That's where you're wrong," I said, pinning her against the pillar. "I walk around on this earth owing everything to someone else."

Lyla searched my eyes, and when I tried to turn away, she gripped my jaw tightly and forced me to look at her. "There's more to it, isn't there?"

"More to what?" I asked, loving the way her hand felt against my skin.

"More to your pain. It's not just about losing your boxing career. There is something darker, something deeper." She paused. "Who is the present for? Who are you shopping for, Kace?"

The way her eyes cut through me, the feel of her skin on mine, her proximity that had always made me feel so safe were breaking down my walls. The answer rested on the tip of my tongue.

"Tell me, Kace. Who are you shopping for?"

I danced with the possibility of telling her when Pepper joined us, holding a bag.

"Got the gift...." She trailed off when she saw how close Lyla and I were. "Oh, sorry, was I interrupting something?"

The concerned look on Lyla's face soured.

"No, I was just leaving," Lyla said while separating herself from me. "Pepper, give me a call for a girls' night." Lyla looked at me. "See you around, Kace."

With sorrow in her eyes, Lyla walked away, leaving Pepper and me alone with a bustling market behind us.

Tourists and locals flowed in and around the pillars that

held up the roof of the French Market, but like a parting in the sea, I had a clear view of her retreating beauty, reminding me I wasn't privileged enough to hang on to such a life-altering woman.

"You love her, don't you?" Pepper asked, tilting my whole world upside down.

Love was a foreign concept. Love wasn't on my radar. That was what I'd convinced myself. "No," I answered, even though the thought had crossed my mind.

"Bullshit," Pepper responded.

"Sorry to disappoint, but I don't know what love is, Pepper." Taking a deep breath, I nodded at the bag in her hand. "What did you get?"

Letting the moment pass, Pepper reached into the bag and pulled out a green voodoo doll that was sporting a purple and pink dress. The twisted-looking doll was hideous.

"I'm not fucking giving her that," I stated, not even letting Pepper explain her reasoning for getting it.

Laughing, Pepper said, "This is for me." She handed a small locket to me. "This is for your friend. There's a gray stone inside."

I opened the locket and saw the small polished stone nestled inside. It was simple but beautiful. Simplicity went a long way at times.

"Gray?" I asked.

Pepper grabbed my hand and squeezed it. "It's the color of repentance. I don't know what you're searching for or trying to accomplish, but maybe someday you will be able to forgive yourself, Kace."

If she was looking to hammer a stake through my bleeding heart, she'd fucking nailed it on the head.

Forgiveness was something you earned; it wasn't granted

to you. It took a strong person not only to forgive but to accept forgiveness. I would like to say I would be strong enough to accept Linda's mercy, but I knew I was a weak, broken, and battered man. Her mercy wouldn't be enough to set me free.

CHAPTER TWENTY

My present...

"Rough day?" Blane asked as he sat next to me.

"You could say that," I said, lifting my beer bottle to my lips.

We sat off to the side as Diego practiced an act with one of the girl performers he'd just hired. Watching the whole thing made me realize Diego was nowhere near being ready for his club to open.

Cirque du Diable had an appealing vintage circus feel to it with a touch of erotic flair. It was a novel concept I was excited about but nervous at the same time for the time constraints Diego was in, given how quickly he wanted to open the club.

The main ring, where all the acts took place, was scattered with strong ribbons hanging from the ceiling as well as hoop apparatuses. The room circled in its shape while chairs and tables surrounded the edge. In the back were raised seats that mirrored the feel of stadium seating, and lifted highboy tables were strategically placed near the bar. Behind the main section of the club, themed rooms were available for couples to take advantage of.

When I'd talked to Diego about his club during the early stages of construction, he'd told me he wanted to establish a safe haven for those living the same erotic lifestyle as him, a place where they could practice their craft, their love, and find solace. It was a great idea, he just needed to work out some kinks.

"What was so rough about today?" Blane asked, leaning back in his chair and eyeing the new girl on stage. He was not very subtle when it came to the female form.

"Nothing," I said, trying to brush it off.

"You know, we all have our problems, Kace. It's how you handle them that defines you as a man."

"Are you saying I'm not a man?" I asked, growing defensive, remembering all the times my father had thrown those words at me.

"Nope, just stating a fact."

"Seems like you're trying to fucking instigate me."

"Is it working?" he asked with a shit-eating grin.

"You're a fuckwit, you know that?"

"Yup," he smiled. "Seriously though, if you ever want to talk...."

"Got it, thanks," I replied as the song playing over the loud speakers ended.

Diego wiped his brow with his forearm. Privately, he made a comment to the girl. She nodded and took off toward the back, looking rejected. Diego stood in the middle of the ring with his hands on his hips and shaking his head.

"Looks like you're not the only one having a rough day," Blane said while nodding at Diego.

Defeated, Diego walked toward us but stopped off at the bar quickly to grab a handful of beers. He pulled a seat from another table set and sat in it backward while placing the beers on the table for all of us.

"Fuck, she was terrible," Diego huffed while knocking off the cap using the edge of the table.

"Why did you hire her?" Blane asked. "I mean, killer fucking body, but she looks like a robot up there."

"Tell me about it. She said she was nervous with you guys watching."

"She realizes there will be an audience of more than two people, right?" Blane asked.

"You hope there is." I smirked over my beer.

"There will be more than two people, jackass," Diego countered. "When I interviewed her, she was confident and sexy as hell. She has an extensive dance background. Apparently she forgot to put brilliant liar on her resume as well."

"Did you can her?" Blane asked.

"Nah, not yet. Figured I would give her one more shot."

"Didn't know you were running a charity," I said.

Diego smirked at me. "Damn, who chewed on your dick and took off?"

"Your mom," I responded with a grin, swallowing a large gulp of beer.

The floors in the hallway creaked, letting us know someone was approaching. In seconds, Jett appeared with a gorgeous Goldie at his side.

The lucky fuck got to take her wherever he wanted, hold her when he pleased, and live his life with a sassy yet beautiful woman that would turn the head of any man.

I'd had such a crush on her, "had" being the key word.

Hell, she'd turned my world around the first time I held a conversation with her. I can still remember the day Jett came home to the Lafayette Club after a trip to the cemetery. He'd told me I needed to make room for another Jett Girl. There were already four. Adding another would have made things uneven, but he'd been adamant about it. I hadn't understood, but I'd accommodated him and moved Francy to bartender permanently. It had actually worked out because she was more excited handing out drinks than dancing for the city elites.

Jett's constant need to add Goldie to the lineup had been confusing to me. I hadn't understood the urgency, but then I'd met her in daylight, at a restaurant, and she'd flipped my entire world upside down. A little piece of me had hated Jett that day because he'd found her first.

The only shred of hope I'd held on to was the fact that Goldie had to decide if she actually wanted to become a Jett Girl. If she'd decided against signing the contract, then she was fair game and there was no doubt in my mind that I would have gone after her, but she chose to sign, making her off limits.

There were nights when I'd lain alone in my bed, praying she would come find me, come talk to me just so I could hear her sweet little voice ramble on about God knows what. But she chose a different man, a more dignified man.

I knew she wasn't meant for me, but at the time, I'd wished for once I had been able to hold something positive in my life.

And then came Lyla.

I'd thought I knew what it felt like to be knocked on my ass by a woman, but damn had I been wrong.

Lyla had swept into my life and grabbed me by the motherfucking balls with a vise grip, never letting up. She still clutched them now, even from so far away.

"How the hell did we get so lucky to have you grace us with your presence tonight?" Diego asked Jett.

Goldie and Jett walked into the main room, holding hands and smiling brightly. Their love was sickening, and I was fucking green with envy.

"I wanted to show Jett all the rooms I painted."

Goldie was a brilliant artist and had painted murals and designs on the walls to coincide with the theme of each room. I'd had the opportunity to look at some of her work and would be lying if I said I wasn't impressed.

Jett nodded in greeting. "How's the hangover?"

"Sitting pretty," I responded with a tilt of my beer bottle. His jaw tensed when he saw the alcohol in my hand. "Don't worry, Mom. It's only a couple of beers."

"That's cute," Blane said. "That you call him Mom. Do you suckle his tit too?"

"Watch it," I warned, not really in the mood.

"Blane, don't you know you can't joke with Kace?" Goldie chimed in, her arms crossed and looking pissed. I didn't blame her. I'd wronged her best friend and was usually a dick to her.

"Calm down, little one," Jett cooed. "He's having a rough day."

"When is he not?" Goldie rolled her eyes and took off down the hall.

Jett gave me an apologetic look and went after Goldie.

"Taming her has got to be a damn good time," Diego said.

"It's not fucking easy," I responded, knowing damn well how hard it was to wrangle her in.

"How's the community center?" Blane asked. "Is it open yet?"

Honestly, I had no clue. It was supposed to be opening soon, but my alcohol-induced coma had left me currently unaware of where the community center stood. Nausea and dread continuously flowed through me, making my days uncomfortable.

It wasn't like me to skip out on my responsibilities,

especially when I was in charge, but the dark abyss I slipped into after my night with Lyla was hard to climb out of. That combined with the fact that I had almost missed Madeline's birthday had my stomach churning at an alarming rate.

"Don't know," I answered.

"Can I be honest with you, man?" Blane asked, looking serious.

"Don't stop now," I encouraged.

Rolling his eyes, Blane said, "Why are you letting your demons win? Why are you letting them run your life?"

"Because I don't deserve a life," I replied, like the Debby fucking downer I was.

"Fair enough." Blane sipped his beer. "I don't understand what happened, and I will probably never know your story, but damn, man, you have to at least give the people around you a chance to include you in their life. You're a good guy, a fucking fun guy when your head isn't shoved up your ass. If you want to grieve, be depressed about the hand you drew, by all means, go ahead and fucking grieve, but when you're around your friends, people who care about you, just fucking lighten up for an hour or so, because damn, you're disheartening to be around."

The motherfucker had a serious point, and I hated it.

I nodded at Blane, drained the rest of my beer, and got out of my chair. "Sorry about killing your buzz, dude."

I walked away while both Diego and Blane called after me, but I ignored them. I wasn't leaving because I'd been told I was being a giant pussy. I left because what Blane said was so right.

It hit me like a fucking sucker punch to the liver. The people in my life were important to me, and even though I was living a different kind of life than they were, that didn't mean I had to be a dick to them. They weren't the ones who'd fucked up. They were just the unfortunate souls who had to deal with my moody ass.

Contemplating what Blane said, I walked down the hall toward my space. Jett and Goldie stepped out of one of the rooms.

"Hey," I said as they spotted me.

"Where you off to?" Jett asked. Goldie stood next to him, avoiding eye contact with me, and acting defiant. I wouldn't expect anything less from her.

"Can I talk to you two in my room?"

"Trying to cash in on that threesome now?" Goldie asked sarcastically.

Grinding my teeth together so I didn't make a smartass remark, I led us to my room, which was still destroyed from my drunken tirade.

"I see you've tidied up," Goldie said, kicking some of my clothes aside.

I pulled the mattress from the floor and haphazardly placed it on the frame, then kicked it into place. It would do. I pointed to my bed and said, "Sit."

Jett was calm and cool, but Goldie was ready to start shooting shit from her mouth. I could see it in her eyes. She was gearing up for a fight. Her hands were sharpened and her claws were ready to strike.

"I want to apologize."

"About time," Goldie huffed. "You know, Kace, you can't go around acting like an ass whenever you want just because of something that happened to you years ago. It's bullshit. Hell, I lost my parents to Hurricane Katrina, and you don't see me walking around with my dick shriveled up between my legs."

Jett placed his hand on her thigh. "Goldie, let him talk, and please, don't ever refer to yourself as having a dick. The visual is too much."

"Is it because you know my dick would be bigger than yours?" Goldie asked, deadpan.

"Even though I would like to hear how you figure you would have a bigger dick than me, I think we need to shelve that conversation and listen to Kace."

"It's because I take my fish oil vitamins and you refuse to," Goldie responded, not caring to acknowledge what Jett had suggested.

"Yes, I've heard fish oil produces giant dicks," Jett said with sarcasm as he pinched the bridge of his nose. "Can we proceed?"

"Say it. Say I have a bigger dick than you."

"For fuck's sake," Jett said, exasperated. I smiled inwardly from the struggle. "You have a bigger dick, Goldie. Happy?"

"I am," she said with a bright smile. She then turned to me, crossed her legs, and gestured for me to proceed.

"You sure you don't want to talk about dick size anymore?" I asked.

"Just get the fuck on with it," Jett replied, frustrated as hell. Jett was a dominant man in every facet of his life, and to have such a strong-willed and stubborn woman at his side was comical for me to watch.

A small smile made its way over my lips from seeing my best friend be topped by his girl.

As I gathered my thoughts, they waited patiently for me to speak. I grabbed the back of my neck and looked at them, trying to find the words I wanted to say. Would it always be this hard to convey my emotions?

Most likely.

Taking a deep breath, I said, "I'm sorry for always being a jerk to you, Goldie. You have to understand, there was something I did in my past—"

"The steroids? I don't believe it," Goldie interrupted me. "Jett's actually been—"

"Goldie," Jett said sternly, shutting her up.

"Jett's been doing what?" I looked at my guilty best friend. Neither of them spoke. Jett avoided eye contact while Goldie bit her bottom lip, knowing full well she'd let the cat out of the bag.

"What have you been doing?" I asked Jett.

"He's finding justice for you," Goldie spat while slapping her hands together, as if she'd just told the best secret she's ever heard.

Irritation seethed through me.

"Why can't you stay the fuck out of my business, Jett? I told you, I don't care about my boxing career. I don't care what Jono did. It's over and done with. Let's move the fuck on."

"If that's the case, then you need to move the fuck on from everything," Jett countered, giving me a pointed stare.

Taking a deep breath, I shook my head. "You know that's something I can't move on from."

"There's something else?" Goldie asked while looking between the both of us. "Is this the reason why you are so distant with Lyla?"

Throwing her a bone, I nodded. "Goldie, I want you to know I honor the friendship you've given me, but this is the one thing I can't talk about with you, not because I don't want to but just because I can't. I'm not a good guy."

"It was one night," Jett cut in. "One drunken mistake, and it wasn't your fault."

Lost in the thoughts of that evening, I said, "I lost control." I shook my head in disappointment. "I let him provoke me."

"Who?" Goldie asked, leaning forward.

"Shit," I muttered, having temporarily forgotten Goldie was there. "Goldie, can you please just accept my apology and not ask me again? I promise to make a better effort to be a friend when I'm around you guys, but I need you to not dig around in my past. Can you please do that? I just want to move forward."

It was a lie, but she didn't need to know that.

She took a moment to process what I was asking of her, but after some deep thought, she agreed and stood up. She walked right up to me and wrapped her arms around my waist. Behind her, Jett tensed from the intimate contact but then nodded at me as if granting me his blessing. I wrapped my arms around my best friend's girl and, for a brief moment, reveled in the feel of her pressed against me. The distinctive aroma of vanilla and citrus floated into my nostrils as Goldie squeezed me tighter. Instinctively, I placed my cheek to the top of her head and squeezed her just as hard.

I'd once confessed my love for this woman. I'd once asked her why she'd chosen Jett. I'd once wished I was the one who got to hold her hand, but now, even though she stirred the slightest arousal inside of me, it was nothing compared to what Lyla did to me. Goldie had tilted my axis, but Lyla shook me to my fucking core.

"I will always be by your side, Kace, rooting for you and praying that one day, you're able to find peace with whatever is eating you alive."

"Thank you," I replied, pulling away and walking to the door. "I've got to get out of here. I will see you guys around."

Before they could say anything else, I left the house. Breathing in the musky air of New Orleans, I took a walk to clear my mind. Starting tomorrow, I needed to get back on track, beginning with my responsibilities at Justice.

CHAPTER TWENTY ONE

My past...

This wasn't where I wanted to be, waiting outside a restaurant for Goldie Bishop to arrive. Jett was adamant about making Goldie a Jett Girl, and I had no clue why.

Well, that wasn't true. I knew she had the basic requirements to be considered. She'd lost her parents, their business, and their home to Hurricane Katrina. She was thousands of dollars in debt, working at a shady strip club named Kitten's Castle, and living paycheck to paycheck, barely making ends meet. There were a lot of women like her in New Orleans. What I didn't get was why Jett was so transfixed on helping her. She wasn't even his type.

She was my type. Spunky, stubborn, and fucking fine.

After seeing her at Kitten's Castle, she'd buried herself inside my skin, and I itched to see her once again, but on my own terms, terms where I could claim her as mine, not recruit her for another man.

I placed my foot against the pillar I was standing next to and rested my hands in my pockets. The hood that hid me from the outside world cushioned my place against the pole.

Routine in my life offered me little chance to think about anything outside my little world. I appreciated the monotony of my daily activities. The girls knew their roles. They worked seamlessly with each other, so I didn't understand why Jett wanted to disturb that peace. It was rare enough to see four women get along with zero drama. Adding a fifth into the mix was only asking for trouble.

But I didn't make the fucking decisions,—Jett did. That was why I found myself standing outside of a café waiting for Goldie to arrive.

Growing irritated from waiting, I looked down at my watch and then back up in the direction I knew Goldie would come from. As if she appeared from nowhere, I spotted her walking toward me. Her steps faltered as she looked up to find me staring her down. The grip on her purse tightened and her chin lifted as she continued to stride toward me.

Every inch of her was covered in clothing, clearly making a statement she was not to be ogled. She could cover herself up all she wanted. I still knew what kind of curves she was sporting under her clothes. They'd been burned in my brain from seeing her at Kitten's Castle.

"Goldie," I said more as a statement rather than a question.

"Uh, yeah. And you are?" she asked, not relaxing the death grip on her purse.

"Let's get a table," I said as I released my stance and nodded toward the door.

I walked inside without giving her a second glance. I knew she would follow me. She was desperate, at her wit's end. She needed this meeting.

We were seated at a table in the back against a wall, giving us an optimal amount of privacy. I'd arranged the table with the host early on.

Goldie fidgeted as a waiter took our orders for water. Her hands shook, and I wondered if I made her nervous.

Of course I made her nervous. What was I thinking? I was a strange man trying to convince her to perform for the city elites. If I'd been her, I would have run all the way back to my apartment and locked the doors.

Ignoring how nervous she was, I proceeded with the meeting.

"What took you so long to call?" I asked, leaning back in my chair and crossing my arms.

"Why don't we start off with a little introduction, eh? You know, the old 'hi, my name is...'." she motioned her hand for me to continue.

"What took you so long to call?" I asked again, ignoring her attempt to get me to talk casually.

Blowing out a frustrated breath, she said, "Sorry I didn't jump at the chance to call a number from a stranger who contacted me three times after following me around the fucking French Quarter."

I stilled a small smile and continued. "Why did you end up calling?"

"Because apparently I'm a masochist." She got up. "This isn't working out. Thanks for the... water."

I sat casually in my chair, not worried about her departure. "Your tens of thousands of dollars in debt aren't going to just disappear, Goldie."

As if on cue, she swung around in shock. I casually played with the straw in my water and eyed her from under my lashes. It didn't take a genius to figure out how to press this little hellion's buttons.

Quickly sitting down again, she said as quietly as possible, "Where did you get that information? That is a violation of privacy."

Her blue eyes blazed with fury as she stabbed her finger against the table and demanded answers.

God, she was beautiful, even when she was mad. Her eyes were full of life, an attribute I was greatly lacking. The blush on her cheeks showed how young she was despite her old eyes.

Why had Jett found her first? Right about now, I would have given anything to grab her hand, pull her onto my lap, and bury my head in the sweet smell of her skin.

Every orifice of my body prickled with the need to pull her into me, to make her mine. I didn't know her, but just after one interaction with her, I was sold. There was something about her, something special that was infectious. I knew she was going to make a mark on me.

She waited for me to answer about her invasion of privacy, but instead I continued with my tactic of reminding her about the destitute life she was living.

"Do you want to escape the hole you're living in now, Goldie? Do you want to feel safe, taken care of, and debt free?"

"No, I want to live in the gutter while being fucked in the ass by Bourbon's hobos," she shot back sarcastically.

I couldn't help myself. The corner of my mouth tugged to the side from her comment. She was feisty. *Good luck, Jett.* "That mouth is going to get you into trouble."

"Oh, is that right? Well, frankly, I don't give a fuck." She leaned closer and said, "Stop bullshitting me; just tell me what the hell a Jett Girl is and what it entails."

I admired how tough she was. "Fair enough. Have you heard of the Lafayette Club?"

"Only from what my friend Lyla, told me, and it was

practically nothing."

Lyla was her roommate. That I knew. I also knew she worked at Kitten's Castle as well. I'd been so transfixed with Goldie that first night, I wasn't able to scope out the roommate. From what I understood, Lyla was in the same situation as Goldie but not as desperate. She could handle her own.

"It's a high-class gentlemen's club where very important men go to conduct business. The Jett Girls are the in-house entertainment, ranging from still art and choreographed dances to serving drinks. The girls are never touched, they are never completely naked, and their personas are entirely anonymous. They go by aliases and wear wigs and masks during their presentations. If they were ever seen on the streets of New Orleans, you would never know they were a Jett Girl."

"Okay...," she dragged on skeptically.

I could tell my little elevator pitch had scared the crap out of her, but I continued. "All Jett Girls are required to live in the club and get an education, which is fully paid for, so when they're ready to move on, they have something to move on to. All debt a Jett Girl accumulated before she signs on is immediately erased the minute she comes into the club. You are completely taken care of: food, clothes, housing, etc. Every Jett Girl gets the feeling of being safe and sound while living in the Lafayette Club."

"What's the catch?" she asked, not buying it.

How did I go about this without making Jett seem like a total creep? He wasn't. He just liked sex, like I did. Nothing wrong with a healthy libido. I understood Jett's reasoning for being monogamous with the girls. His mom had passed from AIDS. She was very cautious, but he wanted to please the girls as well. That's why he offered them the chance to go up to the Bourbon room with him, his playroom.

"If you're a Jett Girl, you're required to keep yourself for Jett and Jett alone. Outside relationships are not permitted, and you must submit to Jett."

"Submit?"

"Yes, submit to him."

Yup, I'd scared her. I could see it in her eyes, but she was trying to put on a good show for me, show me how tough she was. I was a little excited that she was freaked out because honestly, that meant I might possibly have a chance with her, even though I had no room for a relationship in my life.

She contemplated what she was going to say and then said, "Man, this Jett guy must be one ugly fuck if he has to spend thousands of dollars 'saving' women just to get a little ass. Doesn't he know there are willing prostitutes on every corner who would only charge him a hundred dollars to suck his dick?"

She had it all wrong, but damn it if I was going to correct her. I was a selfish bastard. I wanted her.

"Well, that's a nice little, uh, establishment you've got going on there, but I have to say... not interested."

I mentally fist pumped as my phone vibrated in my pocket. I knew who it was. Jett was checking in to see how the meeting was going. My conscience battled with me. Even though I wanted Goldie, at least for a night, she needed Jett more than she needed me. Jett would be able to give her everything she needed for a second chance in life. I couldn't give her anything.

With regret, I said, "Don't be an idiot, Goldie. You and I both know you don't have a choice in the matter."

She spat back quickly, fire in her eyes. "That's where you're wrong. I do have a choice. I have a little more self-respect than whoring myself out at some creepy man's brothel so I don't have to live sad paycheck to sad paycheck."

Time to drop the bomb. "Is that why you get paid for sex by

Rex Titan?"

My words smacked her in the face. Rex Titan, also known as Jett's arch nemesis, paid Goldie occasionally for sex. It was an act of desperation on her part, to help make ends meet. For Rex, it was a way to fulfill the needs his wife ignored. Rex was a sick man, someone Jett and I kept tabs on but refused to acquaint ourselves with.

She pointed at me. "You're a sick fuck, you know that? Get another hobby and stop stalking innocent girls. Fucking creep."

I liked everything about this woman, from her gorgeous body to her filthy mouth.

"The offer stands until midnight, Goldie."

"You can take your offer and shove it up your dick hole. See ya, psycho." She took off.

I hadn't expected anything less from her.

CHAPTER TWENTY TWO

My present...

For the last week, I'd worked my body ragged, getting
ready for the opening of Justice. After I returned to the
community center, I assessed what needed to be done and was
surprised to see that in my absence, the girls had stepped up.
The center was ready to open to the public, and the only thing
that needed a final once-over was the Haze Room. Naturally,
the girls left that to me.

If I was going to spend most of my time in the room
teaching, I wanted it organized to my liking. I moved bleachers
and bins around and added more equipment, along with
chalkboards and more mats.

It was nine in the morning, and the center was set to open
in half an hour. I wasn't sure if I was ready. I was still reeling
from my demons, trying to overcome the ache in my chest I'd
been living for years. Could a damaged soul try to save another
damaged soul? Was that even possible?

"Looks good," Jett said as he walked in and surveyed my
changes. "I'm proud of you, Kace."

"For what?" I asked, wondering what he could possibly be proud of. This center had been his idea. We used his money to create a safe haven. He'd been the mastermind, and I was the follower.

"For putting your reservations on hold and helping develop this center with me. I couldn't have done it without you."

"The girls did a lot."

"With your guidance," Jett added. "Don't discredit what you were able to accomplish here. Accept the compliment and be proud of yourself."

It pained me, but I nodded and accepted Jett's commendation. "Thanks, man."

"You're welcome." Jett smiled brightly. "I've got to admit, you've changed in the past week. I haven't spoken to you much, but does this new you have to do with the apology you gave us the other day? Goldie is still dazed by it. She thinks she changed you with her dick talk."

"Of course she does," I shook my head. "She's a piece of work, you know that?"

"Don't have to tell me that. So what's with the change?"

I shrugged and stared at the punching bags, wondering if I could get a quick workout in before the center opened.

"Blane said something to me that made sense. I was the one who made the mistake of punching Marshall. I am the one who decided to punish myself. I shouldn't punish the people around me. You've all been accepting of me and my faults. It's about time I treated you all the way you deserve to be treated."

"Does that mean you're going to start kissing me goodbye?" Jett asked with a grin.

"Both cheeks," I joked, pointing to my face.

"The only way I like it." Jett paused and put his hands in his pockets and rocked on his feet. "I know you're dealing with a lot, Kace, but I need to tell you, your friendship over the years has been the best thing in my life. Well, until Goldie."

"She does have the pussy."

"Watch it," Jett smirked. "Seriously though, the guilt you live with on a daily basis might not ever go away, and I understand that, but thank you for keeping my best friend around. I don't know what I would do without you, Kace. I don't say it enough, but you're my fucking brother, and I would do anything for you."

"I know."

We exchanged a knowing look that spoke volumes about our friendship. No matter what came our way, we would always have each other's backs. We might not have been brothers by blood, but we sure as hell were brothers by soul.

"Mind if I get a couple of quick hits in before we open up?"

"Go ahead," Jett replied while eyeing the punching bags. "Break it in. This is your room now, Kace. Make it worth it."

With pressed lips, I nodded and shook Jett's hand. He pulled me into a brief hug then briskly walked away. It wasn't Jett's style to show much emotion, not even toward Goldie, but the woman had softened him, and it was a big day. I would take his exchange and hold it close to me. If anything, I would die knowing my past crime wouldn't deny me a true friendship.

Without taping my hands, I quickly slipped on the boxing gloves I now kept stored in the Haze Room and went to the closest bag. I circled it once and bounced on my toes, looking for the perfect spot to strike. With a quick jab of my right hand, I punched the bag, causing it to swing.

The feel of my fist connecting with the sand bag enthralled me. Excitement coursed through my veins as I circled, stopped, and threw a couple of jabs at it. I bobbed to the left, bobbed to the right, and threw an uppercut straight into the bag, my signature move.

Heavy concentration settled over me as everything around me turned black. Like a couple, I danced with the bag, letting the swing from my punches turn into a rhythmic tango of sweaty athleticism. In a few short minutes, a sheen of sweat skimmed my skin just as my arms started to loosen up, allowing my punches to strike at full force.

Right hook, left hook, uppercut.

Upper cut, upper cut, bob to the left, jab with the right.

Move, Kace, move.

From a distance I heard a crowd roar with every punch I made. My coach called, guiding me from the corner. Blood pounded in my head, and my punches became heavier. I focused and was instantly in the zone.

The smell of my opponent's sweat came roaring back, the feel of my feet bouncing around the ring attacked my senses, and then and there, I felt the euphoric pleasure of being in the spotlight with my gloves taped to my wrists and a sorry-ass sucker bobbing in front of me.

Right hook, left jab, right uppercut, bob, right uppercut.

Cheers erupted, and clapping echoed in my mind, a clapping that seemed all too real.

"You look good."

I was mid-jab when I stopped, my vision cleared, and the lights from the room fogged my vision. Even though I had a hard time adjusting, I knew that voice like it was a constant record playing in my head. "What are you doing here, Lyla?"

"Wanted to wish you good luck on the opening," she answered nonchalantly.

I stepped away so the punching bag was no longer in my way and glanced at the woman who'd burned herself into my soul.

Fuck me, was she gorgeous.

Her long hair was curled in light waves that hung over her shoulders. She was wearing a pair of skinny jeans that were cuffed right above her ankle boots. But it was her top that was really grabbing my attention. She was wearing a loose-fitting tank top that opened at the sides and dipped low in the front, giving me an eyeful of her navy blue bra that showcased her breasts to perfection. Her skin glittered under the lights, and I wondered if she thought of me often like I did of her.

I was weak around her; my brain scrambled whenever she was near. She crippled me, mind, body, and fucking soul.

"Thanks," I replied, really not knowing what else to say. I shed my boxing gloves and tossed them to the ground. I grabbed a towel and wiped the sweat from my forehead. "You're looking good yourself." I nodded at her outfit.

Good didn't even come close to describing how she actually looked.

"Thanks." Her hands rested in her pockets and she looked around the room. When she was done scanning the room, she took a deep breath and took it upon herself to step closer to me.

"What are you doing, Lyla?" I asked, wondering why she kept coming back to me even though I treated her terribly every time we were together.

"It's hard to get you out of my system, Kace. It's hard to just let go."

"It would be best if you did."

"I know," she replied, grabbing one of my belt loops. The heat pouring off her was instantly absorbed by my body, turning me on to an uncomfortable state. "I wish I could stay away, Kace. I told myself I didn't need you, that I should move on, but I see the trouble in your eyes, the hurt, the need for someone to save you, and for the life of me, I can't walk away from that."

Did she know I secretly wanted her to save me? Could she see how much I needed her? Begged for her at night? Could she really see the desperation in my eyes, the heart-stopping ache I had in my chest to live a normal life?

"I know you don't want me, Kace. I know you want to sequester yourself from the outside world. I get that, I've been there, but I just want you to know, no matter how many times you push me away, no matter how many times you're awful to me, I will always be there for you. I want you to be happy, even if that means you're not with me."

My pulse raced in my chest. I pulled Lyla into my space by her hips. Her hand ran up my chest to my jaw where her fingers traced my rough scruff. Her fingernails ran across the bristly hair as her soft green eyes bored into my soul.

"You're my addiction, Lyla."

Distraught and confused, I pulled her head toward mine and gently glided my lips along hers. I was an addict, a junkie, a self-mutilator. This woman in my arms was all I'd ever wanted but everything I couldn't have.

Blood pounded through me from the contact, and I wished in that moment God would decide to take me, because I would die a happy man. I could die feeling like the luckiest son of a bitch to grace this fucked up world.

But life wasn't fair.

I pulled away and stared at her swollen lips. Gorgeous, so fucking gorgeous.

"It's best if you move on, Lyla. I want you to move on."

"How can you say that when your eyes speak another truth?"

"Because I know what's best for you. You think you know me, you think you can handle my past, but you can't. It's not like there is some easy solution."

"Excuse me?" A tall woman with brown hair walked into the room, looking a little confused. I glanced at my watch and saw that it was now past nine thirty. Shit.

I turned to Lyla and said, "Thank you for accepting me, but there is no future with me, babe. Best you move on."

The pained look in her face gutted me once again, but I ignored the searing agony and switched my attention to the woman who'd interrupted us. Anguish ran up my spine as I tried to place the familiarity in the woman's features.

"Can I help you?" I asked.

"I'm looking for Kace Haywood."

"That's me. How can I help you, ma'am?"

"Mom, this place is awesome," came a small voice. Running into the room and hugging her mom, a young girl looked up at her with adoring eyes.

My breathing stopped, my lungs seized, and my vision went dark.

It was Madeline and Linda, the family I'd destroyed.

CHAPTER TWENTY THREE

My present...

"Kace. Kace, are you okay?" Lyla shook my arm, trying to knock me out of my fog, but I couldn't move.

I was numb, paralyzed, crippled from the sight before me. This couldn't be real. I was living in a fucking nightmare. God wasn't this cruel, was he?

"Kace," Lyla called after me again.

"Mommy, I'm scared," Madeline said, snapping me out of my stupor.

"Sorry." I shook my head, trying to clear my disbelief. Gathering my strength, I said, "You reminded me of someone I used to know." I lied, knowing fully well who was standing right in front of me.

Madeline visibly relaxed and gave me a giant toothless grin. Her two top front teeth were missing, freckles were scattered over her nose and cheeks, and her hair was pulled up in a ponytail, but little wisps of hair stuck to her delicate face, giving her an angelic look.

She was a beautiful child.

Assessing her quickly, I caught a glimpse of a necklace that graced her delicate neck. My heart leapt from realizing she was wearing the necklace I'd recently given her. But it wasn't just the necklace. She was using the purse I'd given her, as well as a T-shirt that was still large on her. She was using everything I'd given her...all the fucking gifts from years past.

Not only had she received my gifts, but she'd kept them and utilized them.

In an instant I felt weak, like I couldn't possibly stand on my legs anymore.

"Do you need some water, Mr. Haywood?" Linda asked.

"Yes," I replied, gathering myself. "Let's get some and talk." I turned to Lyla and pressed a chaste kiss on her cheek. "Get out of here, babe. Go live your life." She didn't need to get tangled in the sick and fucked up web I was living. Confusion furrowed her brow as I walked away, trying to gather myself for the conversation I was about to have with Linda Duncan.

What could she possibly want? Did she know it was me dropping off the gifts? Had she seen me in the daylight this last time? If I hadn't been such a drunken mess the night before, her gift would have been properly dropped off like all the other times.

Had she found out I was the one who'd killed her husband? Was she here to air out my past sin? Was she here to turn me in?

Every possible thought I could think of for her being here ran through my brain as I made my way to the water, wondering if this was my final moment before I was sentenced. I grabbed a paper cup from the dispenser next to the cooler and poured myself some water. With a shaky hand, I brought the cup up to my lips.

Taking large gulps, I finished in seconds and then crushed it in my palm, slightly easing some of the tension in my body.

"Sorry about that. The weather changed quickly this year. I wasn't ready for the heat," I said, coming up with some kind of excuse for my weird and awkward behavior.

"Not a problem. I know what you mean. I wasn't ready for such a heat wave right away either, plus the humidity. It can be suffocating at times," Linda agreed.

"Exactly," I responded, feeling uncomfortable.

Linda was sweet. She was nice and very easy to talk to, almost too easy to talk to. I didn't want to get familiar with her because knowing me, I would let go of all my past transgressions in a matter of seconds, thanks to the massive guilt weighing on me.

Last time I'd seen Linda in person was when I'd gone to see Madeline play tee-ball. At the time, Linda had been lankier. She'd seemed okay from afar, but I'd seen the weight of the world on her shoulders. Madeline was as cute as ever but a little more grown up. Linda had gained some weight. She looked healthy now, full and curvy.

I wondered if she had remarried. Had she even dated since she lost Marshall? What was her love life like? Did she even have one, or was she still devastated from what I'd done, from what I'd stolen from her?

"I'm sorry. How rude of me not to introduce myself. I'm Linda, and this is my daughter Madeline," Linda said.

Linda held out her hand, and I took it in a quick shake and then glanced at Madeline, who was holding her hand out as well, showing off that toothy grin.

Damn, she was adorable.

"Hi, I'm Kace." I took Madeline's hand in mine, and she wrinkled her nose and looked at Linda.

"He's all sweaty, Mom."

"Madeline!" Linda reprimanded.

"Nah, that's okay," I said. "Your hands get sweaty in those boxing gloves. Should have warned you."

"Well, that's nice of you, but we need to mind our manners. Right, Madeline?"

"Right. Sorry, Mr. Kace."

"Not a problem at all." I chuckled.

Those freckles and that smile were going to be the death of me. Madeline was so dainty, so petite. The shirt she was wearing was one I'd bought her a few years ago with a map of New Orleans on it. Clearly it hadn't been my best purchase since she was just fitting into it now, and because it was a shirt with a map of New Orleans on it, but apparently she liked it. Choosing presents was so out of my realm but, buying for a little girl was in another fucking galaxy of comprehension. Buying for a little girl just added pressure that resulted in crap purchases like the shirt she was wearing. Although she seemed to like the purse I'd gotten her since she still used it. It was ragged and torn in spots where little patches of ladybugs and rainbows covered up the holes.

Even though I didn't want to feel happy she still used the items I bought her, I couldn't help but feel slightly elated. She loved my presents.

She loved them. Either that or….

Shit, maybe she hadn't been given anything else besides my presents because her mom couldn't afford it.

That thought sent my stomach into another flip.

"Kace, are you sure you're okay?" Linda placed her hand on my shoulder, and it almost felt like her skin was burning mine, burning me for my past sins.

"Fine. Umm, what can I help you with?" I asked, needing this little conversation to end sooner rather than later.

In the background, the community center bustled with excited patrons observing the different classes we offered as well as taking a tour of the facility, led by Goldie, of course, because who else would be more entertaining? Voices started to flow down the hallway, and I knew the tour would head my way soon, which meant having to get my shit together. I wouldn't do the center any good if I was practically hyperventilating on the floor. Yeah, that would get people to sign up for my class.

"And this is the Haze Room," Goldie said, opening the door and allowing a few people to come in.

A family walked in as well as a couple. They looked around in awe. Goldie made eye contact with me and gave me a questioning look. I shook my head for her to not ask anything, and thankfully she didn't pursue it..

"And this is Kace. He is our instructor in the Haze Room. Rumor has it he's ready to work his athletes hard, so if you come here, get ready to sweat."

I smiled and said, "We accept all levels of athletes. No judgement here. I will work with you and your level of fitness."

"He says that now." Goldie winked and led the group out of the room.

"She's so much fun," Linda said, speaking of Goldie. "She was so sweet at the front desk, especially when directed us down here."

"She's pretty amazing," I said, speaking the truth.

"Mom, can I go play on the mats?" Madeline asked, a pleading look in her eyes.

Linda looked at me for approval. I bent down to Madeline's level and said, "Run wild, kid."

"Awesome!" She threw her purse on the floor and ran around, doing somersaults and cartwheels on the mats.

"She has a lot of energy," I pointed out.

"Tell me about it. That's why we're here. I want her to use that energy for good. I want her to learn how to work with others, take instruction, and apply herself."

"She will definitely be able to learn that here. Do you have any classes in mind?"

"Self-defense," Linda said without skipping a beat.

"Okay, well, we have a class she could join. It will probably be more adults than anything."

"That's okay," Linda said while looking at Madeline. "The earlier she learns, the better. I'd also like to see her build confidence and put some meat on her bones. She needs to be able to defend herself."

The way Linda was talking had me worried. Was Madeline being picked on at school? The mere thought had my blood boiling and my hands itching to take care of whoever was picking on her. No matter what their age or size was, I was ready to teach someone a fucking lesson.

"I know this is none of my business, but is she having trouble at school?"

Linda was lost in a daze, watching Madeline. "I'm sorry, what did you say?"

It was as if Linda was just living in another world, completely lost in her thoughts. What was she thinking about? Was she trying to teach Madeline self-defense because her father had been attacked in a bar? It would make sense, but would Linda be all right with me teaching her daughter self-defense when I was the man who had murdered her husband?

I was getting nauseated, but I ignored it, needing to get this conversation over with. Repeating myself, I asked, "Is Madeline being picked on at school?"

"What? No. Why would you ask that?"

"Oh, I just...The way you asked about self-defense, I thought that maybe she was going through something right now."

"Just taking precautionary measures."

Precautionary measures. Linda was trying to protect Madeline from people like me. Little did she know, she should stay as far away from me as possible.

"Do you think Madeline would be able to join the class? It's very important to me that she learns to defend herself at a young age. I want her growing up to be a strong, confident woman."

"Yup," I said, swallowing bile. "We can get her into today's class if you're interested in starting right away."

I was talking, but I really wasn't understanding what I was offering. Was I really accepting Madeline into one of my classes?

"That would be great. What time does it begin?"

I looked at my watch. "Half an hour."

"Perfect. I brought her gear. I can go get her changed and then we'll be back."

"Sounds good," I replied. "Make sure you get a free water bottle up front."

"Thanks. Can I sit and watch?"

"Yup, that's why we have the bleachers. You can join in as well if you would like."

"I'll think about it," Linda said a little shyly. "Come on, Madeline. We have to get you ready for class."

"Awesome!" Madeline called while fist-pumping the air. She skidded across the floor, grabbed her bag, and headed out of the room with her mom.

"See you in a few," Linda called out.

"Yeah, see you in a few, Mr. Kace," Madeline said, waving

and walking away with her mom.

The minute the door closed, I locked it and ran to the trashcan, where I threw up all my past sins and regrets.

How the fuck was I going to get through today without losing my shit?

***

My heart hammered in my chest, sweat dripped down my back, and my throat was clogged with emotion, a fucking unyielding feeling that was making it hard to breathe.

Watching Madeline prance around the Haze Room, wearing boxing gloves entirely too big for her noodle arms, smiling and waving at her mom after every punch she made to the bag, caused me to be physically nauseous.

I didn't know why I felt so ill. I should have been happy she was a well-rounded little girl with a heart of fucking gold and a smile that made me want to give her the world.

But all I felt was the sick need to bury myself in a case of Maker's and wash away the smiling image of Madeline Duncan.

I could feel myself drowning, gasping for air, wondering when the burning ache in my chest would cease to exist.

This pain I was feeling, I'd brought upon myself. I couldn't get over God's sick plan to bring Linda and Madeline into my life.

"Looking good over here," Jett said as he clasped my shoulder. "You got them working hard."

It was a small class of five people. Linda decided to join in and they were all working on their jabs right now while I tried to calm my racing heart.

"Yeah," I said, not knowing what else to say.

Madeline threw her little arms at the bag with horrible

form, and I knew I had to correct her so she didn't hurt herself, but my feet were cemented in place, permitting me from moving forward.

"You all right?" Jett asked, knowing me too well.

"No," I answered honestly. "I'm not fucking all right."

Jett leaned closer. "Want to talk outside?"

"Can't. Teaching a class."

"Are you really? Because it looks like you're standing here in absolute—"

"Madeline, stay on your own bag," Linda called, interrupting Jett. Madeline was running around punching all the bags in the area, causing a fucking adorable ruckus.

Jett swung his gaze to where Madeline and Linda were, assessed the mother-daughter pair, then turned his back on them and got in my face. "Is that…"

I confirmed his suspicions, not letting him finish.

Jett ran his hand over his face and muttered, "Holy shit. What are they doing here?"

"Linda wants Madeline to learn self-defense. She thinks it's important. Given the way her father died, I don't blame Linda for forcing her daughter into the class."

"And you said you were going to help? What the hell were you thinking?"

"What was I supposed to say? 'Sorry, can't help you since I'm the one who killed your husband.' I didn't have many options, Jett."

"I guess you didn't," he said, turning to look at Madeline. She was leaning against a wall, wiping her forehead with her forearm and catching her breath. "She's kind of adorable."

"I fucking know," I admitted. "What do I do?"

I was at a loss. I had no clue how to handle this situation. I needed a lifeline. I needed someone to tell me how to handle this, because right about now, I couldn't breathe, let alone figure out how to talk to Madeline.

"Do the right thing," Jett answered. "Swallow your demons, step up, and teach the girl. What happened in your past was not your fault, but you have a responsibility now to see it through."

Jett was right. I had a responsibility, and it was to take care of Madeline. If that meant pushing past the bile that rose from the mere thought of forming a bond with this little girl, then I would.

"You're right," I said while pushing past Jett and heading over to Madeline, who was still leaning against the wall with her arms at her sides and her head pressed back.

"Hey," I said while squatting down to her level.

"Hi there, Mr. Kace," Madeline said, perking up. "These gloves are heavy."

"Well, they're the wrong size. I told you they wouldn't work for you." She'd insisted on wearing them.

"I just wanted to wear the ones you were wearing when you demonstrated. You looked so tough."

A numbing tingle started to crawl up my back. *I can do this*, I repeated over and over in my head.

"To get tough, you have to start from the beginning. How about we take off the gloves and put on the little hand-wraps instead," I suggested. "Then we can work up to the gloves."

"Those gloves are black." She crinkled her nose. "Don't you have pretty ones?"

I looked over at the hand-wraps and shook my head no. "Sorry, kiddo. I only have black ones right now, but I will see what I can do for you for future classes. How does that sound?"

"All right." She flashed me that toothless grin, melting me on the spot.

For that smile, I would have given her the fucking world.

We walked over to the gloves. She was like a shadow I couldn't shake ever since my fist had connected with her father, and right now, that shadow was stronger than ever.

I pulled out the smallest hand-wraps we had and bent down. She placed her hand on my shoulder. With a serious look, she held out her other hand and said, "I'm glad you're here teaching me, Mr. Kace. I like you." She paused for a second and then continued talking when I helped her put the hand-wraps on. "I don't have a dad, but if I did, I would want him to be like you."

Sweat broke out on my skin, self-loathing started to eclipse my thoughts, and pain erupted from the backs of my eyes as I tamped down the tears that wanted to flow.

"You're quiet though," she continued. "And you make funny faces."

"Funny faces?" I asked, barely able to work my vocal cords.

"Yeah, you're always like this." She put her fists on her hips, curled her lip, and squinted her eyes at me.

If I hadn't been feeling like someone had picked me up and ripped me into shreds, I would have laughed at her impression of me. "I don't think I look like that."

"Well, not exactly," she answered, now with both wraps on her hands. She swatted at the air and bounced around me. "Stinging flowers and floating bees," she said, punching some more.

"What?" I asked, confused.

"You know, Mamala-ladi."

"Mama-what?"

"Boom, boom, boom," she said, striking my thigh. "I'm floating like a bee. Look at me go." She bounced around some more and then it clicked.

"Do you mean Muhammad Ali?"

"Sure," she said while dancing around some more, adding some pathetic kicks to the mix.

"I think you meant you 'float like a butterfly and sting like a bee'."

"Sure. Pow, pow, pow. I'm a champion."

I steered her to the hanging bags as she continued to bounce. "Easy there, killer. Let's get you punching correctly first."

I spent a good ten minutes with her, ignoring the overwhelming feeling of discomfort and violence. Violence for the position I've put Madeline in, a life without a father, a life comparing other men to what she thinks she would want when it came to a dad.

The pain was consuming; the heartache was too much. There was only one way I knew how to get rid of this all-encompassing feeling of complete hatred for myself. It was time to call the boys.

CHAPTER TWENTY FOUR

My past...

Humidity seeped into my pores as the early morning light started to peek through the alleys of New Orleans. Sanitation crews ran up and down the streets, washing away the sins from the night before, preparing for a fresh start of a new day. Musky trash and bile scattered the curbs and moisture glistened on the brick walls, displaying the rough heat of Louisiana in the summer.

I could smell the bloodshed waiting for me. The air electrified with violence as I waited in my normal spot, my selected spot where no one would dare disturb what happened in such an area.

Evil lurked in the dark and dreary alley I'd chosen. Malevolent and ugly crimes were conducted in such alleyways, and that was what I was here for.

It was the anniversary of Marshall Duncan's death. It was the anniversary of my biggest regret. It was the anniversary of the day I'd let my soul slip away from me and the day I'd sworn to the heavens above I would punish myself until my last breath.

There was only one way I celebrated this day, only one

way I knew how to, and that was by getting lost in pain.

Heavy footsteps padded along the cobblestone streets. I knew those footsteps. They belonged to large, intimidating men with steel-toed boots and iron fists. They belonged to the men I'd paid to come beat the shit out of me.

Like usual, they rounded the corner, wearing black pants and shirts, cracking their knuckles and looking hungry. I paid them well to attack to me, to make me forget. I fought back sometimes, putting in a few punches here and there, nothing too damaging. I saved that for the bags, something I should have thought of when I was standing face-to-face with Marshall Duncan.

I was leaning up against the wall of one of the buildings that flanked the alleyway when they came up to me.

"Looking good, Mr. Haywood. Another year has done you well."

I observed Vinny's appearance and said, "How's the wife?"

"Just had twins."

"No shit." I shook my head. "They yours?"

Before I saw it coming, Vinny cocked his fist back and hit my jaw straight on, sending me to the ground. Pain ricocheted through me—intoxicating pain, welcome pain.

"You know damn well they're mine," Vinny replied with mirth in his voice.

I stood up and gripped my jaw. "Fuck, wouldn't have guessed you had time to work out if the wife just had twins."

"Got to stay in shape for the missis." Vinny flexed, showing off his bulky body. His bulk wasn't defined since he loved his wife's Italian food way too much, but beneath a thin layer of lasagna was some muscle that could do quite a bit of damage. I nodded at the other two men Vinny had brought with him. "New goons?"

"Meet my nephews, Johnny and Marco."

I tilted my chin at them and then turned back to Vinny. "Nice that you're keeping the business in the family."

"We're all about familia," Vinny answered, laying his Italian accent on thick. "Are you done with the tea time?"

"Yeah, make it good. They know the rules?"

"They've been informed. Only a few head shots, mostly body, and they are aware of your ability to fight back."

"Then take me fucking out," I replied, opening my arms wide.

Marco and Johnny were hesitant, unsure how to comprehend the situation. They most likely thought of me as some crazy fuck who paid to get his ass kicked, and yes, that was true, but most of the time, people liked to be provoked in order to get into a fight, so I did what I did best on this day: I provoked.

"You just going to stare at me, you little bitch?" I asked Marco. He tried to fake me out with a little step forward, but I stood strong. "Fucking amateur, you really think your little juke move would work on me?"

Marco looked at Vinny, who was standing back, waiting for his turn, wondering if he should just come at me.

"Fucking Christ," I said while I charged at Marco and pinned him against the opposite wall. Johnny was instantly on my back, defending his cousin. Just what I'd expected.

Marco squirmed underneath my grasp, and Johnny clawed at my back but left no impression on me, so I continued to hold on to Marco, slamming him against the brick building until a knee pelted itself in my liver.

"Fuck." I let go of Marco and leaned against the wall. That was when a fist flew into my eye, shooting my head straight back into the brick. In a matter of seconds, my eye swelled shut, making the fight that much harder, that much more entertaining for me.

Call me a masochist, but I lived for this day, the day I was able to endure more pain than humanly possible.

My head was reeling, my pulse was rapid fire, and my will to fight was gone as I tried to navigate where everyone was but there was no hope. They surrounded me and used my closed eye to their advantage.

Blow after blow, I was tossed around the circle, kicked in the side, pelted in the arms, in the ribcage, in the chest.

Vinny's tall frame hovered over me as his fist rammed into my side, making me buckle over just as his knee came up and knocked me in the head, sending me backward to the ground. One of the nephews straddled me and pinned my arms down with his legs, sending blow after blow into my sides and then one to the other side of my jaw.

Sharp pangs ran through me, my vision started to fade, and the slow warm drip of blood crept across my face. The person pinning me down fled, and when I thought they were done, they started taking turns kicking me with their steel-toed boots.

Kick after motherfucking kick had my stomach revolting and my chest heaving for air. The pain was excruciating, and even in my numbest state, I still felt every knock they threw my way.

Everything around me became hazy, and I started to slip into a dark delirium when I heard the distinct sound of Jett's voice.

"I think that's enough, Vinny."

Why was Jett here? He never came down to the alley because he didn't agree with my punishment, he didn't believe it was a way to live my life, but what the fuck did he know? He had no idea of the kind of pain I went through on a daily basis.

"Mr. Colby, what a pleasure."

The guys backed off as Jett approached. "Vinny, congratulations on the twins. How is Theresa doing?"

"Great, thanks for asking. You should see the size of her tits. Doc says I can't go at her right now, but shit is she making it hard on me."

Jett laughed shortly. "Listen to the doc. You don't want to do any permanent damage."

"You know I will," Vinny replied. "I think we're done here. Are you going to collect the mess?"

"Yeah, unfortunately. Maybe next year, you don't show up."

"He pays me too well to let that happen. Sorry, man."

"I would pay you more not to do it."

Silence filled the alleyway as I assumed Vinny thought about Jett's offer. If I hadn't been in so much pain and my voice might reach them, I would have protested but there was no use.

"You make a compelling offer, Mr. Colby, but I couldn't do that to Mr. Haywood. I see an empty man inside him, a hurting man. I know what this kind pain can do to him. I know it helps him forget. I don't want to take that away from him. He needs this."

Vinny was my kind of people.

"I'm sorry to hear that. Maybe I can convince you another time."

"Don't count on it."

Vinny stepped over me, giving me one last kick to the hip. "Until next year, Mr. Haywood. Take care of yourself."

Vinny and his nephews retreated, leaving me aching on the ground of New Orleans.

Jett crouched next to me and turned me so he could see my face. "Fucking hell," he muttered. "Why do you do this, Kace?"

I rolled to my stomach and pressed my hands against the ground to lift myself up. I stayed there on my hands and knees for a bit, trying to catch my breath and watching the blood drip from my face with my one good eye.

Small crimson droplets flooded into a puddle seeping into the cobblestone, soaking the streets with yet another sin that would be washed away later.

I coughed a few times. The feeling of glass shards ripped through my lungs, and I knew they'd broken at least a few of my ribs. It would be a long recovery with no painkillers. I looked forward to it.

"Take me home," I muttered, allowing Jett to grab my arm and help me up.

"Why, Kace?" he asked again, lifting my arm over his shoulders to help me walk. I had tunnel vision, only able to see a few feet in front of me.

"It's too much," I said, coughing again.

"What is?" Jett asked, bringing me around the corner to an idling car. Before Jett helped me into the vehicle, he made me look at him and answer his question.

"The memory, Jett. The memory is too fucking much."

He understood and helped me into the car, where towels and ice were waiting for me.

I knew my best friend loathed this day. I knew he hated seeing me like this, and I knew he hated the fact that he couldn't alter my decision-making process on this day.

Jett was a man who strived to save lives. This was one fucking life he wouldn't be able to save, no matter how hard he tried.

CHAPTER TWENTY FIVE

My present...

I rolled to my side and looked at the clock just before it started ringing, letting me know it was time to get up. Every last inch of my body burned as I threw the covers off me.

There was a lack of energy in my body and an abundance of pain throbbing down every inch of my frame.

Shower. I needed a hot shower.

Exerting my muscles, I lifted my body off my mattress and slowly walked to my bathroom where I turned the water to the hottest setting. I stumbled to the shitter where I pissed a liter worth of whiskey while steam from the shower started to billow from the top.

Flushing the toilet, I carefully walked over to the shower where I stepped in and allowed the searing hot water to run over me. The water was so hot, it almost felt cold. With my face in the water, I pressed my hands against the tile and let the water run over my aching body.

Vinny had been surprised to get a call from me last night, but with a little coaxing, he'd met me in the alley and taken care of business. There had been a concerned look on his face, but I knew he wouldn't ask questions. He was just there to do a job. He'd left me bruised and battered, making sure to stay below the neck since I had to teach a class that morning.

I never doubled up in a year, ever, but after seeing Madeline and Linda yesterday, I'd needed the pain. I'd needed a release, and Vinny was able to deliver.

Water continued to run down my back, reminding me that in fact, I was still alive, a privilege I shouldn't be granted but that also shouldn't be wasted. I gathered up my soap and washed and thought about yesterday.

It'd been one of my most fucked up days to date. Not only had Linda and Madeline tilted my entire fucking world, but Lyla had shown up, letting me know she would never truly let go.

How the hell was I supposed to push away from a woman who wouldn't let me? She was making this entirely too difficult, but it wasn't like I fucking helped any. No, I went and told her she was practically my fucking crutch.

Christ.

What possessed me in that moment to say that to her was beyond me. Maybe it was because all I could think about was how beautiful she was, how her skin looked so soft under the gym lights and how her lips were calling out to me, to fucking make her mine, brand her with my shameful dysfunction.

With the soap, I lathered up my hand and washed my stomach as visions of Lyla kept passing through my mind.

I thought about her face, her breasts, her body.

My hand found my growing erection and without remorse, I stroked myself to the image of Lyla writhing underneath me, an image that had been branded in my brain.

I heard her little cries of pleasure, felt her grabbing hold of my ass, urging me deeper inside her. I growled and pumped my rigid cock. I just needed to think about her, and I was fucking hard.

Her laugh echoed through my head as my sore arm exerted itself by pumping my cock. I shouldn't be thinking of her this way. I was only torturing myself, allowing myself to picture her in my mind constantly, but her beautiful face granted me little reprieve in this fucked up life of mine. She made me forget for a single moment in time.

I clung to the moment, riding it until I developed a new one. It was the one thing that made me not let Vinny push me over the edge, to finally take my life.

A groan escaped me as my stomach coiled, my balls tightened, my breathing hitched, and I came. With a couple more strokes, my orgasm eclipsed me, relieving me of the pressure that built up in my core. A short amount of relief fell over me but was quickly washed away when the slightly euphoric state I experienced ended.

In disgust, I placed my head on the tile of my shower and thought about my life.

Could I really go back to the Haze Room?

It wasn't like I had a choice. If I didn't show up to work on time, Jett would be at my door faster than I could shove a bottle of whiskey to my mouth.

Even though my mind was elsewhere, I knew there was only one place I could go, and it was the last place I ever wanted to be.

It was time to go back to the Haze Room.

***

The community center was already crawling with people signing up for a free membership and going on tours with the girls, who were dressed in khaki shorts and polos. It was almost comical to see the Jett Girls walking around in such normal clothes rather than their presentation outfits that consisted of bras, thongs, and smaller-than-scarves costumes.

Goldie sat at the front desk, greeting me with a smile, but instead of engaging in conversation, I just nodded and headed to my room. She really was the perfect person to greet people, a fucking ray of sunshine. Even though I hated to admit it, her smile had eased the tension in my shoulders.

She got up and followed me. "Hey," she called, grabbing onto my shoulder to gather my attention.

"Ahh, fuck," I mumbled while trying to pull away. Maybe I had spoken too soon about her easing some tension. Her grip on my arm sent shards of pain screaming through my body, thanks to Vinny's thorough work.

"Whoa," Goldie said while backing up a step. "What's wrong?"

"Nothing," I replied, holding on to my cup of coffee a little tighter while the burn in my arm started to settle.

"Don't lie to me," Goldie said with her hands on her hips.

"Mind your own business," I shot back, not wanting to get into it with her.

"You are my business. You're my employee."

"I'm you're employee? How do you figure that when I'm the manager of this damn place?"

I was actually rather interested in hearing Goldie's explanation.

She bit her lip while she tried to nail down her train of thought. Her eyes lit up the minute she realized what she was going to say. I geared up for what I could only imagine would be an obnoxious response.

"You might be the manager, Kace, but Jett is the boss of

this facility, and do you know who owns Jett? I do," she said, pointing at herself. "That man can't function without me turning his head in the right direction. Therefore, I control Jett, and that means I control you—"

"You control me, little one?" Jett asked, walking up behind her undetected.

"Gahh." She gripped her chest, startled. Whipping around, she pushed Jett and said, "Don't sneak up on me like that."

"I have to if I'm going to keep you in check." Jett smiled at her while he pulled her in by the waist.

They were so fucking nauseating.

"Keep me in check? As if I'm a loose cannon?"

Jett just raised an eyebrow, letting Goldie know he meant what he'd said. Surprisingly, she didn't oppose but instead agreed and pulled him into her embrace.

She turned to me and said, "Still, I want to know what's wrong even though you might not be my employee," Goldie succumbed.

"You're damn right I'm not your employee."

I'd started to walk away when Jett called my name. I stopped and waited for him to say something to me. "See Vinny last night?"

"Who's Vinny?" Goldie chirped.

"Don't worry about it, both of you," I responded and then took off to the Haze Room.

The lights were off, and the room was silent, almost eerie looking after the day we'd had yesterday. Outside of the room, kids bustled around me, their mothers chasing after them, throwing out warnings that were sure to be forgotten.

The smell of leather and wood hit me first. My senses were knocked to the ground, memories clouding my mind, vivid images of my boxing days flashing in an instant. That smell would always break me. It would always send a pang of regret, of what could have happened if I hadn't put all my trust in another human.

"Why did you see Vinny?" Jett asked, shutting the door behind him. I turned around to see that he was sans his little minion and let out a long breath as I walked toward the bleachers, feeling every little ache and pain.

"Needed to get lost. Seeing Madeline yesterday was too much."

"Did you make an agreement to stay away from your face?"

"Couldn't entirely scare the new members of Justice, now could I?" I joked, but Jett didn't find it the least bit funny.

"You still look like shit."

"Tell me how you really feel," I responded, sitting and sucking in wind when my side tightened around my ribs.

Jett sat next to me, resting his arms on his legs with his head bent as he spoke. "When are you going to stop beating yourself up?"

"Christ, Jett. Give it the fuck up. Just let me do my own thing. I promised I would be different around you guys, but what I do on my own time should stay my business."

"You're killing yourself," Jett's voice caught in his throat as his hands ran through his hair. "I can't fucking lose you."

Silence filled the room as Jett's confession sunk in. He was the reason I was still on this earth, the reason I kept moving forward, but how much longer could I really go on? I felt my days were numbered.

"You need to let me go," I admitted. "Life has become too much. My time is just around the corner. My fucking grave is calling out to me." I dipped my head as my throat choked up and my eyes burned with tears.

"I can't," Jett whispered. "It's selfish of me, but I can't let you go, Kace."

"Don't you see I'm a shell of the man I used to be? Fuck, look at me, Jett." He did as I said as a lonesome tear fell down my cheek. "Why would you want a sorry excuse for a man like myself to hang around? You're hanging on to the past, to who I used to be."

"You're hanging on to the past." Jett got up and stood in front of me. "If taking your life is what you want to do instead of fighting back, then do whatever the fuck you want. I understand what happened was a mistake, I know that your boxing career was stolen from you, and I know you've been seeking justice, but at some point you have to let it all fucking go. There is a beautiful girl waiting for you, wishing to be a part of your life. There are friends who want to see you happy. You've done your time. Live your life."

I was about to respond when the door flew open and Madeline strode in with a towel over her shoulder and a water bottle in her hand.

"Hi, Mr. Kace," she shouted, waving at me, not picking up on the awkward silence between Jett and myself. Quickly, I wiped my face and cleared any remnants of sadness.

"I got to go," Jett said over his shoulder as Madeline stepped up in front of me.

"I'm ready for a workout, Mr. Kace," she said while taking her water bottle and squirting it on her face and then wiping the water with the towel. She was outrageous.

"I can see that," I replied, wiping my cheek one last time.

"You're sad," she stated, placing her hand on my knee, looking past my fake veneer.

I looked at Jett and he shrugged and took off, leaving me alone with Madeline.

"Where's your mom?" I asked, ignoring her question.

"She dropped me off. She wasn't having a good morning. She was sad like you." Madeline draped the towel over her head and started swaying back and forth. The girl had too much energy. "She was sad last night too. I heard her crying."

I shouldn't have asked. I needed to distance myself, but morbid curiosity won out. "Why was your mom sad?"

Madeline started doing the boxer shuffle I'd taught her yesterday while holding her tiny fists up next to her face. "I don't know. When I asked her, she said something about the past and how she was thinking about it."

Bingo.

Fuck!

Of course Linda was upset. How could she not be? She was putting her daughter into boxing and self-defense classes so the past didn't repeat itself, so she didn't lose another person she loved to violence.

"Are we going to box?" Madeline asked, shaking me to my core.

"Yeah, uh, let's wait for the rest of the group."

"All right. Can I do some cartwheels?"

"Get at it, kid," I responded while I headed over to the stereo to turn on some music. It was going to be a long day, especially with Madeline at my side.

CHAPTER TWENTY SIX

My past...

The melodrama between Jett and Goldie was really starting to get on my nerves. Jett was so fucking in love, but he had no clue how to handle his feelings. Instead of talking to Goldie like a normal boyfriend would, he tried to protect her from harm, but all that had led to was miscommunication and a frustrated Goldie.

The feud between Jett and his father had gotten out of hand to the point that I was afraid it was going to destroy my best friend and everything he'd ever worked for. That was why I found myself standing outside of Goldie's room, about to break her door down with my knocking. I would do anything for Jett, and if that meant inserting myself in the middle of his relationship, then I would.

Without her permission, I blew through her door. The shocked look on Goldie's face was priceless.

"What the hell?" she shouted.

"Are you seriously just waking up?" I asked, taking in her position on the bed.

"Are you seriously barging into my room again? For the

love of God, get a hobby."

Sassy fucking woman. "It's noon and you're not answering your phone," I stated, pointing out why Jett had panicked and made me check on Goldie.

She was living in the Lafayette Club with Jett, diving head-first into their relationship until Leo, Rex's father, threatened the safety of Goldie, making sure to point out he knew Goldie was Jett's crutch. Jett had made it his mission to make it look like he'd cut all ties with her. That was why she was staying with Diego and helping him out with some of the paintings in his club. It was a temporary solution, but it was putting a strain on their relationship.

"It's noon?" she asked. "God, that phone sex must have really taken it out of me."

Even though Goldie was my best friend's girl, I still couldn't help the way she made me feel, like the dark life I was living had some ray of hope. She wanted to be friends, but I wanted to stay as far away as possible because hearing about her having phone sex with my best friend only tightened my heart and irritated me.

She scanned my body and saw the bandage wrapped around my arm. Thanks to Jett's dad and his take-no-prisoners attitude, I was nursing a gun wound.

She stumbled out of bed, so off balance she flew forward, but I caught her before she face-planted into my sternum. Wincing from the pain, I steadied her.

"God, I'm sorry." She straightened up. "Are you okay?" she asked while eyeing my bandage.

"Just a scratch," I replied, not wanting to draw attention to me. "How come you're not answering your phone?"

"Uh, just a scratch? A fucking bullet went through your skin."

"Why aren't you answering your phone?" I ignored her, knowing I was pushing her buttons.

Frustrated, she threw her hands up in surrender and grabbed her cell.

She looked at it and pointed the screen at me. "It's dead. I guess I didn't plug it in last night." She plugged it in quickly and then turned back toward me. "Why? Do you have a secret you have to tell me? Did you finally lose your virginity last night, and you want to talk about it?"

"Cute," I said while blowing out a long breath. "Jett was just trying to—"

Before I could finish my sentence, a whirlwind of black hair and caramel skin stormed into the room, running directly into my back.

"Goldie, did you see—" The woman stopped in place when she slammed into me. She looked up at me as I turned around to see who had just barged in. Her bright green eyes widened at the sight of me. "Oh my God, who's the Adonis?"

The woman standing in front of me was every man's wet dream. Her body was toned from her long legs to her shapely ass to her mouthwatering breasts, which were on display in the form-fitting top she was wearing. Even though she was gorgeous, probably the most fucking gorgeous woman I'd ever seen, it wasn't her exterior that was making my heart pound a mile a minute. It was the way she looked deep into my eyes. It was stupid to think something so deep about someone I had just glanced at, but in that moment, I knew the woman in front of me saw right into my soul. She looked past all my indiscretions and saw me for who I was. The realization hit me like a pile of bricks and a small smile twitched at the corner of my lips. I couldn't help but smile. This whirlwind took my fucking breath away.

I knew she was feeling the same way about me by the way she looked into my eyes, the way she licked her lips and perused my body. I didn't believe in love at first sight—I thought it was a notion for daydreamers and romantics—but I was at least believing in lust at first sight because I knew I wanted this woman. I needed her. She had a cure for the pain coursing through me. I could feel the pull. She was going to be dangerous to my well-being.

The heat in the room turned up dramatically as we looked at each other, not saying anything.

Goldie cleared my throat and said, "Uh, hello. You can eye-fuck each other later. Why are you both here?"

Ignoring Goldie, I introduced myself. "Kace," I said while holding out my hand to her.

"Lyla," she said back, placing her small hand in mine.

I held on to her hand as our connection grew deeper. Too bad the attention-grabbing Goldie was standing a few feet away.

"Oh, so you just give her your name as if it's nothing, but I had to agree to be a part of your little gentleman's club world before you introduced yourself to me?" It was true, she been allowed to know me until after she'd agreed upon coming onboard. It was just a form of torture that I took pleasure in, especially with a mouthy one like Goldie.

Keeping my eyes on Lyla, I answered, "It's not my club."

Growing more frustrated by the minute, Goldie broke the electric pull between Lyla and me by poking Lyla in the side. "Why the hell are you here?"

Slowly turning away from me, she held out a magazine to Goldie. "Just delivering the news."

Fuck!

I quickly reached for the magazine, but Goldie's little

paws were quicker than mine, and she snatched the magazine from Lyla before I could.

"Give me that," I said sternly.

"What are you going to do about it?" she asked as she jumped up on her bed, distancing herself from me.

Not wanting to play her games, I walked over to her, grabbed both her legs, and pulled them out from under her, making her fall ass first onto the mattress. I grabbed the magazine from her, rolled it up, and stuffed it in the back of my jeans.

"Hey, that's mine!" she said while trying to regain her balance.

"Call Jett," I said to Goldie, and then I eyed Lyla up and down and said, "Let her call Jett."

"Give me your number, and I'll keep my mouth shut." Her gaze spoke future promises if I did.

"Say nothing, and I'll think about giving it to you," I teased, wondering who the fuck the man was who was living in my skin right now.

"Good enough for me," Lyla responded as she followed me out of Goldie's room.

"Traitor!" Goldie shouted as I shut her door.

Lyla walked in front of me as we descended the stairs. The minute we exited the back door, the thick Louisiana air hit me hard. Lyla stopped at the edge of the sidewalk, her hands in her back pockets, and spun around to face me. Her breasts were propped up from the position of her hands, making it impossible to look away.

"Do you have any plans?" Lyla asked, looking confident and sexy.

"No," I responded, running my hand through my hair.

"Treat me to lunch?"

"That's awfully presumptuous of you to think I would buy you lunch."

She gave me the once-over, a smirk crossing her lips. "By the way you eye-fucked me upstairs, pretty sure you'll be buying me lunch. Let's go, beefcake. I'm hungry."

Without me agreeing to her terms, she grabbed my hand and started walking me toward Jackson Square. I should have known Lyla would be trouble. She was friends with Goldie, and right now, it was looking like Lyla was more of a sassy counterpart than Goldie.

If that was the case, I was in for a world of trouble.

***

I sat back in my chair at the café and studied Lyla as she placed some sugar in her tea. She stirred the straw in her cup and her eyes shone bright. She leaned forward, her legs crossed under the table, her toe dancing intimately with my knee, letting me know she was close enough that if I wanted to make a scene, I could grab her from across the table and pull her onto my lap.

"Tell me, Kace, what's your story."

"Not much of a story to tell," I responded vaguely. I didn't know this woman. Therefore I wasn't about to tell her about my life, especially given my horrid past.

"Enlighten me," she smiled.

"Tell me about your life first," I countered.

Her smile turned into a knowing smirk. "All right. No questions about the past."

From her brush-off, I could tell she was hiding something as well, but I wasn't about to pressure her to tell me because I'd just gotten a free pass. I wasn't about to have it taken away.

"Fine with me," I responded as we came to a standoff.

Our waitress brought over our food, replenished our drinks, and then took off. Lyla got a shrimp po'boy, same as me. I was impressed with her candidness about eating in front of a guy, ordering a sandwich just as big as mine. Most women I ate with were dainty with their meals, but not Lyla. I surveyed her as she picked up the loaded sandwich and took a giant bite out of it. You would think I'd have gotten sick of the food in New Orleans, but that wasn't the case. I couldn't get enough of the traditional cuisine. When I was in a good mood to appreciate things, I knew when I was fortunate enough to experience some good cooking.

"All right, so no past questions. Then tell me, what do you like to do on a typical Saturday?"

I took another bite of my sandwich and then wiped my mouth with a paper napkin that shredded under my sauce-coated fingers. "Well, when I'm not trying to wrangle up your friend at the club, or preparing for a presentation in the Toulouse Room, I like to spend time in the gym." It was an honest answer. Wasting away my life in my room didn't seem like something she would have liked to hear, and for some reason, I felt like trying to impress this woman.

"Workout? Seriously? You don't have to tell me you work out. I can tell."

"Ah, so you've been checking me out." I smirked at her.

"It's hard not to when I have fear that one of your muscles will poke me in the eye while we're eating."

"You would only be so lucky if my muscle poked you in the eye."

Lyla eyed me and said, "Are you referring to your penis?"

I almost choked on my sandwich from her brazenness and grabbed my water to help the spurt of coughing that attacked me. I should have expected her to say something so crass. She did hang out with Goldie.

"You always this forward?"

"Yeah. Do you have a problem with it?" she asked as she took a giant bite of her sandwich.

"Nope, just want to know what to expect."

She shook her head at me and leaned over to pat my arm. "Sorry to say, Kace, but you're never going to be fully prepared when hanging out with me. I'm a loose cannon."

"Fair enough," I said, leaning back in my chair.

She continued to eat her sandwich in silence, devouring it quicker than me. She licked her fingers, showing me exactly what she could do with those gorgeous lips. I wondered what it would feel like to own those lips, to have them on my body, to feel them against mine.

I adjusted in my seat as my thoughts turned dirty.

"You have that glazed-over look. What are you thinking about?" she asked, tossing her napkin on her plate.

"What your lips would feel like on my body," I answered honestly.

Her eyebrow rose. "And you think I'm forward?"

"Just evening the playing field, babe."

"Fair enough. Tell me, do you believe in ghosts?"

I could tell her question wasn't complicated, but for me, it was a loaded answer. I did believe in ghosts because right now, I felt like a walking ghost in the streets of New Orleans. "I do," I s

"I think there is this whole other world we don't know about, that we won't know about until we breathe our last breath. A place where we can make up for what we've done in life, a place where everyone gets along and where your biggest concern is who are we going to spook that night."

"Who would you spook?" I asked, wondering who she would want to freak out in the mortal world.

"Isn't it obvious? I would haunt the fuck out of Goldie. She is an easy target. It would be too much fun to freak her out."

I laughed, a foreign noise to me, but the image of Goldie freaking out from Lyla's ghost was too comical. Goldie would be an easy target, hands down.

"Damn, I might have to join you on that one."

"All right, shark diving, skydiving, or bungee jumping?"

A lightness ran through me as I realized I was enjoying my lunch with Lyla more than I'd expected. Yes, I was attracted to her, like I was desperate to be inside of her. I thought she was so beautiful, but as I sat here in the café with zydeco music playing in the background, staring at her exotic face, I felt euphoric from her company. I allowed myself to engage in the feeling. It was rare for me, but I allowed it this day.

"Not much of a swimmer. I've been parachuting, which was fun, but bungee jumping is more of a thrill."

"Sign me up for swimming with the sharks. Those beasts are just some toothy assholes who act like they own the water. I would show them a thing or two."

I believed her. "You've heard of shark attacks, right?"

"Eh, not scared. A little punch to the schnoz, and those fuckers would be gone in two seconds."

"Where the hell are you getting your information?" I asked. "You know you have to avoid their mouths to get to their nose."

"You would be surprised by my accuracy," she responded nonchalantly. "Sweet tooth or savory?"

"Do vegetables count?" I asked.

"Oh Christ, don't tell me you're one of those neurotic eaters. Is that why you're nursing that sandwich? Just eat it. Your figure will be fine."

"I'm fucking with you," I laughed. "What do you think I am, sweet or savory?"

Lyla studied me for a second before answering. "I would say savory. You look like a hard liquor kind of guy who enjoys a beer every once in a while, but I think you would grab a chip before a cookie. Although, I would have really hoped for you to be a sweet person."

"Why's that?" I asked.

"Because I have a sweet pussy."

I shook my head at her. "How would you know?"

"I've been told. Plus, I've heard that whatever you crave is the opposite of what you are. So, I wish you liked sweet because I like salty." She winked at me, and I about sprung out of my fucking jeans.

Clearing my throat, I played with my water glass while looking at her from under my lashes. "I think your theory might be wrong."

"Only one way to find out," she said while licking her lips. "But we have time to do that. I want to know, what is your favorite Disney movie?"

The fact that she was able to change the subject so quickly from sex to Disney was slightly disturbing, but I went with it. "*Beauty and the Beast*," I said, not skipping a beat.

Lyla genuinely looked shocked. "Seriously? Wow, I never would have guessed that."

"Why?" I asked.

"Well, I would have expected a burly man like you to have picked something like *The Lion King* or *Aladdin*, but *Beauty and the Beast* really surprises me."

"It's a classic love story of looking past the outer beauty and into the person's soul."

She sat there silent for a second and then crossed her legs, a position I would never dare attempt.

She tilted her head to the side. "Well, fuck, I'm crushing pretty hard on you right now, Kace."

The feeling was fucking mutual. Ignoring her confession, I asked, "What's your favorite Disney movie?"

"*The Emperor's New Groove*," she answered without skipping a beat.

"What's that?" I asked, not familiar with the movie.

"Are you kidding me?" she shouted while placing her hands on the table. "You can't be serious."

"Never heard of it."

Lyla shook her head at me in disappointment and raised her hand. "Check please!" She stood up, grabbed me, and said, "We're going to remedy that."

The waitress brought us our check. I laid some cash on the table and allowed Lyla to pull me to my feet. She escorted me out of the café toward Bourbon Street.

"Where are we going?" I asked, letting this feisty woman drag me around.

"My place. You have a movie to watch."

She linked her arm through mine and leaned into me as we walked to her apartment. Her hair swayed with her steps, brushing against me, sending the subtle scent of vanilla my way. I was starting to become addicted to everything about this woman, from her brash attitude, to her exquisite body, to her sweetness. It scared the fuck out of me.

***

"You are such a Kronk!" Lyla protested, referring to the dumb but muscular character in *The Emperor's New Groove*. The movie credits were scrolling across the screen as we sat on Lyla's couch, talking about the movie. It had been funny.

"I am not Kronk," I countered.

"You're so Kronk. How can you deny that?"

"If I'm Kronk, then you're Yzma," I replied, referring to the villain in the movie who was a crotchety old hag looking to take over the empire. I had to admit she'd been the most entertaining villain I'd ever watched.

"Oh, fuck you." Lyla laughed, throwing her head back. "I am not Yzma."

"If I'm Kronk, then you're most definitely Yzma."

"Fine, you can be the quiet hero, Pacho."

A quiet hero was most definitely not me. Maybe I was actually the male version of Yzma, with evil running through my blood.

"Hey," Lyla said. "Where did you go?"

"Nowhere," I lied.

Lyla eyed me suspiciously. "So, be honest. What did you think?"

"*Beauty and the Beast* is better." I smiled.

"Horse shit!" Lyla said while slapping the couch. "That is complete horseshit. *The Emperor's New Groove* is by far superior."

"Clearly you lack good taste in movies," I joked.

"Wow, way to nail a girl where it hurts," she teased.

"Believe me, you would know if I nailed you."

Lyla put her arm across the back of the couch, scooting even closer to me. "Is that right?"

Her voice was seductive, practically whispering in my ear, enticing me to lean in to her.

"It is," I responded, not really sure why I wasn't pulling away.

She stroked my forearm. I looked down at her fingers running across my tan arms, wondering where she planned on taking it, praying she would move her fingers across my entire body.

"There is something about you, Kace, something different, something dark that kind of scares me but also intrigues me. You're not like any other man I've come across."

"That's because most of the men you come across are foaming at the mouth, just waiting for you to strip naked," I replied, referring to her job at Kitten's Castle, Goldie's old workplace.

"That's not it. You're honest, you speak your mind, and you know how far you can go, how far you want to go."

"You act like you know me," I stated, needing to feed off her energy.

"I don't." She shook her head. "But I want to get to know you. You fascinate me."

The comfort she was giving me was overwhelming. I wanted to confide in her. I wanted to fucking rip my heart out, lay it on a platter, and let her watch it bleed. I wanted her to know all my sins, but the thought of her not understanding me, not getting my situation, was too overpowering. This afternoon had been one of the best I'd had in a really long time, and if I ever let her in, if I ever let her see my bleeding heart and she didn't accept me, she would wreck me. There would be no recovering from that.

So instead of sticking around, I said, "I should probably get going."

The hurt look on her face let me know I'd insulted her after her confession. Guilt washed through me but it was better this way, better to cut her loose before anything serious happened between us, before she could reject me.

"Thanks for the movie," I said awkwardly as I got up.

As I moved toward the door, I heard Lyla's feet pad across the uneven hardwood floors. Her heat pulled at me, practically tore me in the other direction, but I denied myself the pleasure of turning around. I couldn't. I couldn't see her hurt eyes again.

"Wait," Lyla said, grabbing my hand. She pulled me around and shoved me up against the door. She stood on her toes and leaned into me, still holding my hand around her hips. "I don't get you, Kace. I don't understand what has happened to you in the past that has made you so quiet, so reserved, but I like you. I want to see where this goes, and I know you feel the same way. I can see it in your eyes."

Closing my eyes tightly, I placed my head against the door and tried to gain the courage to say goodbye, to put distance between us, but I found nothing. I was gutless.

"You don't have to say anything," Lyla coaxed. "Just know that when you're ready, I'm here." She caressed my jaw and pulled my chin down, where her lips pressed against mine.

My entire fucking body melted into her and I held tightly onto her hips, pulling her closer so I could feel every curve of her body. Her soft lips glided across mine until I opened my mouth and licked across the seam of her lips, begging for admittance.

She obliged with a moan and opened her mouth. I rolled her so she was against the door instead of me. With my hips pressed against hers, I pinned her against the door and ran my hands up her ribcage, dancing terribly close with her breasts. Her hands found the belt loops of my jeans and pulled me in closer.

A low moan escaped her throat, clouding my thoughts, encouraging me to take things further, to truly explore her body, but a small voice in the back of my head prevented me.

I knew I needed to step away. Guilt for what I'd done in the past stopped me. I didn't deserve her sweetness, her kindness, her sexiness.

Frustrated with the shell of the life I had left, I pulled away and pressed my hands against the door, framing her face. Her lips were swollen, and her eyes were glazed from the heat blazing between us. She looked so fuckable, it took everything in me not to take her up against the door.

"I have to go," I said softly, lowering my head so she couldn't see the want in my eyes.

"I don't want you to go."

"Don't make this harder, Lyla."

"How am I making this harder when you're the one walking out?"

"You don't know me, Lyla. There is a whole lot of fucked up attached to me, and I won't let you to associate yourself to that." I took a deep breath and met her eyes. "Thank you for one of the best afternoons I've had in a really long time."

Gripping her chin, I placed a soft kiss on her lips and then gently moved her to the side to let myself out of her apartment. Each step I took that put distance between Lyla and myself pained me, but I knew I was doing the right thing.

Lyla was the type of woman who stuck around, who could ruin a man with just one look, and if I let her in, if I let her past my walls, I knew she would fucking destroy me. Even though I was living a life of regret and pain, I wasn't ready to endure the crushing blow she would deliver to me if she ever left. That was one kind of pain I knew I wouldn't be able to recover from.

CHAPTER TWENTY SEVEN

My present...

The community center was silent. The lights were shut off besides one that shined down on the bleachers of the Haze Room and one boxing bag. All the girls had left, and I was the last one left to lock up.

The day had dragged, the thrill of teaching the sport of boxing to others stolen from me the minute Madeline had joined the practice.

No, that was fucking wrong to say. I shouldn't blame that innocent girl for taking anything from me. She'd done nothing wrong. It was my own fucking guilt eating me up.

I'd thought the pain would slowly ease, that walking this earth would be easier after a few years, but seeing Madeline, looking into Linda's eyes, it was just too fucking much.

I rested on the bleachers, my head in my hands and my elbows relaxing on my legs. I was at a loss, probably the lowest point of my life. For once in my life, I truly felt like I was at a crossroads. When I'd thrown my last punch at Marshall, I didn't really have options because Jett had been so desperate to keep me around, but now that he had Goldie. There was really no reason for me to stick around.

I'd made a commitment to Justice, to staying here and helping the center succeed, but what was I really doing to help? I was empty, I was lifeless, I wasn't helping anyone.

It was time for a change.

A soft knock rang through the silent room, startling me for a second. Linda was standing in the doorway, clutching her purse. Taking a deep breath, I stood and said, "Hi Linda. Did Madeline forget something?"

"No," she said while looking around nervously. "Um, do you have a moment to talk?"

"Yes," I said warily. The nervous tension coming off her threw me for a loop.

With her purse held closely to her body, she walked up to me and visibly shook. The hand holding the strap rattled against her shoulder, and she scanned the room as if she was checking for someone to pop out of the corners.

"Are you okay?" I asked, feeling a tingle crawl across the back of my neck. What was in her purse that was so important that she was clutching?

"It was you, wasn't it?"

My stomach bottomed out, my pulse quickened, and I instantly felt ill. "What are you talking about?" I asked, sweating.

"You were the man at the bar, the man who killed my husband."

I could feel my skin turn white, my breathing grew at a rapid rate, my body became a complete void. I was physically unable to answer.

"You don't have to admit to anything. I can see it on your face." Her hand continued to shake as a tear ran down her cheek. "I knew it was you. I didn't know at first. I had no clue who would kill my husband, but I saw someone who resembled you at the funeral, and I had an inkling. Then on Madeline's birthday and at Christmas, I saw you sneaking presents to our doorstep for Madeline. You thought you went undetected, but I knew it was you. The moment I heard about Justice and the classes you were offering, I knew I had to make contact."

Alarm bells were going off in my head. I stepped back and bumped into the bleachers. Linda didn't look well. She looked almost sick, like she couldn't believe she was going to do something out of her element.

"Linda—"

"Don't, please don't speak." She held up her hand. She reached into her purse and I felt like I was going into shock. I'd waited for this moment, for my last breath, but I didn't want my life to end. I didn't want this to be my last minute on this world.

In slow motion, I watched Linda whip something out of her purse, and I flinched as she pointed it at me.

"Take them," she said, pushing what was in her hand in front of me.

My vision blurred as I tried to figure out what she was handing me. I looked down and saw a pile of construction paper. At closer work, I saw crayon marks drawn across them in a child's writing.

"Take them, Kace," Linda repeated herself.

Obliging her request, I grabbed the folded pieces from her and then sat down on the bleachers. She sat next to me, still shaking but letting go of her purse. Relieved she wasn't here to take my life, I started sifting through the papers.

Colors ranging from pink to blue to green were scattered over contrasting paper and each were addressed to "Dear Sir."

They were homemade cards from Madeline.

"What are these?" My vision started to blur from the tears that clouded my eyes.

"They are thank you notes from Madeline. She wrote one for every gift you've ever gotten her. She would give them to me to mail to the man who gave her such precious gifts. It's time that you read them."

I pinched the bridge of my nose, my eyes burning from holding in my emotions. I opened the cards and read what was inside.

Dear Sir, thank you for my mini purple horse figurine. I named him Clyde. I love him.

Dear Sir, I like purse. Thanks.

Dear Sir, baking with mom is fun. Thank u for the apron.

Dear Sir, I like my shirt. It's big now but mom says I will grow.

Dear Sir, magnets are fun, I like to hang things on the fridge, thanks.

Dear Sir, I wish I could thank you in person. I love my necklace. It's so pretty.

There were tons of cards, but the last one I read was what allowed the tears that clouded my vision to finally fall. I set the cards to the side so I wouldn't get them wet, placed my head in my hands, and let my emotions overtake me.

Kindly, Linda rested a hand on my back, rubbing me soothingly like any mother would. I'd never truly cried, never let myself feel so much emotion, but at this point, I couldn't block it out. It hit me all at once.

Shame, anger, and regret sent me into a tailspin of depression. I didn't want these cards. I couldn't justify having them, not after what I'd taken away from Madeline. I could give her everything in the world except the one thing she deserved: a father.

"I'm sorry, Linda. I'm so fucking sorry."

"Why are you sorry?" she asked, still rubbing my back.

I looked at her as if she was losing her mind. I pulled away and ran the backs of my hands over my tear-soaked cheeks.

"Why am I sorry? You just said you know I killed your husband, and here I am, living a perfectly normal life. I should be rotting in fucking jail right now. Why haven't you called the cops?"

"Kace, why would I call the cops on you? You protected us."

Confused, I sat up and asked, "What are you talking about?"

Linda reached into her purse again and pulled out a thin leather album. She handed it to me and nodded for me to open it. Curious, I flipped open the page and was met with ghastly pictures of Linda, beaten and battered to the point where she was almost unrecognizable. Bile rose in my throat as I continued to turn the pages. Flip after flip, there were pictures of Linda with bruises, burns, cuts.

"Why are you showing me this?" I asked.

"He abused us, Kace. He had a temper and would come home and take it out on me. The night he was killed, he struck Madeline for the first time. Those pictures are from that night as well. He left me practically lifeless on the floor and went to the bar. I had nothing, no family, no friends to support me because they couldn't understand why I stayed with Marshall.

They knew what he did to me. But I stayed with him because I thought that maybe, just maybe he would change, but he never did. His punches got harder, his cuts ran deeper, and his verbal abuse got stronger."

My fucking head spun with the realization that Marshall Duncan wasn't the perfect father figure I'd pictured in my mind. The man I'd built up in my head was the complete opposite of who I thought he was.

Linda gripped my hand and forced me to look at her. "Kace, you saved us. You're our protector, our provider. I can't tell you the kind of freedom you have given both of us."

I shook my head and tried to scoot away, but she held on to my hand tightly.

"Why are you telling me this?" I asked, confused.

"Because I see the way you walk around here, lifeless, not really experiencing this beautiful world you have in front of you. I wanted you to stop punishing yourself. You didn't commit a sin, Kace. You relieved us of a lifetime of pain."

"But... you enrolled Madeline into self-defense classes."

"Yes." Linda squeezed my hand. "So she can learn to protect herself from men like her father. I don't want her to end up in a relationship like mine. I want her to know that she can fight back, that she should fight back. I want her to be a strong, confident woman, and I knew you would be the perfect one to teach her."

I continued to shake my head as my hands ran through my hair. Confused and dazed, I stood up.

"No, this is too much. I can't handle this."

"Kace...." Linda called out as I walked away from her. "Please, don't leave. I want to thank you...."

"Don't!" I shouted, practically running out of the Haze Room.

She chased me down. "Take this at least." She handed me the cards from Madeline, as well as an envelope. Reluctantly, I accepted the items and took off.

I ran out of the center, not bothering to lock up. I sent a quick text to Jett to let him know. He would need an explanation later, but right now, I had a mission and it was to get as far away from Justice and Linda as fast as I could.

As a human, there were situations you conjured up in your head, ideas you thought were so set in stone, nothing could ever change your mind about them. But the minute those ideas were changed, it was hard to comprehend, hard to switch gears. You formed a sort of denial. That's where I was right now. I'd spent the last few years of my life punishing myself, living for someone else, providing for someone else, remembering the strong words of my father, that I would never amount to anything. I'd set out on a mission to find repentance for my sins. Finding out I was seen as a hero rather than a fucking murderer was almost impossible to comprehend.

I needed to get away. I needed to forget.

CHAPTER TWENTY-EIGHT

My past...

"You dumb whore, I did not suck him off. You have lost your fucking mind!" Babs shouted as she ran down the hallway past Lyla's bedroom in the Lafayette Club.

"You did too. He told me," Francy called. They must have stopped in front of Lyla's room because their conversation was easy to hear.

"He told you. Well, then, let's believe the little fucker. There is no way I would have sucked him off. He had some creepy yellow shit down there."

I cringed at the thought.

"Oh, that's nasty," Francy replied. "What did it look like?"

"I'm not reliving that," Babs said, moving away from Lyla's door.

Francy's voice trailed off as she said, "Was it chunky?"

"I think I'm going to throw up," Lyla said into my chest, her hair tickling my skin and her soft body pressed against mine.

I had just had sex with Lyla in her bedroom at the Lafayette Club, where anyone could have heard us. What the fuck had I been thinking?

I rubbed her back, my eyes closed, wishing I would have been smarter about my choices, but after the day we'd had together, I couldn't help it. I'd had to be inside her. She was a breath of fresh air, a short intermission in this cold, dark world I'd been living in.

"You shouldn't be shocked. You've been here for a while. You should know the conversations that go on in this house."

"True." She nuzzled me, making all violent thoughts fade from my mind and warming me to my toes.

It was the anniversary of my dad's death. It seemed like yesterday when I talked to him for the last time on the phone, listening to the bitterness in his voice when he'd spoken of my boxing career, of my accomplishments. I could still feel the blow to the gut of my father not believing me, not listening to my side of the story, telling me he wished I wasn't his son.

Lyla had caught me at a weak moment and asked me to hang out. I'd been frantic for some human interaction, and she'd taken advantage of a rare occurrence. I was the one who'd taken our day too far.

She was making me feel, she was breaking down my walls, and I was letting her. We'd spent the day walking around New Orleans, talking about the city we'd grown up in, talking about Goldie and Jett, talking about whatever came to mind. We'd eaten dinner together and ended up sharing a serving of bread pudding. I'd fucking shared a meal. Christ, I was letting my guard down and had no clue on how to go about resurrecting my walls.

With a flash of her brilliant smile, she had me on my knees, begging for more. Lyla had been at the Lafayette club for a reason, to help fill in for Goldie temporarily, but instead of treating her like all the other Jett Girls, I'd fallen for her hard. I liked Goldie, actually loved Goldie, but Lyla was different. Lyla had the sass like Goldie, the quirkiness like Goldie, but she was also raw, exposed. She showed you who she was and didn't bullshit. She was concerned, she got me, she cared for me. She saw right through me, to the true person I was. She wrecked me with those eyes and debilitated me with her kisses.

Now, she was lying by my side, her arms wrapped around my waist, occasionally brushing kisses against my chest and filling an empty void in my life.

I'd promised myself I wouldn't let it get to this point. Not after the first time we met, not after that afternoon at her apartment, but when Jett had needed someone to fill in, I'd chosen Lyla. I'd asked her to help out, knowing the kind of confusion it would bring me. I'd asked her because deep down, I needed her to be here, to help me, even though I wouldn't accept her help.

"How long have you been living here?" Lyla asked casually, running her fingers along my abs.

"Too long," I answered honestly.

"You say that as if you resent the place."

"I don't," I answered. In fact it had been a sanctuary for my sins. I would forever be grateful for the Lafayette Club.

"Don't elaborate or anything," she teased.

"Probably won't."

I was drawing away from her. I had to. She was making me want things I wasn't allowed to have. She was making me rethink everything I'd set in stone after I killed Marshall Duncan. She was trying to offer me a life and I didn't fucking want it.

I'd started to move when she pinned me down with her arms. She sat up and hovered over me. I averted my eyes from her swaying breasts and tried to focus on the ceiling. If I looked down, I would give in. I knew I would. I was desperate for another taste.

"Where are you going?" she asked.

"I have things to do," I replied, knowing I sounded like an ass.

"You're not going to stay the night?"

"Can't," I responded, pushing her aside and sitting on the edge of her bed with my head in my hands. A pulsing started to develop behind my eye, letting me know a raging headache was lurking around the corner.

"So you're going to fuck me and leave?" she asked, angry.

"Pretty sure you fucked me," I said, knowing there was a double meaning behind my statement.

"You can't be serious. Not after the day we had. Not after the connection we shared."

"What connection?" I lied. "We shared a dessert and then fucked."

I was being cruel. I hated saying such vulgar things to her, but I was in self-defense mode. My heart was bleeding, yearning for the woman behind me, begging for her to take my heart into her possession and save it from self-destruction. It was a feeling I wasn't comfortable with. I hated being vulnerable, and I'd never felt more exposed in my life.

"Fuck you," she said while getting off the bed.

My briefs were at the foot of the bed, so I grabbed them, threw them on, and turned around to see Lyla charging at me with a robe half-tied around her and fury in her eyes. I braced for impact.

She poked me in the chest. "If you want to act like nothing happened between us, fine. Believe what you want to believe but I felt it, Kace. I see the way you look at me, the heat in your eyes. I know there is something you want to tell me, but you refuse. Why? What are you hiding?"

"It's none of your business," I said while walking past her to find my other clothes.

"Taking the pussy way out? Fits you well," she taunted.

"Excuse me?" I shot back, grabbing my jeans and putting them on.

"You heard me," she said with her hands on her hips, in a feisty position. "You're a pussy. Fact, it takes more of a man to admit his feelings than to hide them."

"It's not feelings, Lyla." She was right. I wasn't the man she wanted me to be.

"Then what is it, Kace?"

Taking a deep breath, I said, "I'm not who you think I am. I'm a monster, a demonic man who ruins the lives of others. I'm not sentimental, and I'm not caring. I don't want to talk about my life and I don't care to hear about anyone else's. I'm in this world to do one thing and one thing alone—live with this all-consuming, burdensome guilt until I take my last breath. There is nothing you can say to me that will change this, so stop trying. Like my father told me, I'm not a true man."

Lyla was speechless, her eyes searching mine, looking for answers I didn't want to give. I grabbed the rest of my clothes.

I was just putting my shoes on when she crouched in front of me so we were eye level. She balanced on her knees as she spoke.

"Why do you want to bear the weight of the world on your shoulders all by yourself, Kace? Why don't you want to share some of it? Let me help you."

"I don't need your help." I stood up, nearly knocking her over. Running my hand over my face, I helped her to her feet. "Lyla, this is non-negotiable for me, okay? I'm not looking for a partner. I'm not looking for someone to share my burden. I did this to myself, and I'm paying for it, no one else."

"Why won't you tell me?" she asked, tears welling in her eyes.

"Because...." I trailed off. "It's my dad's death anniversary." The words popped out of my mouth faster than I could take them back.

Her eyes widened from my confession. "I'm sorry, Kace. I'm sure today must be hard on you."

I shrugged. "He was a difficult bastard to please. Never did anything right in his eyes. It's best I forget."

"Clearly you can't if you're acting like this, like a true asshole at his finest."

"Better you see it now."

"Tell me about him," Lyla prodded. "I want to know about your father."

"Not going to happen," I replied, not ready to rip that wound open. I was also afraid to see what Lyla might truly think of me after she heard of my dad's opinions on my life.

Truthfully, I didn't want to lose that spark in her eyes she got whenever I walked into the room. I didn't want to see that vanish once she found out I was a murderer, a loser, someone who couldn't amount to anything. Call me a selfish bastard, but that little spark she gave me every day helped ease the pressure on my lungs that restricted my breathing.

"Fine," she said, moving away. "That's fine. Take your guilt with you and get the hell out of my room, but just so you know, I'm the best thing that will ever happen to you, Kace. The pull between us that you try to ignore, that's real. There is something between us, a deep connection that you keep pushing away, and one day you're going to wake up, alone and wishing you had let me inside your little world. You think what you did in your past is your biggest regret. Wrong, fucker. Walking out that door, out of my life, will be the biggest regret you ever have. Have fun living with that one."

I stormed out of her room, more angry at myself than anything. Jett and Goldie were approaching. Goldie was in Jett's arms and they were headed to her room. Not surprised. The love birds were practically naked with Goldie in a robe and Jett in his briefs.

"Get out of my way," I stated gruffly, not wanting to interact with their jovial faces. They both had that annoying "we're in love" sex glow about them that was too nauseating to look at.

Jett easily obliged for some reason, probably because he wanted to get Goldie back in bed, the horny bastard, but she was a different story. She was always butting her nose in my business, especially when I was in the worst of moods, and today was no exception.

"Wait," she said, struggling to get out of Jett's grasp. "What's going on?"

Goldie rotated her body in Jett's arms so Jett was now forced to hold her by her stomach rather than her back. She took the moment to prop her chin in her hands and kick her legs up behind her.

"Trouble in paradise?" she teased, knowing fully well Lyla was giving me a run for my money.

"Drop it," I said sharply, not giving her an inch.

"Oh, come on, Kace. Sharing is caring."

I looked at Jett. "Take care of your woman and get her off my back."

There was a slight tick in Jett's jaw, but I knew he would oblige. He could read me well, and I was giving off the "don't fuck with me" vibe, something Goldie didn't seem to understand.

"Hey!" she shouted, completely offended, as I walked

away. "I don't need taking care of. I can handle my own! Come back here. I dare ya!"

From a distance, I could hear Jett Coax her as he said, "Easy, killer."

Vibrating with irritation, I went to my room and slammed my door, looking around for something to punch. The urge to demolish every inanimate object in my sight was overwhelming.

I fucking hated my life. The pain was too much, the guilt was far too heavy, and the unhappiness I experienced on a day-to-day basis overpowering. Something had to give, and I was afraid to find out what it was going to be.

CHAPTER TWENTY-NINE

My present...

I pounded the door, begging for entry. I didn't know where else to go. I needed an escape and I'd ended up here.

A series of locks unclicked and the door swung open, revealing a disheveled-looking Lyla. Her hair was askew. She was wearing a robe, and she looked flustered.

"Kace," she answered while straightening her hair. "What are you doing here?"

Her appearance was suspicious. It was almost like she had someone in the apartment with her. The sickening feeling running through me turned into pure rage as I charged inside. I had no right to be upset. We weren't together. She could do whatever the hell she wanted, but that didn't matter. In my mind, she was mine, no one else's.

"What the hell do you think you're doing?" she asked as I stormed straight into her bedroom. I kicked her door in and was shocked to see no one in the room.

"Where is he?" I turned on her. She was standing right behind me with her hands on her hips.

288

"Who?" she asked, starting to get defensive.

"The man you were just fucking."

"Have you lost your fucking mind?" she practically shouted. "Do you see a man here?"

I looked around again and noticed the hot pink vibrator in the middle of her bed. "Were you taking care of yourself?" I asked her.

"You're offensive!" She stuck her chin up and walked away. I followed close behind. She opened the door and said, "Leave."

I stood in place, not wanting to go. It wasn't the best entrance I'd ever made, but I didn't care. I needed her. The rage left me and in its place was hurt and confusion.

"Lyla," I said softly with my hands in my pockets.

She shut the door and came up to me. She placed her hands on my chest and made me meet her eyes. "Kace, what's wrong?"

I crashed into her, tears flowing as I fell apart in her arms. She clutched my back and pulled me closer. Vaguely, I recognized her moving us to the couch where we sat down and I pulled her onto my lap. She straddled my legs and lifted my chin so she could wipe the tears.

"You're scaring me. What's going on?" she asked. Her robe opened at her chest so I could see the swell of her breast.

At that moment, I needed to lose myself in her. She needed her to help me forget.

Without a word, I kissed her. The combination of my tears with her lips made for a salty chemistry. It was intoxicating.

"Wait." She pulled away, a hand on my chest. "You have to tell me what's going on."

"Lyla, I'm spiraling out of control. I need to get lost in you so fucking bad it hurts. Help me forget, please," I begged.

"Forget what?" she asked, searching my eyes.

"Forget my sins," I replied.

I allowed her to wipe away a stray tear, and when I thought she was going to make me talk some more, she opened her robe and displayed her gorgeously naked body.

"I'm yours," she whispered.

Grateful, I stood up, grabbed her hand, and walked her to the bedroom. I moved her previous entertainment from the bed and laid her gently on the mattress. I went to remove my clothing, but she stopped me.

"Let me," she offered. Unable to take control like I normally did, I succumbed to her request.

She sat on the bed and moved her hands to the hem of my shirt. Instead of taking my shirt off, she lifted it and partially exposed my stomach. My abs rippled when she touched me.

She placed little kisses across my taut stomach. Her tongue traveled each ridge, from the V of my hips to the top of my six pack. She was loving me. With each kiss, I could feel the healing power she was bestowing.

Standing, she removed my shirt and flung it aside. Her hands instantly found my pecs, and she scraped her fingernails down them. The scratching of her fingers across my skin was welcome; I loved the pain and she knew it.

Once her fingers found my stomach, her lips traced kisses over the scratches, trying to heal the open wounds. I wanted to accept that her kisses were all I needed to move forward, to forget everything I believed in, everything I set out for these past years, but I knew that wasn't the case.

I stood rigid as Lyla still tried to infuse understanding through her kisses. Her hands wandered down to my waist where she unbuttoned my jeans and tugged on them. I helped by stepping out of them and toeing them aside. She gripped my ass tightly, making my cock jolt forward. Then she slipped her hands into my briefs and pulled them away from the back, letting them slowly slip down over my rigid cock.

Once I was naked, she led me to her bed, where she pushed me against the mattress and straddled my legs. Her hands ran up my thighs and then to my stomach, where she inched herself down, her breasts hovering over my erection and her mouth just above my belly button. She lowered her lips and started kissing my body once again.

I melted into the mattress as Lyla took care of me with her beautiful lips. She kissed me from the tops of my shoulders, to my pecs, to my stomach, and then hovered right above my cock. She licked her lips, gripped my dick, and put it in her mouth.

A low groan escaped me from the heat. She was gentle, thorough, and took her time, making sure to run her tongue over each pulsing vein. There was no urgency in her touch, no need to get me to the edge. She was loving me, adoring me, helping me escape the dark hole I'd buried myself in.

My arm fell over my eyes, trying to cover the tears that were threatening to cascade down my chiseled face. My life was so fucked up, and right now, this woman would do anything to make it better. If I hadn't already fucking loved her, I goddamn loved her now.

Fuck, I wasn't supposed to let her in, but right now, with her compassion and understanding, how could I not let her break through my walls? I didn't have a chance.

Her lips slowed and her hands ran up my thighs. She looked up at me and then freed her mouth. She leaned over to the nightstand, opened the drawer, and grabbed a condom. Expertly, she rolled it over my throbbing dick and then positioned herself so she was sitting on my thighs but not allowing the intimate connection I craved.

"I want you to take me how you want, Kace. I want you to

lose yourself."

Feeling a little weak, I pulled her down on the mattress and then got up on my knees. I ran my hand over my mouth in awe of the beauty that lay beneath me. Her eyes gleamed with unshed tears and her lips were swollen from the kissing she kindly bestowed upon me. Her hair was fanned out against her pillow.

I kneeled between her legs and placed my hands on either side of her head. I dipped my head so my lips were just above hers. Softly, I said, "I'm sorry for everything, Lyla."

"Don't apologize, Kace."

I shook my head. "I need to apologize. You've been there for me during times when I didn't deserve it, like now," I choked out and quickly pressed my fingers into my eyes, trying to erase the emotions that kept wanting to pour out. "I want you to know I care about you. More than I've ever cared about anyone, and the reason I haven't given myself over to you, why I haven't cashed in on the intense feelings I have for you, is because there has been something clouding my way of living."

"You don't have to tell me, Kace. Just make love to me."

The yearning in her eyes told me she needed this just as much as I did, so I gave us what we were both looking for, a way to forget.

I lowered my head to hers and took her lips with mine. I licked, nipped, and rolled them between my teeth. I made out with her, fucking old-school made out. Our tongues mingled. Our need was greedy as we both matched each thrust of our mouths.

With my cock ready to fucking blow, I grabbed it with one hand and found Lyla's slick entrance. She parted her legs even farther, and I pushed in. I was welcomed in with a tightness that was almost too fucking pure. She sheathed my cock as if we were made for each other.

"You're so perfect," I said as my control started to slip.

"You're perfect to me, too, Kace."

It didn't matter to her what I'd done, who I'd hurt. What mattered was the connection we couldn't deny. For that, she would forever be fucking mine.

I pumped into her, her hips matching my demanding thrusts. We were one. We were connected in every intimate way possible. This woman, this was what I needed, to feel her love.

Lyla gripped my back tightly as she arched into me. A loud cry escaped her as her breathing picked up and her heat gripped my cock more firmly than I could imagine. In seconds, my toes went numb, my stomach coiled, and my balls tightened. I shook violently into her as I came. Lyla's orgasm matched mine as we rode out our pleasure together, not letting go until we were completely spent.

Continuing to kiss her, I rested my body over hers, making sure not to crush her.

She forced me to look her in the eyes. "You may think you don't deserve me, Kace, but the truth is, I don't deserve you. I don't know what you've done in the past, but what you've done present day at the center, helping the girls, and being a friend to Jett, you're a good person. It's about time you saw it."

Deep down, I knew she was right. I'd been denying the acceptance of her truth for so long, I wasn't sure how much it would take for me to finally believe it, to make it my truth.

"There is so much you don't know," I answered, burying my head in her shoulder.

She cradled me close. "Well, then, tell me. I won't run, Kace. I told you, I'm here to stay."

"Why?" I asked. "Why are you choosing to stay?"

She played with the short strands of my hair. "I had a conversation with Goldie. She told me not to give up, that you needed someone to believe in you, to be there for you other than Jett. You needed someone to save you. I couldn't walk away. I want to be the one who erases the demons that haunt you. I want to be the one who brings you back from the dark and shows you the light of this world. I want to be the one who makes you laugh, makes you smile, makes you appreciate this wonderful gift we call life. I want it all, Kace."

I gripped her tighter, letting my heart swell for the first time since I could remember, and I said, "I want you to be that person, Lyla. I want it so fucking badly."

CHAPTER THIRTY

My present...

I lingered impatiently on the sidewalk, pacing back and forth as I waited for Jett to show up. He hadn't been very happy when he answered his phone after the fourth consecutive time I called, but what I had to do was urgent.

I'd left Lyla while she was sleeping, leaving a note that said there were some things I had to take care of. She wouldn't be happy. She hadn't been happy after I told her I didn't want to talk about my past. I was probably destroying the chance of being with her with every brush-off I gave her, but before I could commit myself, I had to straighten my sanity out first.

If we were meant to be, then it would happen.

The door to Jett's hotel opened, and Jett walked out looking freshly fucked and wearing a pair of jeans and a T-shirt, a casual outfit not too many people saw on such a powerful man.

Jett rubbed his eyes and said, "This better be fucking good."

I gestured to the car that was idling with the air

conditioning blasting since it was already eighty degrees at five in the morning. New Orleans in the summer was almost unbearable at times.

We got in the car and buckled up. I pulled out onto the empty street that was lined with palm trees and started driving toward our destination.

"Where are we going?" Jett asked, sounding groggy.

"Linda came and talked to me."

Jett became more alert. "What did she say?"

"She knows," I stated simply.

"What? How?"

"She saw me at the funeral and then saw me dropping presents off all these years. I guess I'm not as stealthy as I thought I was."

"Holy shit," Jett breathed, wiping his hand over his mouth. "Did you confirm?"

"I didn't have an option."

"Fuck, Kace," Jett said, sounding shaken. "What is she going to do? Is she pressing charges? Does she even have any evidence?"

"She's not going to do anything," I responded, trying to calm down my best friend.

"Why not?"

"Look in the glove compartment." Jett studied me for a second and then opened it. "Pull those cards out."

"What are these?" he asked while looking at them.

"They're all from Madeline. They're thank you cards for all the gifts I've given her over the years. Linda gave them to me."

Jett was silent as he looked through the cards, reading each and every one of them, taking time to note the way her penmanship improved by running his hands over it, the way her sentence structure grew stronger and the use of bigger, more descriptive words.

By the time Jett finished, we'd arrived at our destination. He looked up at me, tears in his eyes.

"I can't believe she's kept these."

"She said she wanted to give them to me at some point. They mean the world to me, to see even though I was suffering, Madeline was incredibly grateful and happy about the little presents I gave her. Linda also gave me this," I said while handing Jett an envelope.

"What is it?"

"Take a look."

Jett opened the envelope and pulled out a letter that provided access to a bank account for all the money I had given Linda and Madeline over the years.

"She didn't use any of it," I said softly.

"I don't understand," Jett said, confused. "Why are we at the cemetery?"

Gathering my will to speak the words that had only been spoken to me a few short hours ago, I took a deep breath and said, "Linda wanted to thank me. She was an abuse victim, Jett. Marshall used to beat the shit out of her; she had pictures to prove it. The love I thought I'd taken away from them was actually hate. That night, the night I killed Marshall, he hit Madeline for the first time." Jett's jaw tightened as his eyes narrowed. "Linda brought Madeline to Justice so she could learn how to defend herself if she was ever in a violent relationship. She doesn't want Madeline to go through what she went through."

I steadied my breathing and ran my hand over my eyes as tears threatened to fall. My throat constricted as I tried to speak. "She told me I saved her and Madeline. I saved them, Jett." Tears fell as I cried into my hands. "I didn't ruin them, I fucking saved them."

The demons I'd been hiding for so long surfaced as I spoke the words out loud to the one man who'd been through it all with me. The guilt and remorse that had been woven into my soul started to release from my body as I continued to speak.

"She thanked me for changing her life, for giving her hope, for taking away an evil man. This whole time I thought I'd destroyed their lives when in fact, I bettered them. They were happy without him, Jett. At the park that day, when they looked so normal, it was because they were happy. They were relieved. I'd protected them from harm and ended a nightmare for Linda. All this time, they were breathing lighter while I was grasping for air."

Jett got out of the car and walked around to my side, opened my door, and pulled me out of my seat. He wrapped his arms around me and embraced me as I cried into his shoulder. It was too early for onlookers, but even if there had been people milling about, I wouldn't have cared. The life I once knew was finally evaporating and for once, in a very long time, I could see light at the end of the tunnel. The old Kace, the demon-riddled Kace, was dying.

Linda had released a part of me. She'd lifted my burden and let me breathe. It took me a bit to accept it, but speaking the words out loud to Jett, I realized my wrongdoings had been a blessing in disguise. They gave me a second life, a second chance, a chance I refused to waste.

Pulling away, I looked at Jett and realized we were both crying. I smirked as I wiped my eyes and said, "Fuck, we look like a couple of dickheads."

"The hell if I care," Jett said, pulling me into his embrace again.

He was my brother, the one person who had been by my

side during the darkest of my days, guiding me and protecting me. "I would do it again," I admitted. "I would put up with the guilt, the shame, the sins just to know that in the end, Madeline and Linda would be protected."

"I would too," Jett admitted. "Tell me it's over, Kace. Tell me you're moving on. Tell me this fucking nightmare is done." Jett was pleading. I could tell he wanted his best friend back, the man he used to know. It would take some time, but I was ready to move on.

"I've been waiting for this moment to be free, and I'm fucking taking it. I just have one more thing to do."

A giant smile spread across Jett's face from my confession. I could see the hope, the happiness that ensued him. Not only was I setting myself free, but I was giving my best friend one of the things he needed the most, besides Goldie; I was giving him his brother back.

"What's the next step, then?" Jett asked.

From the very beginning, this hadn't only been my journey. It had been his as well, and it was about time we ended it together.

"Time to bid the fucker goodbye," I answered and walked toward the cemetery, Jett falling in beside me.

I knew where the grave was. The image of Linda standing over it with Madeline was burned in my mind. Now that I thought about it, she'd looked pale and rigid that day, covered from head to toe in clothing that probably hid her bruises. She must have been wearing a heavy amount of makeup to hide her husband's brutality because I didn't remember seeing any kind of abuse on her face.

Passing gravestones and old flowers, we finally made it to Marshall's grave. The urge to take a sledgehammer to the stone itched as I stared down at the inscription.

Beloved husband and father.

"The man got off too easy," I said while staring down at the grave. If I had known who he really was, what he used to do to Linda, I would have taken my time on him in that bar, making him feel every last blow instead of ending his life so quickly. I would have tortured him, I would have ripped him to shreds and then ended it." Malice was heavy in my voice. "I've never despised someone so much in my life, Jett."

"Me too," Jett seethed.

"He took years from my life. He took Madeline's innocence, Linda's freedom."

"And now he's paying for it," Jett countered.

Nodding, I crouched and spoke to Marshall directly, letting him know that the inscription on his grave was a lie.

"You spent your years on this earth intimidating Linda, taking advantage of your role as a father and interrogating complete strangers. You dismissed a life you should have been proud of. You threw away a chance to watch Madeline grow up into the beautiful, spicy little girl she is today, and you abused a vibrant woman who cowered under her marriage to you. You're a coward. You're the monster, not me, and I will never regret my decision of taking you down ever again. I owe you nothing besides a thank-you for bringing Madeline and Linda into my life. I will be the man they need, the man you never were, and will protect them from men like you, instead of men like me." Standing up, I patted his grave. "Have a fun time rotting in hell, you sick fuck."

I stepped back and looked at Jett. He was happy. Bending down to the level of the grave, Jett said, "Thank you for being a beast of a man because you not only strengthened my bond with my brother, but you also proved that justice will always prevail."

An orange light started to brighten the sky as the sun rose. Jett clasped my shoulder. "Ready?"

"Ready," I replied. "I have one more stop. Would you mind coming with me?"

"You know I would go anywhere with you, bud."

We walked away, leaving my demons behind. For once in my fucking life, I was leaving them behind. With each step, I felt lighter, freer, like I was finally starting a new chapter in my life rather than reading the same one over and over again. It was time to turn the page, to move on.

It was time for me to live.

CHAPTER THIRTY-ONE

My present...

"I think the beignets were smart," Jett said as I parked the car.

"Yeah, thanks for picking up the bill." I smirked.

"And why did I do that again?" he asked. "After that little bank statement I saw, I would say you're set for a bit. At least a nice down payment on a house."

"I can't take that money," I responded. "I wouldn't feel right."

"Linda isn't going to take it. It's yours, Kace. You've suffered enough. You lost everything that night, you gave up everything. You deserve to put your life back in order. You deserve that money."

"I just don't feel right about it. I want to at least help pay for Madeline's college."

"An admirable thought," Jett said. He looked down at the pastry box and then back up at me. "You ready for this?"

I nodded, pulled the keys out of the ignition, and said, "Let's do it."

We got out of the car and surveyed the little home that belonged to Linda and Madeline. It was still early in the morning, so condensation kissed the grass and a light fog was in the air, which would soon be burned off by the Louisiana heat. The street was quiet, neighbors only starting to wake.

To someone else, it might be too early in the morning, it might look like a dreary day with the fog still blocking the view of the neighbor's houses, but to me, it was a new dawn, a new day, a new beginning. I felt invigorated for the first time in a while.

Nodding at each other, we walked to the front of the house and gently knocked on the door for the first time. I'd been on this stoop before. I'd wondered what kind of life the residents led, if they hated me, if they despised me, but this time, I was confident I would be accepted with open arms into this quaint little home.

After a few moments of silence, the click of locks opening echoed in the silent morning and then Linda opened the door wearing a long terrycloth robe, her hair in a ponytail. Bunny slippers covered her feet and a pair of polka-dot pajama pants peeked out from under her robe. When she saw me, she flew into my arms and hugged me.

She was warm, friendly. She allowed me to relax. I wrapped my arms around her and returned the gesture. She cried into my shoulder as her hold on me grew stronger. Jett stood to the side, observing like he always did.

I'd never once believed I would be standing on Linda's doorstep with her arms wrapped around my waist, happy to see me. It was hard to believe because I'd spent the last few years instilling in my head that this woman hated me, that she would celebrate the day I died for what I had taken away from her. Instead, I was celebrated as a hero, as a protector, as a savior.

Words I never would have used to describe myself.

I was on a fucking high. Take my boxing career, take the last few years away from me, I didn't give a fuck, as long as in the end, I was the man who came out on top, the man these ladies looked up to, the man who was a blessing in disguise.

Linda pulled away and wiped her tears. "I'm so glad you came by." She laughed. "As you can see."

"Linda, this is my friend, Jett Colby."

"Why yes, you own Justice. Madeline and I are so grateful for your kindness to the community, opening such a center for this city. It was a pure act of selflessness."

"Pleasure is mine," Jett responded while shaking Linda's hand. "Glad you were able to find peace within Justice."

The meaning of Jett's words were heavy. We all felt the weight of them and what he was conveying.

"May we come in?" I asked, feeling the tears she'd shed on my shirt. They were happy tears, tears I didn't mind seeing shed.

"Of course. Please excuse the mess. Madeline and I had a slumber party in the living room, so sleeping bags are on the floor."

As I entered the little house, I instantly felt at ease. The walls were a beautiful yellow color, the same yellow that was in Goldie's room at the Lafayette Club. All the furniture was white, and there were little touches of orange and teal all around the house. I felt calm, my pulse wasn't racing, and my skin didn't crawl. Instead, I felt like I'd found another home, a piece of me that had been missing.

To the right was the living room where there were pillows and sleeping bags on the floor. DVD cases were strewn across the coffee table, *Frozen* being the one that was open. Two cans of soda with straws coming out of them were sitting next to a giant bowl of only kernels left on the bottom. The scene made my heart ache in a good way.

Linda and Madeline were thriving, more than I could have ever asked for.

"Went to the bathroom!" Madeline said as she skidded into the living room, stopping abruptly when she saw there was company. "I mean... used the ladies' room," she corrected herself, looking embarrassed.

She was wearing the same pants and slippers as her mom, but her hair was a wild mess on top of her head, and she was wearing a *Frozen* shirt that was entirely too large on her. In a few short days, I'd learned to absolutely adore this little girl.

"Mr. Kace, what are you doing here?" she asked, twisting her shirt.

"Madeline, is that how we greet our guests?"

Madeline straightened and said, "Can I get you something to drink, Mr. Kace?"

Chuckling, I squatted down in front of her just as I grabbed the box of beignets and opened it up in front of her. Her eyes widened from seeing the deep fried pastries. "Do you have anything that will go with these?"

"Chocolate milk!" she said with excitement. "I would have to make it though. We have powder."

"Would you make my friend Jett and me a glass?"

"I would love to." She took off to the kitchen and started rustling around, opening cabinets and shutting them.

Linda shook her head. "Putting your drinks in Madeline's hands. I would watch out, boys." Linda smiled and led us to the dining room to a small round white table and matching chairs. Linda pulled back a teal curtain so the morning light came in.

"Your house is beautiful, Linda," Jett complimented.

"Thank you, Mr. Colby."

"You can call me Jett." Sincerity laced his voice.

"Thank you," Linda said. "When Marshall passed, I decided to redo the house with some of the insurance money we got. The house was so dark and dreary before. It had his decorations, he was everywhere, and I needed to be rid of him. Madeline helped me pick the paint color, and we went to work. I couldn't imagine this house any other way."

"It's so cheery and inviting," I praised.

"Thank you. It's what we were going for."

Before Madeline reappeared, I pulled out the envelope Linda gave me before I left the community center the other day and handed the envelope to Linda, who refused to take it. "Linda, take this, please."

"No." She shook her head. "That is your money, Kace. Start over with it."

"Linda, I gave this to you for a reason."

"Yes, and even though your reasoning was very sweet, we don't need it. We are doing just fine. I have a well-paying graphic design job that allows me to work from home. We are good, Kace. We are taken care of."

"But what about Madeline's college? Can I put it toward that?"

Linda shook her head. "She's set. This is your rebirth. Do me a favor and use it. Start a new chapter."

"Got the drinks," Madeline said as she carried in a tray with four glasses of chocolate milk on them. She moved carefully to avoid spilling. Her tongue was sticking out as she concentrated on trying not to spill.

She set the tray on the table and then kneeled on a chair and started handing out the glasses.

"I put extra chocolate in yours, Mr. Kace. You look like a chocolate kind of guy."

"Is that right?" I asked.

"Mom says milk makes you strong and you have lots of muscles, so I figured you drank a lot of chocolate milk."

"And I don't have muscles?" Jett asked in a teasing tone.

Madeline looked Jett up and down. "Hmm, I think Mr. Kace just wears smaller shirts."

A snort escaped Jett, and Linda warned her daughter to be polite. I knew Jett would never let that comment drop, so I looked forward to a future teasing.

"Madeline, why don't you get plates and napkins as well?"

"Sure thing," Madeline said, scurrying off to the kitchen once more.

"I'm sorry about that," Linda apologized to me.

"Totally fine," I said, taking a drink of my chocolate milk. Chunks of chocolate hit my tongue, and I about spit it back in my glass from the surprise of having a chunky chocolate milk, but I swallowed, despite my stomach revolting.

"Told you to look out," Linda chuckled as she grabbed a spoon from the tray and stirred her drink, breaking up the chunks.

"I'm going to need that spoon after you," I said, wiping the thick layer of chocolate off my mouth.

Linda laughed and handed it over. I quickly stirred my drink and Jett's before Madeline returned. I didn't want her to feel insulted that she didn't do a good job.

"Do you like your drink, Mr. Kace?"

"Very chocolatey," I complimented.

"I knew you would like chocolate." She smiled that toothless grin at me.

Madeline handed out plates and napkins and then opened the box of pastries. She divvied those out as well, giving us each one. She continued to kneel down on her chair and started to dig into her breakfast. With one bite, she had powdered sugar all over her face.

She was too cute with her morning hair that rivaled Albert Einstein's, her powder-covered face, and her oversized shirt. How could anyone else raise their hand to this precious little girl? The mere thought had my stomach buckling. Marshall Duncan was exactly where he belonged, six feet under.

"These are good," Madeline said before she picked up her glass of milk with both hands and took a big gulp. When she put her glass back down, she formed a chocolate and powdered sugar paste ring around her mouth. "I'm excited to hit the mats today," Madeline said in between bites, using one of my terms.

Linda shook her head and shrugged her shoulders at me, as if to say, girls will be girls.

I chuckled and said, "Yeah, you going to throw down today?"

"I've been practicing my jabs." She closed her hand into a fist and punched the air while saying, "Pow, pow!"

"Honey, remember, we talked about how you don't have to make sound effects while punching," Linda said with a motherly smile.

"But it's so much cooler with saying 'pow,' Mom. People take you more seriously if you make a noise. If you just jab the air, people will think you're crazy, but if you say 'pow pow' while doing it, they will be sure not to mess with you. Isn't that right, Mr. Kace?"

"They'll definitely back away." I laughed.

"See, Mom? Boxing is my second nature. Put me in the ring, and I will do some damage."

"You won't be going in a ring," Linda said protectively.

"Ah, come on. Have you seen my footwork? No one can catch me."

Visions of Madeline bouncing around me in the Haze Room clouded my brain, making me smile.

"We will consider it when you're older," Linda answered.

"Sounds like a plan." Madeline looked around. "Why am I the only one eating?" She pushed her hair aside, leaving powder in her wake. With a ring of chocolate on her face and powder all over her, she was one adorable hot mess.

"Sorry," I said, smiling and taking a giant bite. "Beignets are my favorite breakfast."

"They're my second," Madeline said, reaching for another. "I love French toast."

"So do I," Jett chimed in. "Bananas Foster French toast is my favorite."

"That's good," Madeline nodded. "But I like peanut butter and Fruity Pebbles on mine. Oh, and marshmallows."

Both Jett and I looked up at Linda, who was resting her head in her hand. She laughed and said, "Remember, Madeline, that's our French toast surprise that we keep between us."

"Oh yeah, well, Mr. Kace and Mr. Jett won't tell anyone. Right, fellas?"

"Right," Jett and I said at the same time while chuckling.

We finished up our breakfast while chatting with Madeline about her "summer plans" and listened to her tell us all about the "good values" a movie like *Frozen* had. She was so entertaining, I could have listened to her talk for a days.

In the middle of her telling us all about her favorite Disney Princess, Mulan, she looked at the clock and screeched. "Mom, I need to get ready for class at Justice."

I had about half an hour before I had to start teaching. This go around, it was going to be much easier.

"Well go get ready, honey, and I will take you. And please, wash your face," Linda said.

She took her dishes to the kitchen and went to her room. She tore out of the kitchen and down the hallway to her room. Her door slammed shut and Linda exhaled loudly.

From down the hall, we heard her call out, "Sorry!"

"She is a beautiful little girl, Linda. You've done a great job raising her," Jett complimented.

"Thank you. She can be a handful at times, but I can't imagine a day without her." Linda turned to me and said, "Why are you here this morning, Kace?"

I knew the question was on her mind the entire morning, but speaking in front of Madeline would have been inappropriate, so she waited for a time when we were alone. I knew it was coming.

Taking advantage of Madeline's absence, I sat back in my chair and said, "I wanted to thank you for coming to me last night. I didn't handle your news well at first. It was all a bit of a shock. I needed to let it soak in, but after I let it soak in and after I gave myself some closure, I wanted to thank you. I've been walking around in this world so focused on my past sins that I never realized how you might be fairing. I was convinced I ruined you, convinced that I destroyed any chance of Madeline having a normal life, but I was wrong. You gave me the gift of opening my eyes yesterday, and I have to thank you for that."

"I have to thank you as well," Jett cut in. "Kace and I have been friends since grade school, and I know the man he can be. You brought him back, Linda. With your forgiveness, your grace, you brought my best friend back."

Tears streamed down Linda's face as she listened to us. You don't need to thank me," she replied. "You gave me hope, Kace. You gave me freedom and you protected Madeline in a way I never could have. You're a blessing to our family, and I hope you will continue to make us a part of your life. Madeline is quite fond of you."

"I would be honored," I said, getting up and pulling Linda into another hug. "I'm quite fond of the both of you too."

Jett was right; justice always prevailed.

CHAPTER THIRTY-TWO

My present...

"Gahhh! Are you going to propose?" Goldie hopped up and down and clapped her hands together as I washed down the mats in the Haze Room after a long day of forgiveness, acceptance, and of course training Madeline and the other patrons of the community center.

There was one more thing I had to do, and it was going to be the hardest part of all. It was the one thing I was dreading but looking forward to the most, if that made sense.

"No, Goldie, I'm not proposing."

"Why not?" She crossed her hands over her chest like a child.

"Because life doesn't work like that."

"Yes it does," she countered. "Let's go pick out a ring."

"I asked you when Lyla worked, and you have me picking out a fucking ring? Don't you see where you're exaggerating here?"

Goldie thought about it for a second and then shook her head. "Nope, I think we're on the right path."

312

"Just tell me when the hell she's working."

"God, you're no fun. All I'm asking is for a little proposal. It's not like I'm asking for little Lyla and Kace babies, but oh my God, can we talk about how cute they would be? Ahhhh, you guys would make beautiful babies, all mocha skinned and pretty eyed. Hopefully they don't get your temper though because holy hell, could you imagine five of you running around, moody as fuck?" Goldie used a little person voice and said, "Dada, I shit my pants. Whatcha gonna do about it?"

"There is something seriously wrong with you," I said while getting up and taking the cleaning supplies back to the cabinet. The Haze Room was good to go. Now I just needed to shower and prepare for tonight. "So when does she work?"

"She's on stage at nine," Goldie finally admitted.

"Thank you," I said while walking to the locker room and grabbing the duffel bag Diego had brought by for me since I had been too busy to stop at home.

"Does this have to do with that other woman who brings her daughter here?" Goldie asked, seeming nervous about my answer. "Is she a love child?"

"Ask your fiancé," I responded, not in the mood to tell the nosey Goldie everything. Knowing her, she would ask a million questions, and I would never get out of here.

"Ugh, he doesn't tell me anything when it comes to you."

"Well, he has permission. Tell him that."

Goldie chased after me. "Can you text him that? He wouldn't believe me if I told him."

"Maybe it's because you lie too much," I said, turning to face her.

"I do not! I just embellish things. It makes for a better story."

"Say it how you want; it's still lying."

"Whatever," she responded defiantly. "Can you just text him for me?"

"Why does it matter that much to you?" I asked, the bag slung over my shoulder.

"Because I'm nosey! I need to know what's going on in everyone's lives. Do me a solid and text Jett, then I won't bother you anymore."

"That's a giant fucking lie, and you know it." I laughed.

Goldie gave me with a questioning look, as if she was confused by the person standing in front of her.

"Umm, I'm sorry, did you just laugh?"

"I'm leaving." I turned but heard Goldie clapping behind me.

"You laughed. It was all throaty and sexy too. Lyla is a lucky girl."

"Drop it, Goldie," I warned but with mirth in my voice.

I spent the next thirty minutes showering and getting dressed. Diego had packed a pair of my worn grey jeans, black chucks, black shirt, and black sock hat. The V-neck of the shirt showed off some of the muscles in my chest and for once in a long time, I actually appreciated the reflection in the mirror. For once, I was proud of the man who stood before me.

I drove over to Kitten's Castle and parked the car on one of the back streets near the club since cars were blocked off at night from going down Bourbon Street.

Nerves settled in as I walked to Kitten's Castle. In my head, Lyla would be happy to see me, but after I'd left her this morning without saying goodbye, I could see it being the last straw. There was only one way to find out.

As I approached the club, one of the girls was standing outside the door, calling to men who walked by to come and enjoy the atmosphere of the club. She wasn't wearing a bra and had kitten-shaped pasties over her nipples. Her garter belt and thong kept her cool in the steamy night air, and her heels had scuffs near the bottom, letting me know the woman was struggling, like every other female working Bourbon Street.

"Hey, coming for a lap dance?" she asked as I approached.

I didn't answer her as I walked past her through the door and into the darkly lit club. It was just dark enough so you couldn't see what men were doing under the tables and so you couldn't see the grime in the place. I kept my hands in my pockets and walked toward the stage, where acts were in the midst of a change. I checked my watch and saw it was nine. Lyla would be on any minute.

Quickly approuching the stage, I looked around before going behind the curtain. Cigarette smoke immediately smacked me in the face. Barely covered women walked around with their hair half done and their false eyelashes hardly attached to their eyelids. Lyla was by far superior to these women in every department.

I looked around for Lyla but didn't see her. It wasn't until I heard the crowd cheer that I realized she must have snuck past me. Music ripped through the club, a heavy beat with a sexy undertone.

Lyla was on stage.

I peered past the curtain and saw her, strutting around in a thong and a T-shirt that scantily covered her breasts. The men watching her could no doubt see the underside of her boobs. Rage filled me as men started to slip bills in her thong and cat-called for her to take her shirt off. Lyla grabbed the pole in the center of the stage and dipped low then slowly rose back up, sticking her ass out for everyone to see. That was all it took. She was done.

Tearing across the stage, I gripped her by the arm and

started dragging her away.

Shock was her first reaction, followed by anger.

"What the fuck do you think you're doing?" she hissed.

Two bouncers jumped up on stage and grabbed me by the shoulders. I released Lyla. I elbowed one of them in stomach, making him instantly back down and then elbowed the other in the jaw, sending him backward into the crowd. I grabbed Lyla again and forced her behind the curtain.

"Kace!" she shouted. "Let me go!"

"Nope," I responded, leading her to the lockers. There were a few ladies in the locker room, and when they saw us enter, they quickly exited, giving us some privacy. Once they were gone, I slammed the door, turned on Lyla, and crossed my arms. "Get your things."

"Excuse me?" Her nipples were hard and poked the thin T-shirt.

"You heard me. Pack your things, Lyla."

"The fuck I will. You don't order me around."

"Lyla, I will not ask you again. Pack your fucking things, or I will do it for you."

She didn't move. She just stood there, tapping her foot. Stubborn fucking woman.

"Fine," I said. I walked over to her locker, cocked my elbow back, and plowed into the middle of the flimsy medal, sending the lock across the room. I opened the dented door and grabbed her purse, shoving her items inside.

"Hey!" she shouted while she rushed over to me. I tossed her regular-sized shirt and shorts at her, then grabbed the bills from her thong and put them in her purse.

"Get dressed."

"No. I'm not leaving. You can't just come in here after last night and be all controlling and try to tell me what to do."

I got in her face and lifted her chin so she was forced to look in my eyes. With a serious tone in my voice, I said, "You're not working here anymore. So get your ass dressed, because we're leaving."

"No."

"Lyla," I warned.

"What are you going to do? Man-handle me out of here?"

I grabbed her around the waist, showing her I wasn't kidding. "Do not test me."

"Ugh, you're infuriating!"

"Lyla, get your ass back on stage," Marv, the owner of Kitten's Castle said as he bustled into the locker room, breathing heavily and purple from anger.

"Let go of me," Lyla threatened.

"Who is this?" Marv asked, poking me in the back.

I turned quickly on the man, towering over him. He backed up and held out his hands defensively.

"Whoa, don't want to start trouble."

"Then I suggest you find someone else to cover Lyla's shift."

The puny man backed away and practically ran out of the room, closing the door behind him. Even though I was easily able to scare away her manager, the overbearing tactic wasn't working with Lyla, thanks to her stubbornness, so it looked like I was going to have to open my heart right in the middle of the locker room.

I grabbed her hand, and she tried to pull away, but I laced our fingers together. "Lyla, please come with me. I'm sorry about this morning. I had some things I needed to take care of, but I'm ready to talk and I would rather not do it at Kitten's Castle."

"That's all you had to say, idiot," she muttered under her

breath as she dressed. She slowly took off her stage shirt and walked over to her purse, naked besides her heels and thong, and dug around for her bra. She then grabbed the neckline of my shirt and pulled me closer so I could feel her nipples pebble against the thin cotton of my shirt. My hands instinctively went to her hips. Her lips nipped mine as my hands went under the strap of her thong and molded into her ass.

I groaned when her tongue stroked the seam of my lips, looking for entrance. Kindly I obliged and allowed her to explore my mouth.

Just when I was settling in for a make-out session, she pulled away and then tapped my hard-as-fuck erection. "Just making sure it still worked." She smiled and put on her bra.

"Teasing will get you nowhere," I warned.

"Doesn't seem like you have the right to threaten. Pretty sure I have the upper hand at the moment."

I hated that she was fucking right about that. "Just get dressed."

"Don't get pushy with me, Kace. The more you demand, the longer I will take."

"You're enjoying this, aren't you?" I asked while pulling on the back of my neck.

"Just a little." She smirked.

Leaning against the wall of the locker room, I watched as she put her clothes on as slowly as possible. I didn't know what was sexier, watching her put her clothes on or watching her take them off. Both had a deep yearning stirring at the base of my cock.

Once she was ready, she grabbed her purse then grabbed my hand and said, "Let's go."

I led her out the back of Kitten's Castle to the car, where I opened the passenger door for her, trying to remember to be a gentleman. It'd been way too long.

We drove in silence to Woldenberg Park. We should have walked, but luckily, we found a parking spot along a side street.

I walked around to Lyla's side and helped her out of the car, making sure to grab her hand. I brought her to a bench that overlooked the Mississippi River, grateful there weren't many people milling about at night. Imitation gas lamps lit the sidewalks, casting a romantic setting for our walk.

The night sky was free of clouds, and looking up, I could faintly see stars. I chose to bring Lyla to the park because I wanted to start a new chapter, and bringing her to my room at Diego's or going to her apartment to talk to her would just remind me of the life I was once living.

We sat on the bench, facing the river. I put my arms on the back of the bench and she snuggled close. I played with the strands of her hair as we enjoyed the cooler night air.

I knew she was waiting on me to talk, but I had no clue where to start. I'd never told anyone my story, ever, so to try to talk about it was going to be one of the hardest tasks I ever had to face. Her head rested on my shoulder and she caressed my thigh, letting me know she would wait for me, that she was patient. I kissed the side of her head. "I need to talk to you."

"I gathered that," she said with a slight laugh.

"Yeah, I'm not good at talking about things."

"I gathered that as well." She kissed my jaw. "I'm a good listener though, so take your time."

Taking a deep breath, I leaned into her for support as I tried to get through my story. "You know about my boxing career."

"I do. I wish I could have seen you box. I can only imagine how hot you looked."

Chuckling, I said, "Yes, it was the hotness factor that made me so good."

"I'm sure it was, but go on."

"Jono was my trainer, he ruined my career—stole it from me, actually, by slipping me steroids without my knowledge."

"Yes, I read about that. He's been convicted since then though for doing it to other athletes. You're not the only one. You could get your name..."

"That doesn't matter now." I kissed the side of her head and said, "But thank you for caring. That night I found out that I was banned from the circuit, I hit rock bottom. I went to a bar where I knew no one would bother me and drank my sorrows away. Jett was with me. He watched me take drink after drink, convincing me to take action, to fight back, but at that point there was no fight left in me. The one thing I had worked for my entire life for was stolen from me, so I gave up. It was over."

"I'm so sorry," Lyla said, kissing my jaw again.

I shut my eyes tightly and tried to even out my pulse that began to quicken. This was much harder than I thought.

Clearing my throat, I said, "There was a guy there that night. He found out who I was and took it upon himself to provoke me. He started physically attacking me."

"What do you mean? Like he tried to pick a fight?"

"Yes."

"Was he an idiot? Didn't he know who he was against?"

"He did, but he also thought I was some puss bag who used steroids to get to where I was. He never considered the fact that I was actually good at my sport."

"What did he do?"

"He continued to attack me. At first I welcomed the pain, but then he pushed me past my limit and I struck back with four punches. I can see it so vividly now as if it just happened. A punch to the stomach, a right uppercut, then a left jab and right jab to his temples."

"Oh my god." Lyla covered her mouth. I could feel her tense underneath me and panic started to ensue me. I couldn't lose her over this, but I knew if I didn't tell her, if I kept this secret, I would lose her for sure.

My throat closed, my eyes burned, and I could feel myself shake with nerves, terrified that with my next spoken words she would get up and walk away.

"I...I killed him, Lyla. In a matter of seconds, I killed a man and watched him bleed out underneath me."

"No." She shook her head as she pulled away, my gut clenching from her distance.

"I'm sorry," I said, tears running down my face. "I didn't mean to. I lost control. Jett covered it up, and that's when I gave everything up, moved in with Jett, and started working at the Lafayette Club, building it from the ground up with him. I spent my days either getting drunk, reminding myself of the monster I was, or training the girls. I drank until I was numb, I fucked to temporarily forget, and I swore to myself to take care of the ones whose lives I destroyed."

"The person you were buying a present for...," she stated, connecting the dots.

"Yeah, Madeline. She's the man's daughter, and Linda was his wife."

"Wait, Linda and Madeline, aren't they the mother-daughter duo at Justice?" I nodded my head as she tried to grasp everything I was telling her. She scooted away again, and a little piece of me broke in half.

"Lyla, please don't distance yourself. I can't..." I rubbed my eyes and said, "I need you to understand me."

She bent her knee and placed it on the bench so she was fully facing me now. She grabbed my hand with both of hers and scooted in closer so she was only inches away.

"Then keep talking, Kace."

I nodded and said, "Every Christmas and every birthday, I would drop off a present to Madeline since she wouldn't be getting one from her father. I thought it was only fitting to give her something. I also would leave money for them every month in their mailbox. I wanted to make sure they were taken care of. I was so convinced they were struggling, that I had ruined their lives."

"That night after our date, when we went back to your place and you told me about your father, I freaked out because all I could see was you as the grown-up version of Madeline. That she was going to have to have a tough life like you. I lost it. I should have comforted you, but instead, I ran because your story hit too close to home."

"I didn't have anyone, Kace. Madeline at least had her mother."

"I know that now," I replied. "This whole time, I haven't allowed myself to have feelings for people, to live a normal life, because I didn't think I deserved one. Up until yesterday, I was ready to let go, to finally slip into a dark place, to end my fucking misery..."

"No," Lyla said, crawling onto my lap and grabbing my head in her hands. "Don't say things like that." Her eyes welled up with tears and her lips kissed away the trail of tears on my cheeks.

"I had nothing left in me, Lyla. I was at a point where the pain was too excruciating. Having to teach Madeline how to box on a daily basis, watching her in person, her fiery spirit, it was debilitating. From a distance I could deal with my remorse, but up close, I could barely function."

"What changed your mind?" she asked, gripping me tightly.

"Linda did," I answered honestly. "She knew it was me."

"She knew you killed her husband?"

"Yes."

"How?" Lyla asked, confused.

"She saw me at the funeral and dropping off gifts, and she put two and two together. When she saw me at Justice and the pain I was living with, she knew for sure."

"And she confronted you?" Lyla questioned.

"No, she came to thank me."

"For killing her husband?"

"For ending her misery," I corrected. "He abused her on a daily basis, he terrified her, and that night I killed him, he went after Madeline. Linda wanted to thank me, to tell me how grateful she was for protecting them, for saving them..."

"Oh, Kace." Lyla pulled me into a hug, and I buried my head in her hair, getting lost in her cherry scent.

"I didn't ruin them, Lyla. I saved them."

"You did, baby," Lyla said, pulling me closer and kissing my neck. "You're a good man, Kace."

Relief spread through me. A final weight was lifted off my shoulders, and I relaxed into her embrace.

"You believe me?" I asked.

"Of course I do, Kace. You're a good man and I know you wouldn't lie to me. I told you, there is nothing you could say that would push me away. I knew from the moment I met you, there was something special between us. You were meant for me, Kace, faults and all."

I slowly looked up into her green eyes and grasped the nape of her neck. I pulled her forward and placed my forehead on hers.

"I've fallen in love with you, Lyla. Somewhere along this journey, I allowed myself to feel for you, and no matter how hard I tried, I couldn't get you out of my mind. Every day, I fell harder and harder until it was impossible for me to forget your soft lips and your beautiful heart. You were made for me, babe, and I will be damned if you get away."

Lyla kissed my lips softly and said, "I've fallen for you too, Kace. I've fallen hard."

"I just had to let go of my demons before I could commit to you because what I want with you is something I never thought I could have, but now I can. I want to start fresh. I want us to live together. I want us to work together. I don't want you leaving my sight. I'm so fucking gone when it comes to you, Lyla. I want everything with you."

"I want the same, Kace. I love you."

"I love you, babe."

Smiling, she pulled my lips to hers and kissed me senseless. My hands fell to her hips as I let her take control of our connection. We were both needy and desperate for each other. It had been a long road to get to where I was now, but I wouldn't give up the journey for anything.

Like the song "Blackbird" by The Beatles, I'd taken my broken wings and waited to fly. I'd waited for my time to rise. With broken and bandaged wings, I was ready to fucking soar. The blackbird was now free.

I'd finally paid my repentance.

EPILOGUE

"Ketchup on a hot dog?" I asked Madeline with a disapproving glare. "Didn't your mother teach you anything? Its mustard and relish, not ketchup. Ketchup belongs on hamburgers."

"Oh, Mr. Kace, you don't know what you're talking about. Have you ever tried it?"

"No. have you ever tried it my way?" I countered.

She looked at my hot dog and shook her head. "It looks funny."

"How about this...." I grabbed her hot dog off her plate and replaced it with mine. "I will try it your way if you try it mine."

"Okay." She smiled, her front teeth now peeking past her gums.

"Cheers," I said, bumping my hot dog with hers.

We took big bites of each other's hot dogs and watched each other as we chewed. After we swallowed, we both cringed and shook our heads, grabbing for our original hot dogs.

"That was yucky," Madeline said, taking a huge gulp of her grape soda.

"Tell me about it. You have no taste," I joked.

"You don't." She laughed and pushed my shoulder.

"Who doesn't have taste?" Lyla asked as she sat next to Madeline with a hot dog doused in ketchup.

Madeline lit up and looked at me with a giant smile. "See, Mr. Kace. I have taste. Look at Lyla's hot dog."

I shook my head as two of the most important girls in my life ganged up on me. It happened quite often, and I wouldn't trade it for anything.

Now that I had my own house near Justice, Madeline came over often to hang out or enjoy a girls' night with Lyla. The relationship between them had grown into a real friendship, and watching them together fucking turned me into a puddle of emotion. Linda was as close to us too. Recently, Lyla and Linda had formed a real bond, and their new mission was finding Linda a man. Little did they know the lucky bastard was going to have to go through a series of tests from me and Jett first. To hell if Linda was ever going to have to suffer again.

Justice was thriving. Each and every day, someone new came along, a new soul we could touch and help. The housing was almost finished, offering a whole new branch of Justice. Linda had become more involved in the community center, designing a website for us as well as some great handouts about our programs.

We'd become a family, and I couldn't be more grateful for the odd turn of events in my life.

Recently, Jett had cleared my name with the professional boxing league, expunging the mark on my record. I'd been approached by many trainers and media outlets, begging me for a comeback, but like the day I'd hung up my gloves, my boxing career was over. Providing a healthy athletic outlet to those in need was way more important to me than any title I could win. All it took to realize that was seeing Madeline bounce around on her toes, jabbing around her little noddle arms.

"Love the built-in grill," Jett said as he sat down next to me, mustard and relish on his hot dog.

"Look at that." I nudged Madeline. "Looks like we're tied when it comes to who has taste."

Madeline looked over at me to see what Jett had on his hot dog and she cringed. "Gross, Mr. Jett. Where's your ketchup?"

"In the bottle," Jett said with a smile. "Where it belongs when it comes to a hot dog."

"Noooo," Madeline said, dragging it out. "Mom doesn't eat hot dogs, so that leaves Goldie. Where is Goldie?"

A couple minutes later, she waddled in, showing off her pregnant belly. Jett lit up and held out his hand. She walked into his embrace and sat on his lap. Jett protectively wrapped his arm around her stomach and kissed her shoulder.

"What's on your hot dog, Miss Goldie?" Madeline asked, leaning over to catch a glimpse.

"Peanut butter, bacon and marshmallows. What's on yours?"

Madeline studied Goldie for a second before saying, "All right, we were both wrong. Goldie doesn't have taste."

I threw my head back and laughed. "You got that right, kiddo."

"What's wrong with my taste?" Goldie asked, her mouth full of her foul-looking hot dog.

"Don't worry about it, little one," Jett replied. "Your hot dog is perfect."

"No, yours is." Goldie wiggled her eyebrows.

"Ewww," Madeline said, making everyone laugh.

I went over to my grill to check on the rest of the meat. Lyla joined me. It was our first barbeque after buying the house, and we were surrounded by everyone we cared about. The Jett

Girls were in the pool, catching some sun. Blane and Diego were playing cornhole in the back. Linda, Jett, Goldie, and Madeline were at the picnic table, and the love of my fucking life was sauntering toward me with a dangerous look in her eyes.

"That look will get you in trouble."

"What look?" she asked, her bathing suit blocking my view of her delectable body.

"That heated look."

"Don't walk around shirtless, and you won't have to worry about the way I look at you."

"We've got company and hot dogs on the grill."

"Come on, a quickie in the pool room. No one will notice we're gone."

"I will," Goldie said, leaning in.

"Jesus." I startled and looked at her. "You have a belly and now you can be stealth. Does that thing give you magical powers?"

"Didn't I tell you? Jett's mom was part unicorn. His seed is full of wonderlust kinds of things. This isn't just some pregnant belly. No, it's a magical orb where unicorns plant eggs and I crap them out into a special toilet where leprechauns harvest them for glitter bombs."

"You're so fucked up." Lyla shook her head, and I pulled her into a hug. Her warm skin pressed against mine made me wish we didn't have company.

"So, when are you going to propose?" Goldie asked.

"Yeah, when are you going to propose?" Lyla asked,.

I ran my hand to the back of my neck and said, "If you keep asking, it will never happen."

"But it will happen?" Lyla asked, hope in her eyes.

"Damn right it will happen." I smiled. "You're the best fucking piece of me."

"Me and Madeline," Lyla countered.

"You're right about that." I kissed Lyla's head and looked over our backyard, loving the hodge-podge of family I'd sewn together. We all came from different backgrounds, but the one thing we had in common was we'd been granted second chances in life and for that, we would always be grateful. We might be a mix of odds and ends from the city of New Orleans, but we were each other's odds and ends. We were family.

Thank you for reading Repentance! If you enjoyed reading Kace's story, check out some of my other books...

The Bourbon Series
Becoming a Jett Girl
Being a Jett Girl
Forever a Jett Girl

The Hot-Lanta Series
Caught Looking
Playing the Field
Warning Track

The Love and Sports Series
Fair Catch
Double Coverage
Three and Out

The Warblers Point Series
Beers, Hens and Irishmen
Beers, Lies and Alibis

The Addiction Series
Toxic
Fame

The Virgin Romance Novelist

Newly Exposed

ABOUT THE AUTHOR

Born in New York and raised in Southern California, Meghan has grown into a sassy, peanut butter eating, blonde haired, swearing, animal hoarding lady. She is known to bust out and dance if "It's Raining Men" starts beating through the air and heaven forbid you get a margarita in her, protect your legs because they may be humped.

Once she started commuting for an hour and twenty minutes every day to work for three years, she began to have conversations play in her head, real life, deep male voices and dainty lady coos kind of conversations. Perturbed and confused, she decided to either see a therapist about the hot and steamy voices running through her head or start writing them down. She decided to go with the cheaper option and started writing... enter her first novel, Caught Looking.

Now you can find the spicy, most definitely on the border of lunacy, kind of crazy lady residing in Colorado with the love of her life and her five, furry four legged children, hiking a trail or hiding behind shelves at grocery stores, wondering what kind of lube the nervous stranger will bring home to his wife. Oh and she loves a good boob squeeze!

Made in the USA
Las Vegas, NV
22 February 2024

86001689R00184